DECLAN TUCKER'S GRAND DEBUT

William Wodhams

AOS Publishing, 2024
Copyright © 2024

William Wodhams

All rights reserved under International
and Pan-American copyright conventions

ISBN: 978-1-990496-69-1

Cover Design: Chanelle Poupart

Visit AOS Publishing's website:
www.aospublishing.com

For Ann, Patrick & Scott

One

The sad truth is that I had sent my résumé to 147 of the top graphic design houses in the world and not heard back from a single one.

I'd explained to each of them how my personal artistic vision had been shaped, my extraordinary success in the industry (starting with an art contest I'd won in fifth grade), my belief in taking risks and breaking rules, and my recent graduation from the Laurentian Academy of Graphic Design. My introductory letter stretched to just over thirty-two single-spaced pages. It included how I had received a B- at Laurentian Academy and why it should have been an A. I underlined—three times—that I had no paradigms when it came to my chosen art. No paradigms at all. Still, I heard nothing from any of them.

C'est la vie. Their loss.

"Maybe you should think about applying for a job at the local paper," my mother suggested at least once a day.

"Just have to get your foot in the door, my man!" my father repeated often enough that he must've thought it was one of the original holy mantras.

The local newspaper? A crude and despicable suggestion, in my mind, eclipsing mere insult and verging on threat. I should've had my parents arrested. After all, these were the same parents who had called me a prodigy every day since fifth grade, had raised me to believe I was an artistic genius *sans précédent.* But as they were providing me with shelter, sustenance, and spending money, I was forced to reconsider. So I did my familial duty, completed and submitted the *Georgetown Herald*'s online application form, and prayed it would go ignored. Within the hour, an email arrived asking me to come in for an interview the next day.

The universe hates me.

I woke the next morning full of anxiety and regret, wishing only that I could stay in bed for a few more hours. But I couldn't. I may have been indifferent, but my parents were as excited as children on the first day of school. I knew there was no way out of this, so I got up, threw on my least wrinkled shirt, tossed back a vanilla-flavored coffee, ran outside, and climbed on the bus. Twenty-eight minutes later, I climbed off and laid a reluctant eye on the *Georgetown Herald*'s gray brick offices. The reception area was empty when I walked inside, and I had to bang on a bell at the front desk to get anyone's attention. A harried-looking middle-aged woman wearing an ill-advised kaftan ushered me into a small and sparsely furnished office beside reception and I sat down.

While I waited for my interviewer to arrive, I went over the standard questions and answers in my mind: *Why do I want to work here? Well, sir, I've always had a great passion for the newspaper industry, ever since I can remember. Where would I like to be in five years? I'd like to be a supervisor in the art department here, at the* Georgetown Herald, *whose high-quality journalism I have admired for years, if you don't mind me saying. That would be a dream come true.* I owed it to my parents to at least try.

A man walked into the room. "Hello—um—it's Declan, isn't it?"

Trying to ignore the missing button on his shirt, I pushed all thirty-two pages of my résumé in front of him with the confident, relaxed smile I had practiced in the mirror only hours before. "Yes, it is, sir."

"Nice to meet you, Declan. Neil Beckwith. Sales Manager. So." He turned the pages quickly, humming to himself, barely glancing at the section detailing my artistic journey and completely skipping over my vision statement before stopping at my work history and education. "Laurentian Academy, design, worked at Three-for-One Pizza, hobbies, art." Neil mumbled through my life story as if it were a sales brochure for a life insurance company. "Impressionists. You like the Impressionists, huh?" He peered up at me. "What's an Impressionist?"

This was going to be harder than I thought.

I started to give Neil a lesson in art history, but had barely covered Manet to Monet when his eyes glazed over like two Krispy Kreme doughnuts. We chatted for another minute or two, trying to find some common ground for discussion and failing, before he put my résumé down and scratched his belly. "Great! Nice. So, anyway. Can you start tomorrow?"

Well, well, well. Despite my misgivings about working here, I felt an unexpected rush of happiness. Or was it relief? The *Georgetown Herald* was a thousand miles from the design houses I had dreamed about working in, and offered a salary that just squeaked over minimum wage, but it was a job. It would give me, as my father suggested, a foot in the proverbial door: international fame could come later.

And it would make my parents happy. Could I start tomorrow? Yes, I could.

The next morning I packed my lunch (roast beef, lettuce, and cheese wrap, can of Coke, small bag of chips) and spent an inordinate amount of time choosing my wardrobe. It took almost an hour, but I finally got it right: the striped pink shirt and black slacks gave me the antiestablishment rebellious nature with a slightly ironic nod to contemporary pop culture look I was going for. I caught the eight-fifteen bus on the corner of McIntyre Crescent and Delrex Court and was at the paper twenty-seven minutes later.

"Good morning, Declan!" The harried woman who had greeted me yesterday appeared in front of me. "Welcome to the *Georgetown Herald* team! I'm Nancy. I'm so excited you're here. Are you excited?" I told her that I was excited, and we shook hands awkwardly. "You're probably wondering where everything is. So, washrooms are over there," she said, pointing across the room. "Your desk is there, photocopier is there, coffee is beside the fridge. Fifty cents, and we use the honor system." Her voice dropped to a whisper that could be heard in Missouri. "Everyone pays but Kevin." She nodded at a middle-aged man in the corner. "And guess what? That's why nobody likes him. It's only fifty cents. Is it worth it?" I shook my head to assure her I didn't think it was worth it and got a big smile in return. "Make yourself comfortable!" She clomped off.

The *Georgetown Herald* was housed in a cavernous, echoing space, with fifteen of us tucked into tiny cubicles spread around an office that could have seated forty. Faded motivational posters dating back to the nineties papered the walls: COMMITMENT. COLLABORATION. VALUES. The posters featured images of men and women climbing cliffs, rowing, and other stock photographs intended to inspire a few extra ounces of effort from the slumbering employees who worked here. The paper was a creaking relic in the internet age, but still, a relic that had stayed in business for over forty-five years, pumping out new editions every Monday, Wednesday, and Friday. The smell of ink and dust filled the air, occasionally combined with the whiff of microwaved popcorn. There was an old-world charm to the office, like an elderly uncle who repeated the same stories year after year and asked for "just one more rum and Coke, please and thank you" and never knew when it was time to leave.

I put my lunch in the fridge and sat down at my desk, pulled my pencils out of my bag, and carefully placed them in the desk drawer: H first, then B, then 2B through to 6B. These weren't just any pencils. I used Pilot Croquis graphite pencils exclusively, renowned for their easy-hold barrels, wide triangular grip, and retractable lead—the ultimate sketching pencils. I settled in, adjusted my chair, took a deep breath, and looked around.

So here I was. A world-class artist plying his craft at a small local newspaper. I was happy and sad, not unaware of the tragic irony: of course I deserved a higher calling, but at least I was working as an *artiste*. It was a beginning. I would not let my future be defined by the chance circumstances of my current employment. Many legendary artists had begun their careers with even humbler prospects—Cézanne started out as a lawyer, poor man. The more modest the beginning, the greater the ultimate achievement. Working at this old newspaper would make a sensational story one day: a badge of creative honor, like Van Gogh's ear or Rothko's suicide. It would make my grand debut even grander.

The first two days were spent learning the craft of the newspaper graphic designer. Standard column width eleven picas wide, headlines twenty-four-to-thirty-point Helvetica font, copy twelve point, don't leave too much white space in the layout, make the logo big, the call to action bigger, that kind of thing. It was late morning on my third day, shortly after I had begun working on my very first ad—for Mabel's Fine Fashions—that I encountered a stubborn artistic block.

While I waited for the muse to inspire me, I took the time to straighten out my desk, wipe down the computer screen, stretch my neck, and flex my fingers. Walked over to the window for a gaze outside and walked back. Moved my pencils to a different drawer, then moved them back. After an hour, still nothing. I got a coffee, dropped fifty cents in the collection cup with a loud clang, wandered back to the window, and stared out at Georgetown's skyline for another half hour. Still nothing. Thought my inspiration might be sparked by one of Monet's great works; after all, the old master had never failed me before. I searched Google for a high-resolution image and clicked on full screen. *Impression, Sunrise.* There it was, in all its beauty. Leaning back, I put my hands behind my head, feet up on the desk, and stared, lost in its sublime brilliance.

There it was. But what was it? What was he trying to say? Was it a prayer, a code, the key to some universal truth? I looked closer, searching for a clue in that holy work of art. The brushstrokes, the light, shadows, air, clouds; the mist in violet, gold, pink, and green; the atmosphere, all burnt orange and blues; the lack of form and structure, the layers and tones, the fog. Oh, the fog. I loved that fog. I could've eaten that fog. Every single droplet filled with oceans of love, passion, and beauty. It seemed as if there was a secret buried in there, something Monet was trying to tell me. What was it?

That's when I felt my boss, Neil, breathing on my neck. "Dec-*lannn*?"

Long dramatic sigh. Here's the thing people like Neil don't understand about the creative process. Art doesn't just happen. It's not like a tap you can turn on and off. Art takes its direction from the muse, and the muse is a strange and fickle mistress. She comes and goes as she pleases and doesn't like it when her efforts are interfered with. Isn't that obvious? After all, did Pope Julius II interrupt Michelangelo when he was working on the Sistine Chapel? No! Well, I don't know, but I doubt it. Yet Neil...

"Yes, sir," I answered. "Working on it right now." Sigh. I said goodbye to Monet, closed the browser window on the old Acer computer, and opened my email folder. Neil disappeared while I reread the specs on the ad I was supposed to be working on. One quarter page, two color. A comment attached to the request read "Headline—The Boss Is Away Sale!!! Highlight fashions!!!!!" Due date: noon today. It was already past one o'clock. So that's why Neil was harrumphing me. For a moment, I cursed the uncaring universe that led to my employment at this primitive little newspaper. Then I got back to work.

It required superhuman effort, but I forced myself to look at this menial task as a creative challenge. This wasn't going to be just an ad. It would be a piece of art, an opportunity to put everything I had practiced at home and studied at school for all these years in front of a real, live audience. This was my first big shot, and I wasn't going to miss it.

I went to work searching for new ways to flow space, experimenting with colors and forms. I was determined to create something new and profound. The next few hours raced by. I followed no rules and accepted no paradigms. The headline didn't work for me, so I removed it. Ditto the fashions. There was no place for linen-striped suit jackets or pleated slacks on this canvas. I focused on the shapes, the energy of the piece, the essential emotions it evoked. By late afternoon I had something I truly believed in. It was bold and evocative, paying homage to the great art movements of the past yet introducing something new—a confluence of influences. It had been an emotionally exhausting exercise for me, but it was (I had to admit) beautiful.

Save and Send. From: dtucker@gherald.com. To: nbeckwith@gherald.com.

Approximately eight minutes after I'd hit the send button, Neil banged his door open. He stood outside his office, holding a crumpled version of my ad in his hand, scanning the horizon of cubicles until he saw me. His eyes had a molten look to them. For a sloth of a man with a lethargic sense of personal style, he managed to evoke a surprising amount of anger.

He walked toward me, head down, taking big, clomping steps. A stout man on a serious mission. His two quivering chins and big head of thinning curly red hair shook as he approached. Neil's shirt was partially untucked, there were sweat stains under the arms, and his pants looked like they were held up by sheer willpower. In a way, I almost felt sorry for him. He looked like one of those toys my parents played with when they were children: the Weebles that wobbled but never fell down. Genes can be such a bugger. He wobbled over to my desk, dropped the ad layout in front of me, and stood there, red-faced and huffing, trying to catch his breath.

"Declan, what exactly is this?" His voice was so soft and high it reminded me of Michael Jackson. The image of Neil breaking into a moonwalk popped into my head and I started to grin but held back: he was here on serious business. There was a forced control behind his delivery, like he was expending a lot of energy to sound like he was normal. The voice that psychotic people have when they're trying to sound like they're not psychotic. "What? Is? This?"

I looked up. Very calm and collected. "It's my ad. For Mabel's."

"No. No, it isn't. I'm sorry but—look at it!" He pointed a nail-bitten finger at the layout, still fresh from his printer. "It's not even an ad. There's no headline, no photograph of Mabel's delightful fashions. You—look!—you didn't even... There's no copy, no nothing. It's... I don't know what this is." Neil's eyes were bulging and he was shaking his head, his curly hair waving wildly in the air. "I was supposed to send this to Mabel four hours ago!"

Where could I begin? I had imagined this moment so many times, sitting in my makeshift studio in my parents' basement, drawing, designing, creating *objets d'art*. I had visualized presenting my works to a crowd of respected critics: seeing their shocked looks, their initial hesitation, their wide eyes and shaking heads. Watching them as the radical originality of my work slowly sunk in, and those questioning looks giving way to silent, awestruck wonder as they realized the brilliant reality of what they were looking at. Hearing their applause. And me: sitting back, nodding, hands folded behind my head, not smiling, not saying anything, letting the work speak for itself. Although I don't smoke, I always saw myself lighting a cigarette.

Well. I could see that was not how this was going to work out. Neil was still shaking his head, harder now. I was beginning to worry that it would come loose. I knew my work would require explanation. "I have no paradigms."

He shook his head even harder and shut his eyes, as if trying to rid himself of some Beelzebub that had become attached to his face.

"What? I don't know what that is. What do you mean you have no paradigms? What paradigms?"

"It means no paradigms. There are no paradigms in my work."

Neil's mouth hung open, which was not an attractive look for a man who was already far below the attractiveness median. "I don't know what that means."

I had used that word hundreds of times, maybe more, to describe my work. Loved the sound of it: *paradigm*. It was a solid, important word, a word that carried serious intellectual heft. However, at that exact moment, I realized I didn't know what it meant either. Not really. Had nothing more than a foggy notion. "It's—well, like—it's like something no one has ever... No one thinks about."

Neil's face turned a luminous red, and the sweat stains under his armpits had almost reached his elbows. It was sad to watch.

"I don't want 'no paradigms'"! he said. "I want an ad for Mabel's Fine Fashions. I want to see suit jackets and pleated slacks. And a headline that reads 'The Boss Is Away Sale.' And I want it four hours ago!"

I am sorry to report that I temporarily lost my cool, but at that point I just wished Neil was dead. Standing as tall as I could stretch, I heard my voice go up an octave or two as I responded. "She's not away! She's there every day! And this"—I held up the ad—"is...is...is...it's an abstract interpretation of Mabel's Fine Fashions. That's a kind of art. Don't you know anything about abstract art?" In my defense, even I knew how arrogant that sounded. It was one of those moments during which my therapist would have advised me to Stop, Think, and Reflect before I acted—but it was too late. I regretted that loss of self-control before the words were out of my mouth.

Perhaps I should not have been surprised. Perhaps I should have expected this lack of enthusiasm. That, too, was poor judgment on my part: I had been too hopeful that these suburban newspaper types would recognize true art.

Apparently Abstract Expressionism had not yet reached the hallowed halls of the *Georgetown Herald*. I was angry, hurt, and embarrassed. So I humbly bowed my head, apologized profusely, made excuses, and promised to do better. Neil turned around and stomped away.

I sat down and put together a strictly traditional ad layout, which I knew he would love. Headline in thirty-point Helvetica font. Lots of Mabel's delightful fashions, minimal white space. Copy in twelve-point Helvetica. As a peace offering, I threw in a few extra exclamation marks. An hour later, I was done. I couldn't look at it without throwing up in my mouth.

Save and Send. Save and...save...and... No. I couldn't. My finger touched the button but refused to go any further. No, no, and no. Do not Save and Send. I couldn't do it. How could I? How could I compromise my artistic integrity so quickly? If I hit that send button now, where would it end? Would I end up like Neil, with an expanding waistline and thinning hair, fretting over whether an ad for Mabel's Fine Fashions pushed too many artistic boundaries? Whether headlines should have twenty-four or thirty-point fonts? Michelangelo had fought with the Pope. Raphael had battled with the king! How could I give in so quickly to a pudgy, balding, sweaty newspaper sales manager?

They had laughed at the first Impressionists, called them lunatics. They had called Monet's early works ugly. Now this curly haired barbarian couldn't appreciate the creative forces behind Declan Tucker's *objet d'art*. My work had broken rules, ignored paradigms, created something new. And my reward? Insult upon insult! This was the price one paid for genius. I had to stand up and fight, no matter the cost. I tried to think of an inspirational quote, but nothing came to mind.

Now I was more determined than ever to forge ahead on my artistic journey. This was my big chance, and I couldn't let it go. I dragged my last layout to the trash bin and permanently erased it with a satisfying *whoosh*. A fresh creative fire burned inside me, and I started again. Picked up a clean sheet of paper and my 4B Pilot Croquis pencil, spent hours creating original designs on the page, then recreating them, then finessing them on the computer. I looked up just once and realized the office was empty: everyone had gone home. I went back to work, ignoring the hunger and exhaustion that threatened to overwhelm me. More hours went by. It was almost midnight by the time I finished Mabel Number Three. Then I put my pencil down, sat back in my chair, folded my hands behind my head, and looked at what I had done.

This. This was art. It was passion, beauty, love, all in one two-thirds-of-a-page ad, and it contained not one iota of Mabel's Fine Fashions. No headline, no copy, no jackets or slacks, and no one was "away." Everything was here except for anything Neil had asked for. This layout had elements of Art Nouveau, Dadaism, Impressionism, Futurism, Minimalism, and a heavy sprinkling of pissed-off Declanism.

No emailing this one. I printed it out, laid it on Neil's desk, and went home.

———

When I arrived at work the following morning, an ambulance, fire truck, and police car jammed the entrance to the parking lot. I ran inside. A heavy silence, interrupted only by hoarse whispers and muted sobs, had descended on the office. My colleagues walked around blankly, looking even more zombie-like than usual, or stood in hushed groups with heads bowed, as if in silent prayer. Nancy was sitting on the floor, crying. A group of paramedics stood in Neil's office. Walking inside, I saw Neil lying on the floor, eyes shut. "Heart attack," someone said. His dead hand was wrapped around my ad for Mabel's Fine Fashions.

The next few hours went by in a thick fog. I tried to get back to work, but the layouts on my screen seemed even more nonsensical than usual, the list of urgent requests meaningless. My hands were shaking and my stomach felt queasy. Eventually I gave up and wandered over to the office window, and gazed down at the people walking by. The happy citizens of Georgetown were going about their day as if nothing had happened, the very picture of suburban serenity. Dogs barked, children played, teenagers rode skateboards, young mothers drank coffee with other young mothers. I envied their Eden-like state of innocence, for I was once as happy as they. No more. The pink glow of Declan Tucker's youth was gone forever.

It wasn't that I had any great love for Neil. I didn't even like him. The fact that he was dead was sad, I guess, but he was kind of old, and I guess his heart wasn't in great shape. In the great tapestry of human history, Neil's death wouldn't matter more than a stitch. Rather, it was the cause of his death that provoked such distress. For I, unlike anyone else in that moth-eaten news factory, knew exactly what had killed him. No doubt an official investigation and autopsy would follow, and the authorities would come to whatever conclusion made sense to their scientific proddings. That was a matter of no consequence. They would be wrong. I alone knew how Neil had ended up on that floor.

It was me. Declan Tucker. I killed him. The entire scene kept running in a frame-by-frame loop through my mind. He was expecting an ad with a big headline and lots of fashions. When he looked at the ad I had left on his desk, the shock of seeing all that creative power, all that raw passion, hit his small-town sensibilities with the shock of a thousand volts. It was all just too much for his plaque-filled heart.

Only a few short hours ago, I had been young, optimistic, and innocent. Now, there was only darkness and misery as I sank in an ocean of guilt. I had wished he was dead, and now he was, and it was my ad that killed him. The greatest of all earthly burdens had been placed on my gentle soul. I tried to ease my anxiety by playing SimCity on my computer, but by lunchtime it had dissipated only slightly. I ate my wrap in a state of deep melancholy. After all, I was responsible for the death of a good man, a decent man—even if he was just an old, sweaty, wrinkled newspaper sales manager, he was still a living, breathing human being.

Feelings of guilt, fear, and anxiety consumed me. But as I sat there, wallowing in my self-pity, I felt something else. I tried to pretend it wasn't there, kept pushing it away, but it refused to be ignored. Deep down inside me, another feeling kept rising up through my battered consciousness.

Underneath all that existential angst I felt something that was like—oh, what words could describe it? Like redemption. No, not that. Like a calling. No, something else. It was, well, like I had been anointed. Like a sacred gift had been conferred upon me. Like my hallowed artistic talent had been granted its own sainthood.

I had been blessed with a divine power.

I had a gift, and I had been given this gift for a purpose. Though I had no idea yet what that purpose was, it was most certainly not for the selling of Mabel's Fine Fashions. I knew, as I gazed around that moribund, depressed office, that I was destined for greater things. I packed my pencils in my bag and walked out of the *Georgetown Herald*'s offices, never to return.

<h1 style="text-align:center">Two</h1>

Walking through the wide, empty suburban streets of Georgetown, past the older bungalows and the newer oversize houses stretching to the edges of their tiny lots, the half-abandoned downtown core that housed the old hotels, used record stores, restaurants, and hardware suppliers, past Mabel's Fine Fashions (where I saw Mabel standing in the window—I *knew* the boss was not away), past Fred's Auto Body and Ollie's Bike Shop, I wandered and wondered. It was a cold spring day, and a strong wet wind cut through my thin jacket, but I kept walking. Thinking. There was no way I could go home yet.

Here's the thing I realized about having divine power. It's not like you just naturally know what to do with it. There is no omniscient being with a twenty-four seven helpline you can call and ask for guidance. There are no how-to books you can download, no *The 7 Habits of Highly Successful Supernatural Beings.* You're all alone here, just you and your omnipotent self. I'm not complaining about having supernatural power, per se, but I was wishing there was some sort of guide as to what the next steps should be.

Then I remembered *Impression, Sunrise.* Maybe that was it. Maybe he was telling me what to do. Yes, that had to be it. Monet's message was clear to me now. I knew what he had been telling me in his painting, the secret message hidden in the fog. *Declan,* he was saying, *you must use your power. Go to Paris and become the greatest artist in the world.* Of course he was. It was obvious once I thought about it.

I knew what to do. Monet told me to go to Paris, and that's where I was going to go. That's where I belonged, the city where I would realize my true destiny. Turning around and making my way home down these dreary streets, I felt a true sense of purpose. I had a goal in mind and an inner resolve as hard as steel and sharp as a razor. Now all I had to do was convince my parents to pay for my trip.

As I walked home I prepared my case, carefully honing my arguments, anticipating counterarguments and coming up with counter-counterarguments. My mother was a litigation lawyer; I had learned long ago how important it was to be prepared. By the time I swung open our front door, I was armed with a formidable stream of multilayered points of reasoning and was prepared for hours of debate.

My parents were buzzing around the kitchen, preparing for another grand occasion to celebrate another big something or other. For a couple somewhere over fifty years old, they were both trim and toned, and their dedication to fighting the ravages of age showed well on them. My father was still running marathons, a feat I couldn't imagine myself accomplishing, or wanting to. He was holding on to all his hair and his teeth looked an unnatural shade of white, which I suspected they were. My mother's personal trainer had been spending more time at the house than my father lately, and she could hold a plank for six minutes. I knew that because she challenged me to plank contests every other day. I accepted once, got beaten handily, and had ignored her entreaties ever since.

They also loved to entertain. There was a house full of guests almost every Saturday night, and ever since I was a child, I was part of the entertainment. My mother and father would dress me up and trot me out like a prizewinning pumpkin, where I was fawned over as a brilliant, charming, handsome, polite boy—and such an artist! I didn't mind. I truly believed the flattering comments our guests piled on the artwork my parents had framed and hanged on the walls. "Wonderful" "Incandescent!" "Dazzling!" I was told I was a genius so many times it was permanently ingrained in my psyche.

I took my usual seat at the kitchen island.

"How was work today, Declan?" my mom asked.

"It was alright, I guess. There was one little—"

"Good! I'm glad you're getting settled in already!" she said, sipping her wine. I could see her mentally calculating how many calories she had just consumed.

"Well, yes, I am, I guess, except for this one thing."

"There's always going to be something," my dad chimed in. "The thing is, you have to rise above it. Take the high road. People will respect you for it."

"This was a little bit more than that. You see, I—"

"It's not going to be easy every day. But you're doing it. We always believed in you, and now you're doing exactly what you wanted to do. You're so talented. We're proud of you."

My parents had been strong supporters and encouragers of dream-pursuing and goal-fulfilling for as long as I could remember. Their generation believed in raising children in an environment of positive attitudes and endless encouragement, where awards were given for participation and no one ever failed. They had bought into the doctrine without reservation. The books on our shelves were an ode to inducing self-actualization among the prepubescent: *10 Secrets to Happy Children*, *Raising a Confident Child*, *How to Raise Successful Kids*, *SuperParents! SuperKids!* They had told me, on what seemed like a daily basis, that I was smart, talented, and that I could do anything I wanted as long as I set my mind to it.

Which is why I was certain they would support me on my artistic sojourn to Paris.

"I quit my job today."

They stopped buzzing and looked at me.

"You did what?" They spoke at the same time, their eyes flashing and mouths hanging open in equal amounts.

"I quit my job today. I've decided to go to Paris and become an artist." I launched into my prepared speech. "This trip is essential to my personal growth and sense of self-worth. It will provide me with the opportunity to achieve fulfillment as per Maslow's Hierarchy of Needs." (I knew their soft spots, and I was not above exploiting them.) "And nurturing my talents will assist me in overcoming my special needs, which you have been aware of since I began counseling, and—"

"You didn't really quit. You couldn't. You just started!"

"I did. I quit my job. It wasn't very, um, fulfilling." An understatement, but I knew not to gild the lily. "I have decided that I will—"

"Why? Can you get it back?"

"I have to follow my dreams, like you always said, so that's what I'm doing, and—"

"What the hell were you thinking?" My father raised his voice at me. Not quite a full shout, perhaps, but far louder than anything I had heard before.

"I wasn't—"

"I know! You weren't being fulfilled! So what?" Now he was shouting full-out. It was a shock. No one, in my memory, had ever shouted inside our house before. "You don't quit your very first job after three days because it's not fulfilling!"

"If you'll just let me—"

"No." My father put his glass of wine down, a sure sign he was serious. "No. This is ridiculous. We've been supporting you for years. You're old enough to be on your own now. If you quit, that's on you. It's time you stood on your own two feet." He crossed his arms and raised his chin. "The holiday is over."

My mother crossed her arms and stood beside him. "Exactly how are you going to pay for a trip to Paris? I hope you don't think we're footing the bill. We're not. If you want to go, you can pay for it. And if you do stay here, you're going to be working. As a matter of fact, you can start paying rent. Otherwise, you can find your own place to live."

This line of attack was so unsuspected, I had no defense prepared. Pay my own way? Pay *rent*? Where was the dream-supporting? Where was the growth-fulfilling? More importantly, where was the offer to pay for my trip? I was still in a state of shock when the caterers arrived and took over my parents' attention. It was a welcome distraction for them while I tried to understand what had just happened.

The universe had never been on my side and had launched many dark conspiracies against me in my short life; it would take far too long to catalogue them all here. I had always believed that one of the most malevolent conspiracies was having the misfortune of being born into a stable and loving family of considerable wealth. My father was a well-known architect, my mother a lawyer with an international reputation. We had all the trappings of upper-class society: housekeepers, private schools, soft beds and silk sheets, vacations in St. Barts. The whole catastrophe.

Before you, gentle yet cynical reader, mock what may seem to be a youthful and spoiled existential angst, let me remind you that artists such as myself thrive on pain and anguish—suffering is like oxygen to us. It is the friction that makes the pearl in our oyster. How many times have I lain awake at night, wishing that I was living in a broken-down trailer with flat tires, a stove that didn't work, and a bitter, alcoholic mother crying over my long-lost father? When I think of the inspiration I could have gained from living in that beautiful, broken world, my heart cries. Heartbreak, poverty, misery—that was my *Paradise Lost*. The comfort and luxury of my sprawling suburban home served only to numb the mind and dull the spirit.

All this ran through my mind as I tried to decide what to do next. When my parents so quickly withdrew their support, they probably thought I would give in to their financial and emotional extortion, plead with them for the chance to stay home, and go begging for my job back. I didn't. Instead, I saw an opening. A chance to escape the life of cashmere and silk that had numbed my mind and dulled my creativity for so long. I saw an opportunity to break free from the silver spoon that had been jammed in my mouth the day I was born.

They didn't think I could make it on my own. But they were wrong. I would show them I was made of tougher stuff than they thought. I didn't need their money or their career advice. I'd saved up a little money over the years, for one thing. Also, a credit card company had sent me a personal letter only that morning, informing me that I had already been preapproved for a substantial sum of money. Clearly, the credit card company had more faith in me than my own parents.

I stood up, proud, defiant, and independent. "Have a great party," I said. "I'm going to Paris."

I was on a plane by late the next evening, had taken a seat in a street café by the following afternoon, and had fallen in love before dinner.

Bienvenue à Paris.

Walking through Arrivals and into the great halls of the Charles de Gaulle airport, I was overwhelmed by the scale of it all. There were hundreds of glistening windows with shiny chrome accents displaying the latest Dior, Hermès, Gucci, and Ferragamo designs—alien names on the streets of Georgetown, where we would have sacrificed every child under the age of five for a Banana Republic. It was a new world. A kaleidoscope of people, thousands of them, were covered in all manner of color and style, shouting in a dozen unidentifiable languages as they passed by. I got lost several times. Just finding my luggage was a journey worthy of two Tolkien novels.

I took a selfie standing by the welcome sign in the airport. Typed *Bienvenue à Paris* and posted it on all my social media sites. Read that, my former classmates, and sigh a long, bitter sigh of regret. I am here, and you are not. During my long years in high school, I had been the one who was never invited, the one who sat alone at the front of class pretending to ignore the jeers and smirks directed at me from jocks, cheerleaders, jet-setters, and other intellectually stillborn students behind me. Ha! Take that, you cruel barbarians, condemned as you are to a life of slavish drudgery and primitive amusements! You have insulted me for the last time. As I wander the fabled City of Lights, lounging in legendary patisseries and dining on fresh pastries, I wish you only the worst. Revenge is a dish best served with freshly baked croissants and melted garlic butter.

Post successful. I shut off my phone and threw it into the waste bin. *Au revoir*, phone. Hello, freedom. This was not a journey that would be tracked by the trolls on social media. There would be no likes, shares, comments, followers, or unfollowers. I had been loosed from the surly bonds of social media and was free to experience the joys of Parisian life on my own terms, without judgment.

I waved down a cab, lifted my luggage into the trunk, climbed in, and suffered the first dent in my idealized vision of Paris. I had imagined that everyone here, even the cabdrivers, would be different: more debonair and cultured than in Georgetown. I expected them to be wearing a nice red beret and Vuitton scarf and reading Proust in their spare time. This driver was a grizzled and grumbling old man who smelled of cooked onions and seared meat. I greeted him with a cheery *bonjour*, but he just snorted and lit a cigarette. Before I had fastened my seat belt, he hit the gas pedal and the car jumped forward like a gunshot. He raced out of the airport and onto the highway, the pedal pressed tightly against the floor. The g-forces pressed my cheeks back into my face as the cab filled with smoke. Weaving in and out of traffic, shouting a steady stream of French obscenities, and waving a middle finger at every car that he passed, he drove like he was in the world's angriest race.

"Destination?" he shouted at me, brown spittle covering the glass between us.

I wondered when he was going to ask. "Forty-five Rue Laffitte," I answered.

The driver mumbled a few indecipherable expletives and yanked the steering wheel to the right, turned down a side street, executed a U-turn, and sideswiped another vehicle as he turned the first corner. My stomach went sideways and I was gripping the door handle with all the strength I could summon. Families were chased from walkways, dogs ran for their lives, and cars dodged in last-second attempts at avoiding head-on collisions as he sped down the street.

"I'm in no hurry," I managed to say.

He shook his head and muttered "stupid English" under his breath. At that moment, the car swerved into the other lane and a screaming cacophony of honking horns from oncoming traffic warned the driver of an impending disaster. He cut back into his lane, but too quickly, and lost control of the vehicle. We swerved and skidded around running pedestrians before we came to a stop in the middle of a small courtyard crowded with women and children. I sat in the back, eyes clenched shut, struggling to breathe, waiting for the screams of dying children to fill the air. There was nothing. After a few moments I opened one eye and saw people casually walking around the car, as if it were part of the architecture. Was this normal to them?

"This is fine, thanks." I opened the door and grabbed my luggage.

The driver rolled down his window. "Sixty euros," he barked. I heard him muttering obscenities at me, just loud enough that I could hear every word even if I couldn't understand them. I threw some bills at him and sped-walked away. Perhaps I should not have been so surprised: I had read about French drivers. But it still took me a few minutes to shake the feeling that Paris wasn't exactly what I thought it was going to be.

It took a few blocks to recover, but I settled down and began to feel normal again. I kept walking, and the more I walked, the more I loved. I could see why Paris was Paris. For one: the people. They were so—well, French. *Á la mode!* A bracelet, a scarf, a hat, the cut of their hair, or the material of their shirt, it seemed like everyone had a fashion statement to make and they did it with elegance, simplicity, and personal style. I resolved to up my fashion game *tout de suite.* But it wasn't just the people. It was everything.

I must confess, I had experienced great anxiety on my flight here. From the moment I walked in the doors of one airport to the moment I walked out of the doors of another,

I suffered waves of self-doubt and anxiety that left me sweating and sick to my stomach. There wasn't a minute where I wasn't thinking I should return home to the safety of my old, comfortable life. I had never been on my own before. But now, now that I was here, all that anxiety went away. Every step I took, every breath, convinced me once again that I had made the right decision.

I loved it all. I loved the miniature ladies walking with their miniature dogs down the narrow, tangled streets. I loved the old men who sat alone at small tables in street cafés, hugging glasses of wine and reading heavy books. I loved the scents of fresh croissants, chocolate, flowers, and baking bread that floated through the air as I strolled by old brick buildings, past store windows filled with bundles of cheese wrapped in string, old-school butchers and fishmongers, musicians and street artists, grocers and crêperies, high-end fashion stores and grand hotels. It was all so perfect that I forgot where I was going until I saw the sign for Rue Laffitte.

Why had I chosen Rue Laffitte as my first stop in Paris? There were no ancient monuments, museums, or art galleries here, no fresh markets or hidden patisseries to discover, and no celebrities gazed out from the apartment windows lining its sidewalks. There was only one reason for me to be here, and that was this: Monsieur Claude Monet, the founder of French Impressionism, the creator of light and color, the Master who had sent me to Paris through a secret message hidden in the fog of *Impression, Sunrise* was born here, at 45 Rue Laffitte, on a chilly Paris morning, November 14, 1840.

I looked up and imagined him as a young man, swinging open the old wooden door of his apartment at the top of the stairs all those years ago. His long, thick black hair was pulled straight back and that famous beard was just starting to make its appearance. I could see him scurrying down the stairs, carefully avoiding the father who kept insisting that he should go into the family grocery business. Walking downtown, paper and pencils in hand, where he would sit and sketch caricatures for tourists and sell them for twenty francs apiece. Then, he was just a young kid who wanted to create art. It would be years before he became famous, a century before his works would sell for over one hundred million dollars. He was my inspiration, role model, and career counselor.

The sight of Monet's home filled me with inspiration, and I couldn't wait to get started. My own apartment, reserved with my new credit card, was less than an hour away. I ran all the way there, dragging my luggage behind me. All I wanted to do now was get rid of my bags, go find a street café, and get to work. I found the building and checked in. The room was a bland studio in a bland six-story apartment, no more than five hundred square feet, but it was more than enough for me. I ditched my luggage, grabbed a few pencils and my sketch pad, locked the door, and hurried back downtown.

Heaven and bliss. Every time I turned a corner, I fell in love with the city again. This was not only the City of Lights, it was the City of Love, the City of Food, Culture, Art, and Style. It was the birthplace of Dadaism, surrealism, modern art, Monet, Voltaire, Gauguin, de Beauvoir, Degas, Rodin, the baguette, la raclette and escargot, the mimosa and absinthe, nouvelle cuisine, the Enlightenment and existentialism, Gothic architecture, the bikini, the little black dress, and the guillotine. This was a city with history. It was impossible not to think back to where I had come from and compare. The most famous person I could name from Georgetown was Brian Hayward, a backup goalie for the Montreal Canadiens.

I wandered the streets, happy and content. The depression and anxiety that had become such a regular part of my life vanished. Observing people, studying the covers in secondhand bookstores, the doors on museums and churches, watching old ladies barking at their little dogs, the sausages and pigs' feet hanging in butchers' windows and jazz playing inside the bistros. Four thousand miles from home, I felt at home for the first time in my life.

I turned a corner and came upon Café Le Petit Pont. A faded red-and-white-striped awning leaned over several rickety metal tables surrounded by rickety metal chairs. Chalkboard signs advertised Croques and Oeufs and Gourmand Plats, the scent of butter and smelly cheese floated in the air, and thin, impeccably dressed waitstaff ignored the shouts of customers with looks of amused condescension. Café Le Petit Pont fulfilled every hazy dream I had of what a sidewalk café in Paris should be. The only offbeat note was the flashing neon sign advertising half-price Miller Lite during happy hour—otherwise, pure Paris. I grabbed a seat and waited.

"Hello, *bonjour.* What would you like?"

I looked up and saw the Queen of Heaven, the Madonna, and the Goddess Aphrodite gazing down on me while a chorus of angels sang from above.

Blue eyes the shape of Chinese almonds; long, straight blond hair blowing just slightly, perfectly in the wind, framing a round and exquisitely bored face. Perfect, yes; and yet, not society's version of perfect. She had imperfections, if one compared her to what the beauty experts would have prescribed. Her teeth were bent a little the wrong way, those almond eyes were not quite aligned, her face was rounder, cheekbones lower, and nose larger than the accepted ideal— yes, she had imperfections, but it was those imperfections that I loved more than anything. It was her imperfections that made her beautiful. It is, after all, our imperfections that make the world a perfect place.

I looked into those deep-set eyes, she looked at me, and something passed between us. It seemed as if our spirits had become instantly fused together. I felt like I could feel everything she had ever felt, see everything she had ever seen, know everything she had ever known. As if her mind had been AirDropped into my own.

I could have written her entire life story in one draft, no corrections required. I don't know how, but I knew that she came from an aristocratic French family. Not from the top ranks of royalty, but close. I bet her father was a duke. Yes, a duke. I was sure of it. I could see her in that world, sitting through all those elegant royal banquets, nibbling through luxurious dinners with gentle-voiced waiters and their long, rolled *r*'s and thirteen-course meals and endless gossip while jewelry clinked politely in the background. She had been there, I knew, smiled at all the right moments, but with her mouth only. Missing something, or someone, but not knowing what or who it was. Surrounded by people but all alone. Thinking of other worlds, withdrawn and remote. She was Manet's bored waitress at the Folies Bergère. I also knew, somehow, that her name was Chloé.

Gazing back at her, eyes wide, tongue frozen tightly in place, I struggled to maintain my intellectual-detached-artistic-global-traveler persona.

"A glass of white wine. Chablis. *Merci,*" I managed.

"Chablis?" she repeated, pronouncing it *Chablee.* Wait. Wasn't there an *s*-sound in *Chablis?* It's not pronounced *Chab-liss?* Admittedly, my French was not very *bon.*

"I'll be right back." She placed a napkin on the table. "American?" she asked.

If I had known we would be having a conversation, I would have mentally prepared for it. I wasn't. My mind had already scurried into a series of carnal images of the two of us together and it was impossible to stop. I responded in a voice an octave or two higher than I would have preferred. "Georgetown."

"Georgetown?" She didn't sound impressed.

"Well, yes. No. San Francisco, actually," I added, in a desperate bid to sound interesting. "First Georgetown. Then, whoosh, off to San Francisco."

She appeared justifiably puzzled. "I'll get your wine."

A voice like fresh white truffles. As she floated away, I thought perhaps the universe had finally warmed up to me. She was barely five feet tall and must have weighed under ninety pounds—a miniature goddess in Doc Martens. She wore a T-shirt with a faded New Order logo printed on the front and ripped jeans, but they were the kind of T-shirt and ripped jeans you could wear in the front row at a Vogue fashion show. The former-heroin-addict-turned-raw-foods-and-yoga-addict look. The I-don't-care-what-I-look-like look. The *enfant terrible* of the chattering class.

I pulled out my sketch pad, my favorite pencil (Pilot Croquis, graphite, 4B), and started to sketch.

"Here you go." She placed the wineglass on my table, eyes moving to my sketch pad. "Are you an artist?" There may have been a smile. Was she already falling in love with me?

"*Oui.* Graduated a few months ago," I said with a nod and a casual shrug.

"Congratulations." She nodded and casually shrugged back. "I have two more years to go. I attend the École nationale supérieure des Beaux-Arts. Where did you go?" she asked.

"Laurentian," I said, pronouncing it *low-rent-she-un*, hoping it sounded exotic and exclusive. The look on her face suggested I had not been successful and I panicked: what if she thought I was just some boor from a small town and a small school? In the face of that panic I decided to make it more prestigious and impressive sounding. Fast. "It's in San Francisco," I lied. "Where I lived, after Georgetown, after I ran away from home. Anyway, it's a very exclusive school. There are only five students admitted every year, so it's possible you might not have heard of it."

"Sounds nice." She smiled.

That lie, told in a spontaneous act of desperation, would cost me a lot of anxiety and suffering later. But for now, her smile made it all worthwhile.

After she disappeared inside the restaurant, I sipped my wine and sketched. More specifically, I tried to sketch, tried to put the inspiration I had felt after my visit to Monet's old home onto paper. But there was nothing. I could barely put two lines on the page. It was a line here, a line there, crumple the paper into a ball and start again. Everything felt wrong. Every time I tried to draw, I heard Chloé's voice, her footsteps, her laugh. I would try again, making ever-greater efforts to focus on the blank page in front of me, but my imagination would interrupt with images more carnal than the last. I'd try again, but then I'd catch a side-eyed glimpse of her, and another supernova of exploding stars would go off in my head.

The soul of an artist follows no simple path. My heart had taken off in another direction, found a new passion, and as much as I tried to ignore it and focus on my work, it refused to cooperate. After an hour, I gave up and put my pencil away. What was I going to do? My inspiration had vanished. My muse had abandoned me, left in a jealous rage over the Doc Martens-wearing Aphrodite I had fallen in love with. Which left me with a difficult choice.

There comes a time in the life of every true artist that he or she must make the supreme sacrifice. Art or love. That was it. There was no middle ground. For me, that time was now. I had to leave. It was the most difficult decision in my life, a choice both cruel and painful, but I had to do it. Chloé and I were meant to be together here on earth, but I had a higher power to answer to—Monet had not sent me here to fall in love. So it had to be *au revoir, mon amour.* Perhaps we will meet again. I finished my wine with a heart full of regret. Got up and walked away. Turned around once, in ultra-super-slow motion. If anyone had been watching, they would have been in tears. But I had worlds to conquer and a destiny to fulfill, and couldn't allow myself to be sidetracked by a pair of deep-set almond-shaped eyes.

Three

I wandered the streets, searching for another café to sketch in, passing the ancient landmarks, iconic facades, and statues that lined the streets of Paris. God-like men and women in flowing robes on winged horses and chariots, proud birds and chiseled lions—you couldn't go a hundred yards without running into another ancient marble ode to someone or something. It seemed to me it wouldn't hurt them to send one of these to Georgetown; one statue wouldn't be missed here, and it would easily be the highlight of our entire community.

Turning a corner, I had a fresh view of the imposing church I had seen from the sidewalk of Rue Laffitte. *La Basilique du Sacré-Cœur de Montmartre*, the magnificent Basilica of the Sacred Heart of Montmartre, stared down at me and I stood and stared back. The grand building seemed to be calling me, and I couldn't help but listen. I walked toward it, up the hill, and just when I was getting close, I stopped. Felt something, but couldn't quite tell what it was. Looked around, listened, waited, wondered. There was a sense that I'd been here before. Maybe it was the way the street corner bent, or something about the slope of the sidewalk, but yes, I had seen this place before. Or read about it. Where? I thought and thought. And just when I was about to give up, it came to me. I'd seen a photograph of this street in one of my art books. I was in one of the holiest places on earth.

Catholics have their Vatican, Muslims have their Mecca, and artists have Montmartre. It is the epicenter of the artistic universe, the North Star of aspiring painters all over the world, the cradle of modern art. Montmartre, a village perched high on a hill that rewarded its visitors with the greatest view of the greatest city on earth and artists a place they could call home. This was the neighborhood that provided many of history's most exalted artists with an affordable incubator where they could play, imagine, and create. They came from all over the world, attracted by its low rent, bohemian lifestyle, and flexible moral code. These were the streets where the dreams of Picasso, Utrillo, Matisse, Braque, Modigliani, Toulouse-Lautrec, and so many others turned into the art we still worship today.

My mother always said everything happens for a reason, and for once I agreed with her. My arrival here offered concrete proof that my life had been predetermined, my fate as a famous artist already decided. Monet had sent me here, and Montmartre had made it official. All I had to do was follow the stars unfolding before me.

Of course, Montmartre is not the same rundown bohemian refuge it was a hundred years ago. Today, the streets were crammed with bug-eyed tourists and every foot of the center square was jammed to its borders with dozens of amateur painters. This sacred space had been turned into an outdoor flea market filled with men and women wearing cheap red berets and sketching cartoon caricatures. Still, you can't take the Montmartre out of Montmartre. The bistros, patisseries, and chocolate shops that circled the square back then had new menus and stratospherically higher prices, but in the most important ways they remained unchanged. I walked around the square, feeling the creative air of the place soak into my pores. There was a feeling here, something different about this place. A spirit you could see and touch. It was strong, tangible, and unmistakably real, and I felt it as clearly as the brick sidewalks under my feet.

Grabbing a table in the least touristy café I could find, I found a seat in the sun, ordered a triple espresso, and pulled out my sketch pad and pencils. Fresh inspiration had come over me, and this time I wasn't going to let it go.

Declan Tucker, I wrote on the page. Then I wrote it again. And again. *Declan Tucker. Declan Tucker.* I looked at my signature, compared it with the signatures of other famous artists I had studied: the tidy, loopy doodle of Monet; the stretched, chiseled signature of Picasso; the childlike scrawl of Vincent. My signature suddenly seemed important to me. Simply *Declan?* *DT?* Obviously, *Tucker* would never do. *Declan Tucker* seemed most appropriate, with *Declan T.* a close second. Should I use scrawls and loops? How about a big *D?* I tried a few dozen variations, imagining how it would appear to art students and professors in future classrooms, or under the careful gaze of an art curator's eye a hundred years from now. This is the kind of stuff you have to think about when you're planning for immortality.

"Pilot Croquis?" a deep, drawling voice behind me said. "Ugh."

My pencil. Someone had just insulted my pencil.

I looked around, then gazed at the speaker sitting alone at a table a few feet behind me. He was slightly older than I was, with long, ragged black hair pulled straight back, a thin, dark face, and darker eyes. His dirty jeans and worn black T-shirt contrasted with a red silk scarf that looked like it might have been Hermès. There was a shredded backpack on the ground beside his chair and the faintest smile on his lips. I couldn't tell whether it was friendly or sarcastic.

"Try Staedtler," he said. "6B."

"I prefer 4B," I said. "And just so you know? This pencil has a retractable—"

"It is an awful pencil. Absolutely horrible." He had a thick French accent, and spoke slowly, intensely, and deliberately. Pronouncing every syllable as if it were a complete sentence. *Hore-yee-blah.*

I went back to my signature, ignoring the gross interruption of my work and the insult to my favorite pencil. He didn't know what he was talking about.

"Pilot Croquis is a bourgeois pencil," he said. *Booj-waah.*

What this decrepit munchkin clearly did not know was that the Pilot Croquis was a carefully handcrafted structure, featuring a sleek and durable chrome barrel, a broad ergonomic grip, and confident strokes. Anyone who read the packaging would know that. I started to correct him, but then I thought, *To what end?* What could I possibly achieve by explaining my choice of pencil to this rude street urchin? I decided to ignore him.

I flipped to a blank page and turned to study the figures at the tables in front of me. Yes, that one. I selected one of the older artists as my first subject. A man with a grizzled face and long, unkempt gray hair covering his head. His expression recalled late Monet to me, even if his work recalled early Disney. After a few attempts, I felt that I had a good likeness of his facial outline, including his glasses, nose, and beard.

"What is it you are drawing?" my shabby neighbor asked.

Don't answer this French street punk, I told myself. I checked my jacket for my wallet and kept sketching. Focused.

"Is that a beard? It doesn't look like a beard," the irritating presence beside me weighed in. "Or a face. You should make the eyes smaller."

As if I needed the advice of an itinerant drifter.

"It looks like a cartoon of a fish," he said. "The hands look like fins."

"It's an interpretation," I blurted out, straining to mask my growing hostility.

"Well, it's a poor interpretation. His lips look weird."

That was it. I'd had quite enough. I turned around and stared, unblinking, with my chin up. In Georgetown, I had accepted the insults of my classmates with a silent stare, unable or uninterested in fighting back. But that was the old Declan. The Georgetown Declan. I was a different Declan now. I was The Paris Declan. And The Paris Declan stood up for himself. I would fight him if I had to. "You are irritating and rude. Now go away and leave me alone. I'm creating something important here, and you are interrupting me." Besides, the lips did not look weird.

The ragged young man leaned back in his chair, put his arms behind his head, and smiled. He seemed almost impressed. But he didn't say a word or move a muscle.

I stood up, fists clenched, ready to launch into a new round of insults and more, if I had to. Then something caught the corner of my eye and distracted me. I spun around, unbelieving, doubting what I had seen.

It was impossible. It couldn't be. But it was.

He was sitting on a stool in front of one of the artists, having his portrait done. It was Neil, my former sales manager, the wobbly man himself. The man I had murdered. No, not murdered, accidentally murdered—no, not accidentally murdered even, it wasn't any kind of murder, at worst it was involuntary manslaughter, really just innocent collateral damage. But it was him, sitting, posing, looking as alive as he ever had. He looked over, saw me, grinned his goofy grin, and waved.

No. No. I closed my eyes and tried to shut out the world and swallow my anxiety. Once again, inspiration had been taken from me—first by an angel, then by a beggar, and now by a ghost. I packed up my sketch pad and pencil and got away from there as quickly as I could. Wandered around, down one street and another, walking until my mind was clear and I figured it was safe to go back. After an hour, I returned to the square and looked warily around. Neil was not there. (Of course he had never been there. I had just imagined it. A guilty conscience, perhaps.) It seemed safe to start again, to try and channel the inspiration I had lost. There was an empty table at the far end of the square. I sat down, ordered an overpriced cappuccino, and looked twice at the building I was sitting in front of. For the second time that day, I was struck with a sense that I'd seen this before. For the second time, I realized I had.

His name was Pablo Diego then. He came to Montmartre from Spain, traveling by train, horse-drawn omnibus, and foot. A man with style, dressed in loose sweaters with high collars and long, flowing jackets, filled to the brim with a wide-eyed confidence that stopped just short of megalomania. Montmartre was a squalid wasteland at the time, full of broken-down buildings and dirty streets, but it was a wasteland with a reputation as a sanctuary for artists. It was the place to be, so that's where he belonged. The rent and wine were cheap, the women were easy, and there were many others like him—fellow artists without money, means, or anything but a passion for art and a disdain for the establishment. That alone would make the pilgrimage worthwhile. The local media had been tipped off that one of Spain's leading artists was on his way. This wasn't by chance, for he had done the tipping-off. It was 1900, and Picasso was just a boy of nineteen. In time, his paintings would become some of the most sought-after works of art in history, selling for a hundred million euros and more. But now, all he wanted to do was have fun, chase women, and change the world. And he would do it here, in Montmartre, working in a dilapidated building they called Le Batcau-Lavoir.

The building I was now sitting in front of.

It wasn't the *same* building. The old artists' home had been converted to a modern artists' workshop, complete with air conditioning and elevators, but he had lived here—I could feel some of his original spirit pouring out of those windows. Felt what I thought Picasso must have felt when he first walked through these doors. He was just nineteen. Nineteen! The number kept going through my mind, ringing like the first schoolyard bell after a long and wasted summer. He was four and a half years younger than I was. By then, Picasso had already established a reputation as a genius, had his work hanging in respected galleries, won distinguished awards. And me? I had little to show for over two decades on this earth but a pad full of sketches, a degree, and a dead body.

My attention turned back to the building in front of me. Staring at those holy gates, I could imagine what life would have been like in Le Bateau-Lavoir in 1900. A group of young, starving artists like me. Living in a small, filthy room without heat or insulation, sleeping on a lumpy mattress on the floor, cold and hungry. Mice running along the baseboards, cockroaches crawling on the ceiling. Nothing but a few francs in my torn pockets: just enough to pay for painting supplies, a little food, beer, and a regular supply of opium.

And painting. Painting life on the streets—real life in all its ragged glory. Delivery men in faded topcoats on horses, prostitutes laughing and flirting outside the dance halls, wrinkled men wandering the streets selling fish and cheese, snow-covered children in torn clothes playing on the sidewalks. How happy I would have been to live here then. Yet another slight the universe had bestowed upon me—I had been born a century too late. Still, I would have loved to go inside, just to see it, to get some sense of how they would have lived then.

"Monsieur Croquis. Welcome to the artists' lair."

I looked over to see the beggar who had interrupted me at the café earlier today. He was standing too close, leaning on the metal rail separating the paying customers from everyone else, and for the second time in a few hours he had invaded my space and interrupted my thoughts. He also smelled a bit. Why was this vagrant stalking me? Once again, I tried to ignore him and wished he would go away.

"We should go inside," he said. That slow, pondering voice.

"We are not permitted to go inside," I informed him. "Access to the Le Bateau-Lavoir is limited to those who—"

He shook his head, a thin grimace crossing his face. "Limited? By whose decree? This building is part of history. No one has the right to lock us out. It belongs to all of us. I would like to go inside," he said, "so that's what I'm going to do. You should join me. It's yours, too." Spinning around on his heels, he walked toward the building and disappeared into the side alley.

I didn't want to do it. What I wanted to do was paint for a few hours, then go back to my apartment, read a little, watch some television, consider my future with Chloé, have a glass of warm milk, and go to bed early. Let this street urchin risk arrest and prison for breaking and entering while I prudently walked away. But I couldn't. I knew he was right. That building was history and it belonged to everybody. And besides, I really did want to look inside and see where they had lived, to better imagine what their life had been like. So, some invisible power made me follow him right into the side alley, where I found myself at the rear door of Le Bateau-Lavoir.

I stood back, not quite committed, and watched as he smiled and nodded at me, pushed on the door a few times, and, finding it locked, gave it a series of loud, hard kicks with the heel of his thick black boot. The door grudgingly swung open, a loud screech calling out to anyone within a few blocks that there was a break-in occurring. He turned and looked at me.

"It's open." He bowed and held out his hand, palm upward. A shabby royal butler inviting me into this forbidden castle. "Are you?"

I was.

We walked inside. The lights were off, the halls dark but for the pale glow of the late afternoon sun shining through the windows. I made my way slowly down the empty hallway, my fellow trespasser close behind me. Our footsteps squeaked on the linoleum floor and bounced off the Wimborne White walls. I smelled oil, clay, cleaner, and turpentine. A series of small rooms beckoned with their doors wide open. Everything was in shadows, but I could make out paints, brushes, torches, chisels, and hammers lying on desks and tables; large and small canvases lined up on floors and resting on easels; all manner of sculptures and installations, books, odd objects, and cabinets of curiosities; modern art and classical art and works that defied classification.

It was exciting, liberating, and terrifying. Coming from a long tradition of strict law-followers and social-norms enforcers, the very thought of walking in that building elicited a cold white fear in me. How could it do anything else? My brain had been programmed from childhood to Obey the Rules. The wires had been set firmly in place, and it was too late to unwind them. So, while one-quarter of my brain was telling me I had every right to be here, the other three-quarters began to carefully itemize all the reasons I should not.

One: the most obvious—breaking and entering is against the law. Two: Parents' reaction, should they find out. So disappointed! Remember, my mother was a lawyer. Three: Oh, I could find a thousand more reasons for me not to be here, if I were to dig into the deepest recesses of my inner self. But I wasn't going to do that. My rational self believed what the itinerant drifter had said: this was a historical building and it belonged to everybody, including me. So, I fought every single microorganism of my genome structure and kept walking. My stomach was in knots and my hands shook. But for the first time in my life, I felt like a badass.

"Croquis. In here."

I had almost forgotten my illicit friend. Turning around, I then walked back and found him in a small kitchen that held little more than a round table and an old fridge. He opened the fridge door, pulled out a bottle of wine, twisted the cap off, and drank from the bottle. Then he handed it to me.

"My name is Gaétan. Nice to meet you."

"Declan." I grabbed the bottle, forgetting my fear of germs, and added theft and public alcohol consumption to my ever-expanding crime sheet. We moved to one of the artist's rooms and grabbed a seat on the floor.

"I am sorry about earlier today," he said. "I was just having a little fun with you."

"That's okay. I was just joking, too. Same."

He smiled. "What land do you hail from, Croquis?"

"San Fran." As you are aware, my cherished reader, this was more than a thousand miles from the truth. The fabrication I had used to buff up my life's résumé with Chloé had returned to serve a similar purpose with Gaétan. I was becoming a serial liar. One day I would speak to a counselor about this, but at that moment in time the lie offered a more interesting story than the dull truth. For some reason, I was anxious to impress this thin, young nomad. I drank again and handed him the bottle. It was almost empty. Didn't we just open that?

"Why did you come to Paris?" he asked.

"I came here to be an artist. A great artist. To paint, to create new forms of visual expression..." The more I drank, the more I talked. "My art has no paradigms. It's beyond human expression. It's about our most basic feelings, our fears, hopes, our purest essence." I remember using the word *paradigm* six times in one sentence. He didn't question what it meant. Gaétan seemed to know what I was talking about, even if I didn't. "I'm trying to give shape to a limitless universe, et al."

"What is *et al*? No, please, don't tell me," he said. "But...yes. I wonder what it is that makes an artist great."

"I don't know..." I hadn't really thought of it that way. "Monet is great. Picasso. Van Gogh. Basquiat. Hirst, sometimes."

"Because they're famous? Because people pay millions of dollars to—"

"No! It's because...because..."

"There are many brilliant artists no one knows. Have you heard of Davis? Ali? Greenwood?"

I had never even heard one of those names. Not one. "Absolutely. Are you kidding me? I love Davis, Ali, and Greenwall. You know."

Gaetan had a French accent, Black skin, ragged but stylish clothes and an air of cosmopolitan sophistication. Everything he said sounded like a multilayered metaphor for something deep and important, like the musings of some ancient Greek philosopher. The more wine that worked its way into my bloodstream, the more profound he seemed. He pulled a second bottle of wine out of the fridge, opened it, and handed it to me.

"What do you want to do, Declan?"

I told him about the fame and glory I expected to achieve, all the money I wanted to make, and what I thought my signature should look like.

He smiled and shook his head.

An hour later—maybe two—we were discussing Monet's brushstrokes when a cacophony of screaming sirens and screeching tires came from the front of the building. The sound of car doors opening and slamming shut followed seconds later. The police were here. Hundreds of them, I was certain. We were surrounded. I sat still, eyes wide and hands trembling, unable to move. This was it. The end of my life as I knew it. Busted. I put my hands over my head and shut my eyes, waiting for the police to run into the room and slap handcuffs on me.

A door opened at the front of the building. Feet pounded on the floor. They were in the hall. I opened one eye, expecting them to rush in at any second. What I saw instead was Gaétan stand up, close the door, make his way over to the window, and jimmy it open. He looked back at me.

"We should go for a walk," he said, pulling himself up and gracefully climbing out.

I was shaking so much it was difficult to get off the floor, yet I somehow managed to get on my feet and make my way to the window. I heard the police shouting, getting closer, and just held it together long enough to lift myself up and push myself out. Dropped face down in a garden of thick shrubs and vines. I got up, brushed myself off, and stumbled along after Gaétan. We walked down a pathway that trailed behind the building.

The pathway was bordered with dense trees and hedges, offering a near-complete cover for our getaway. Gaétan walked ahead of me slowly, as if this were just a casual stroll in a friendly park. The pathway ended after a couple hundred yards, and we came upon an alley that led to a quiet street. The sirens faded from hearing, and I started to relax. Gaétan seemed to know where he was going and what he was doing, and for some reason that felt like enough. We walked through the streets, the warm night and soft glow of the setting sun lighting up row after row of Parisian scenes like a never-ending Gustave Caillebotte painting.

Everything had changed. Within forty-eight hours, I had left home, fallen in love with a city and a woman, made a friend, and become a wanted man. Declan Tucker was now a criminal. But did I care? Hahaha. Not a bit. I was free and happy. We'd made a clean escape. It was the perfect crime! I was invincible. So much for normative moral codes and social orders! From now on I make my own rules. My foot slipped out from under me and I fell, but rolled over and got up in one fluid, perfectly orchestrated maneuver. What was I thinking? Oh yes. I make my own rules. I do what I want. Drink when I want. Hahaha! I was Big Badass Declan. More wine, please.

"We should go break ina—ina gallery over there." I pointed across the street to Gaétan, who glanced over but kept walking. He couldn't hear, so I shouted, "Gaétan! We should go and break ina place." I was in the mood for a crime spree, breaking into art galleries all over the city and stealing their wine.

Gaétan stopped and turned around. "I'm sorry. I must be going."

"What? Com'n." I didn't want to stop now. Our career as professional criminals was just beginning. "We shoulda break ina tha place." I was dimly aware that I was nodding furiously, but less certain as to why. Then I got dizzy and fell down.

"Another time, perhaps. For now, *bonne soirée.*" He turned around and walked away.

"Wait, Gaétan." As I sat and watched him leave, it dawned on me that I knew nothing about this strange alien. "Who are you? Where are you from?"

He stopped, turned, bowed, and saluted. "We all come from the same place," he said, and disappeared into the Paris streets.

What the hell was that supposed to mean? Who was he? I got up, and stood on the street wondering what to do when a passerby bumped into me and I fell down again. As an inexperienced consumer of alcohol, this wasn't a familiar situation. I sat on the sidewalk and tried to figure out my next seat. Step. My next step. Why was the sidewalk moving? I shut my eyes, trying to stop it.

I woke up and saw a row of flashing red lights in front of me. My first thought was that I'd fallen asleep on the couch watching *NCIS: New Orleans*, only this couch was concrete and the lights were real. When two men in shadows walked toward me, shining their flashlights in my face and speaking unfathomable French, I remembered where I was. The police helped me up and carried me to the back of their car while I tried to not throw up.

"What is your name?"

"Declah?" I seemed to have developed a slur. "Declan Tucker?" There. That was better.

"Do you have any identification, Declan?"

I felt my pockets for my wallet. There wasn't one. Searched the seats of the car and floor, and it wasn't there either. My wallet was gone, and my shoes were missing.

"It was here," I said. "I don't know. What happened. To it."

"Where do you live, Declan?"

The next thing I remember was being helped out of the back seat of their car in front of my apartment.

"You should be more careful, my friend," the policeman said. "You have made some poor decisions." He got me on the sidewalk and climbed back in his car. "Now drink some water, and get some sleep." The strobe lights shut off and the car disappeared down the street.

Miraculously, I still had the key to the apartment in the pocket of my jeans. I crawled inside and threw myself on the folding bed. I was half drunk and fully hungover. My head felt like it had been cracked open with a sledgehammer, my stomach was in a state of armed rebellion, and my bed felt like it was a roller coaster. My wallet and shoes had been stolen and I had committed a felony. Forcing my eyes shut, I tried desperately to go to sleep and forget everything. It took forever, but when sleep finally came it offered no escape.

To sleep, perchance to dream: and there's the rub. Dream I did, but not of celestial nymphs and heavenly winged horses. I dreamed of Neil. The rotund one kept forcing himself into my dark sleeping subconscious. Neil looked like a flabby suburban poltergeist in casual weekend wear, floating by in a starry blue universe, waving and smiling brightly from the comfort of a lime-green La-Z-Boy chair. He even had the footrest up. If he was a demon, he was the most affable demon I had ever seen. That didn't make him less of a monster. I pulled the pillow over my head and tried to force him to go away, but he wouldn't.

My first day in Paris had turned into a nightmare.

Four

When I woke up, the sun was gazing down at me through the thin white curtains in my suite. My mouth was dry and my pounding head informed me that I had grossly miscalculated my ability to consume wine. It was tempting to stay in bed until I recovered, but I had already lost a day and I wasn't going to lose another. Picasso wouldn't have taken the day off. Monet wouldn't have taken the day off. Renoir might have taken the day off, but look at his work—trees painted with branches that looked like flying snakes, thin girls with bulging biceps that looked like a professional wrestler's—and you would agree that he should have gotten up and gone back to work.

I made my way to the street and grabbed a table at the nearest outdoor café, then ordered a café crème and a brioche. Lucky for me, my passport and credit card had not been stolen, having been stored in the safety-deposit box— traveling with my parents had taught me a few things about security. The waiter, a thin, bored-looking middle-aged man with a tall forehead, nodded and emitted a condescending grunt and sauntered off. I had allowed myself to get distracted from my holy mission here and swore it would never happen again. If I was going to achieve eternal fame and immortality while I was young enough to enjoy it, I had better get started.

I needed to find inspiration fast, and I knew exactly where to look. One more café crème and a second brioche later I was on my way to the Louvre. What better place could there be to get inspired? If Montmartre was the cradle of art, the Louvre was the church. For over eight hundred years, it had served as a testament to the glory of France, as well as their talent for ransacking other countries. Today it stands as the world's greatest art museum, the distinguished resting place of over thirty-five thousand of the most exquisite achievements humanity had created over the last seven thousand years. Da Vinci, Michelangelo, Vermeer, Poussin, Leyster, Botticelli, Raphael, and Rembrandt all had works hanging on these walls. And before long, so would Declan Tucker.

Walking into that famous glass-and-steel pyramid, descending the stairway into the grand lobby, was awe-inspiring. I stood in line, paid my fifteen euros, and made my way inside. Then I stopped and did a slow 360 degree turn. Does anyone do *grand* better than the French? It was so grand that even the word *grand* felt too small to fit comfortably. Every artist I loved had walked these halls, breathed this air, laid eyes on the same walls, looked up at these ceilings. I wondered if they felt the same sense of inspiration I was feeling now.

The Louvre was large enough to seem as if you could spend your entire natural life walking these halls and still not have seen everything. With four levels and over three hundred rooms, it's also easy to get lost. I was looking for the Impressionist Gallery, got lost in the Middle Ages, lost again in the Seventeenth Century, and lost for a third time in Mesopotamia. The Mesopotamia Hall was full of statues of spear-holding warriors, headless rulers, and winged bulls, including a man's bearded head on a horse's body that looked like he was laughing at me every time I walked past. I heard someone say Mesopotamians had ruled much of the earth for over three thousand years. Which is great, I guess, but I just didn't have time for Mesopotamia.

As I searched for the way out, I learned that Mesopotamia invented the wheel, math, and astronomy. Honestly, and with the greatest possible respect, I cared not one speckle of a smidgen. All I wished was that they hadn't invented so much stuff that I couldn't find my way to the exit. Every time I thought I had escaped I would find myself in another hall of winged bulls, and there I was, back in Mesopotamia. After I walked past the same display for the third time, I found a guard and asked for help. She led me out and sent me on my way.

Ah. This was more like it. Back in the main hall, I found myself staring at massive canvases of gods and kings, ancient civilizations and immortal kingdoms of unspeakable gorgeousity. Every single canvas was magnificent, stunning, majestic beyond words, and soon I had no breath left to take away. Walking those hallowed halls, I felt like a young nun on her first trip to the Vatican. For the first hour or two I looked at every masterpiece with a fresh sense of awe: Titian's *Pastoral Concert*, Raphael's *Portrait of Baldassare Castiglione*, studying every detail and brushstroke, feeling the inspired brilliance of these celestial works sink into my bones.

Soon I was full to the brim with inspiration. But before I started painting, there was one more work I had to see. The single most recognized work in the Louvre, quite possibly the most famous, talked about, and visited image in the world. It took some time to figure out where she was, but when I saw a huddled mass of several hundred hushed tourists holding cameras up high and crowded around a small, roped-off portrait, I knew I was there.

She is the subject of thousands of tearstained love songs and epic poems, and over the centuries, critics' reviews have piled the laurels so high there were no more adjectives left to use. I found a spot with an obstructed view and stared— looked deeply into those eyes and studied that famous smile. Kept staring. Waiting. Waiting. And then...nothing. I didn't get it. So I stared, and stared some more, then I found another spot with a different angle and stared again—but I still didn't get it. With all the brilliant works hanging on these halls, why did so many people insist on putting the *Mona Lisa* on the highest pedestal? I had seen copies of that painting a hundred times and thought I must be missing something, that it had to be experienced in person. Now that I was standing in front of it, I realized I wasn't missing anything. It was small, the colors muted and flat, and the famous smile was just a smile. What was everyone staring at? They say her eyes follow you, but they weren't following me.

Making my escape from the jostling, gaping crowd, my inspiration had dropped a notch, so I thought I'd get reinvigorated with a visit to the Impressionists. I walked toward the hall I thought they were in but got lost again and found myself wandering around a room full of marble statues. (Next time, I promised myself I'd buy a map.) There must have been thirty or forty of them, perhaps Greek, possibly Roman. The men all had six-packs, muscled pecs, and tight butts, the women perfectly realized human specimens with taut breasts and flowing robes. It was like a three-thousand-year-old gathering of Calvin Klein models. At first it appeared as if I was the only living person in the room, but as I searched for the way out, my footsteps echoing off the walls of this ghostly archive, I saw her.

She was sitting on a small concrete bench, her back to me, near a statue that could have been *Venus de Milo*—but a lot of them looked like *Venus de Milo* to me. I could see a sketch pad in her hands, and she was so engrossed in what she was doing she hadn't heard me. I stood as frozen as the statues, afraid of breaking her deep state of contemplation, uncertain as to what I would say if I did. I watched her, my hands sweating and heart pounding. It was as if she were one of the statues come to life. I was still trying to figure out what to say to her when she turned around and saw me.

"Well, it's you," Chloé said with a curious smile. "Hello, there."

"Oh, hi!" Dammit. I felt like I had been caught sneaking up on her. And why did my voice always have to go into the highest possible registers of human speech at the worst possible times?

She put her sketch pad on the bench. "I didn't know you were interested in Roman sculpture."

"Oh, I am, I love it, I was just—staring at—the stuff. All the stuff here." Long awkward pause. Dumb grin. Waving hand pointing at random statues. This was not going well.

"Beautiful, aren't they?"

"Yes. Yes, they are. Beautiful. Beauty is truth!" I blurted out. Where did that come from? An icy sweat started forming itself on my back. I was trying to be profound, quoting some line from something I'd read, but I regretted it the second I said it. What a stupid thing to say. What does *beauty is truth* even mean? God, I hated myself.

She smiled and raised an eyebrow. "And truth beauty."

Well then. Okay. Maybe it wasn't so stupid. I remembered where I had read that line. Keats. "Ode on a Grecian Urn". Actually, it was kind of profound. I was amazing.

"Which one is your favorite?" she asked.

With barely a glance, I pointed at the statue nearest me. "I really like—that. That one there."

"Nice. It's—" She looked at it, and then she looked at me, and I looked at her, and then back at it ,and we looked at each other. It was only then that I realized I was pointing at a statue of a short, naked female torso, and a clumpy one at that. Compared to everything else on the floor, it looked like a failed children's school project.

"Sorry, I meant..." I wanted to change my selection, but it was too late. Now I had to find a way to rationalize it. "It's because of the, um, that—you know." Take a breath, Declan. Pull yourself together.

"I do know! I'm so glad you like that. I thought I was the only person in the world that cared about her—honestly. It's beautiful, such an original work for the time. Did you know that was created in the fourth century BC? But that's rude of me, I'm sorry—of course you know that. You're a graduate already."

I didn't know anything, but just nodded, knitting my brow into an expression that I hoped looked wise, or thoughtful, anything but the knot of confusion I was feeling. "Yes. She was—it's crazy. Amazing. I love it." When did I become such a liar? "What are you sketching?" Tone better, more modulated, deeper. I was getting my voice back.

"*The Winged Victory of Samothrace.*" She pointed to a sculpture of another woman, one that was fully clothed and came complete with wings, arms, and legs. It must have been twenty feet high, and she was impressive, even without a head. "It's a homework assignment, but I'm finding it very, awfully difficult. I'm trying to capture the detail in the robes, how it feels like the wind is swirling around her, you see, and the ship she's standing on...it seems like it's floating. But I don't know. I think there's a Baroqueness to it, but I haven't caught that." She held up her sketch. "Does that look Baroque to you?"

"Yes." I kept nodding. It looked brilliant to me, but she could have held up a sketch of Donald Duck and I would have thought the same thing. "Yes, I think you've totally captured...that thing you said. Its Baroqueness."

"Thanks." She put it away and looked back at the statue. "I love her, you know. I look at her and start to feel—I don't know." She gazed at the statue for a moment. "Free? No. More like...hope?" There was a tiny smidgen of sadness on that last word. A little melancholy, a touch of heartbreak. Evidence, perhaps, that everything in this perfect human specimen's life was not so perfect. "I know, it sounds ludicrous. I'm sorry, I've forgotten—what was your name?" she asked.

"Declan. And it's not ludicrous."

"You're sweet. You are from Georgetown, am I right?"

She said I was sweet! Every angel in heaven stood up and cheered. "Well, yes, but then San Francisco," I reminded her.

"Now I remember. The art school. *Low-rent-shun.* It's nice to see you again." She smiled a smile that would have sent Mona Lisa into twitching spasms of jealousy, turned around, and went back to sketching.

I had seen all the beauty I could take for one day. After a quick goodbye I walked away, and had just stepped out of the room when she called out to me.

"Declan?"

"Yes?"

"Would you like to have lunch?"

Yes, yes, yes, a million times yes.

———

Thirty minutes later, we were sitting at a table in Le Café Richelieu, a small coffee shop on the second floor of the Louvre. From its windows we could see the great glass-and-metal pyramid outside. Inside, the elegant charm made up for the high prices and straight-backed steel chairs. Chloé placed her bag on the chair between us—she had her sketch pad and a book titled *Art across Time* with her. The book was about two inches thick and looked like it weighed ten pounds. Dozens of yellow Post-it notes stuck out of the top and sides, with little scribbles on each one. *Florence Cathedral. Ghiberti. Lavinia Fontana.* Several pages were falling out.

"Do you want a café crème? Baguette? Cheese?" I asked.

"Yes, please."

I got a few of everything and set them in front of her. She finished the baguette and cheese in about three seconds. I was too excited to eat anything.

"Whew. I guess I was hungry," she said, laughing.

"Would you like more?"

"No, no, I'm great, thanks."

"Are you sure?"

"Okay, yes, please, if you don't mind..."

"Of course not!" I picked up a few more bagels and set them in front of her. Her art book was sitting on the table. "Who are you reading about?"

"Géricault." She grabbed a bagel and took a large bite. Almost half of it disappeared down her throat.

"Ah, yes. Géricault," I said, nodding wisely.

"Do you know Géricault?"

"Of course. We studied him. Who doesn't know Géricault?" Me. I didn't. That's who.

"And *The Raft of the Medusa*?"

"Oh, no, I'm not sure we covered that one. More his other ones."

"But...that's his most...how could anyone..." She stopped and thought for a minute while she finished her second bagel and picked up another. I was terrified that she was going to ask me which other ones I meant, and that I would have to confess that I had no idea what I was talking about. "Of course. Yes, yes, of course you studied his other ones." She turned the book around and showed me the photo. "Do you like it?"

It was a raft lost at sea, with a bunch of dead bodies on it. A lot of dead bodies. There were also a few live bodies, just barely alive, and they were waving at a ship far in the distance.

"Géricault was a true Romantic," she said.

"Really? How does a raft full of dead people—?"

"A few years before Géricault painted this, a French ship—was called the *Méduse*—hit a reef off the west coast of Africa and sank. The captain and senior officers boarded lifeboats and saved themselves, and all the other passengers were forced onto a broken-down wooden raft. Almost one hundred and fifty of them. Only fifteen survived." She picked up several pieces of cheese and swallowed them. "It was later discovered the ship's captain was an appointment of the monarchy and didn't know what he was doing. He ran the ship aground and the French government tried to cover it up. If Géricault hadn't painted this, they would have gotten away with it."

They didn't teach this at Laurentian. At least, I don't think they did. Honestly, I wasn't paying that much attention. They just kept talking about the history of typography or culture of interaction or something. After the professor started going on about how Helvetica made its debut in 1957 I stopped listening. For the next two years.

She turned a page. "Have you seen this one?"

It was a painting of a building in ruin, set against a gloomy evening sky. "No. I somehow missed that one."

"I believe you would like it. My father owns it. It's in our library." She closed the book. "Maybe I'll show it to you one day."

"Oh. Oh. Your father just happens to own a painting by Géricault?"

"Two, actually." She closed the book and shrugged. "It's not a big deal. He has other ones that are, I think, much nicer. What else have you seen here?" she asked.

The fact that her father owned two Géricaults was a big deal, but that big deal was overshadowed by a much bigger deal—the fact that she had said she might show it to me. That was tantalizingly close to an invitation. "*The Mona Lisa. Et al.*"

"Et al? What is *et al*? Actually," she said, holding her hands up, "please, don't tell me. But you have seen the *Mona Lisa*?"

"Yes, I've seen the *Mona Lisa*."

"Wasn't she beautiful?"

"Yeah, I guess. She was okay."

Chloé scrunched her forehead into a knot of wrinkles. "You think the *Mona Lisa* is just *okay*?" Her plate was empty. I pushed mine toward her and she smiled a thanks and grabbed more cheese. "Hungry," she said, shrugging.

"Honestly, I didn't see what the big deal was."

"Then you didn't really see it. You looked at it, but you didn't see it. It's not the same thing."

"I did see it. I just didn't get it."

"That's because it's not a painting to you anymore— you've seen it so many times, it's just an icon now. To really see it, you need to look closer." She put the book in her knapsack. "Come with me. I'll show you how to see the *Mona Lisa*." As we got up to leave, I turned back and saw

Chloé pick up the leftover bagel and cheese from my plate and drop them in her purse.

She hurried ahead of me with her bag pressed against her chest, out of the restaurant and into the museum hallway. I kept looking up at the artwork surrounding us, finding it hard not to stop. How does one walk past Vermeer's *The Astronomer* without stopping? Every time I slowed down to look at another painting, she would look back and raise her eyebrows and I'd start walking again.

One painting stopped me entirely, and I couldn't just walk past. It was a dead woman laying on a bed. A group of grief-stricken men and women were standing around her while a stark, bright light from above illuminated the scene. *Death of the Virgin* announced a small, somber plaque.

She came back and stood beside me. "Caravaggio."

I nodded. "Caravaggio."

"Do you know Caravaggio?"

"I'm more familiar with Caravaggio's later works," I lied.

"This *is* one of his later—" She shook her head. "Of course, you studied his later works. Anyway. So, you probably know his story; how he used to wander the streets all night, drinking and getting in sword fights. That he hung out with prostitutes and hooligans, may have been a pimp, and was probably bisexual. You also know he killed a man in an argument over a game of tennis."

"I knew that," I lied. We looked at the painting. It was mesmerizing. "She looks dead. I mean really dead, not just painting dead, if that makes sense..."

"He used a dead prostitute for the model."

"Yes, of course. I knew that."

She reached over and rubbed my shoulder. "Of course you did." It was fast, not much more than a touch, really, but it was a touch. Chloé touched me. I would hold onto that moment for a long time. I wanted to put my arm around hers, or hold her hand, or hug her and kiss her madly and tell her I loved her, but I was pretty sure she wasn't ready for that kind of commitment. Not yet, anyway.

"Look at those colors. How black the blacks are," I said.

"Caravaggio was all about contrast. He painted the blackest blacks."

"They are beautiful blacks."

"I love his blacks too," she said. "But now we have to go."

"But look at those blacks!" I said, not quite ready to leave. "Wait. Look at how he—"

She grabbed my arm and pulled me away. Yes! Two touches.

"What other paintings does your father own?"

"Oh, I don't know. Lots of them."

"Name one."

She thought for a few moments. "There's a Morris I like. Or two, or three, I don't remember. Marc Morris, he came to our house for dinner a few times. A very nice man. He and I used to paint together when I was little."

I didn't know anything about Morris either, but I expected there weren't a lot of people who owned his paintings, let alone had him over for dinner.

When we got to the hall where the *Mona Lisa* hung, the crowd was still twenty rows deep. Chloé put her head down and pushed, ducked, and dodged her way through. I tried to keep up, apologizing about six hundred times. Soon, we were standing right in front of the *Mona Lisa*. There was no one in between us and her: Chloé had gotten us front row seats. For a few minutes, we looked without saying anything.

"He—da Vinci—carried it around for years without selling it," she said.

"Why?"

"He didn't want to let it go. He loved it, and he may have loved her. Are you looking?"

"I'm looking. But I still don't get it."

"That's because you've seen it so many hundreds of times. The repetition has dulled its power. That's what I mean when I say you must look again, look at it like you've never seen it before. Close your eyes."

I closed my eyes.

"Now imagine you were standing here over five hundred years ago. You're a bishop, prince, or a rich merchant. Imagine that you haven't been exposed to a lot of art, and if you have, it was strictly paintings of religious scenes or stuffy royal portraits. You've never even heard of da Vinci. Can you imagine that?"

I nodded.

"Now open them again."

I did.

"Can you see it now? Look at it closely. Do you see it?"

I stood, staring. Still nothing.

"Notice how your eye shifts from foreground to background, and how the light in the background seems to shift. Like it's floating. And that smile—happy, sad, perplexed—who can say? So. Anything?"

I still wasn't getting it, so I shut my eyes and tried again. Rewound my mental clock several hundred years. Then I opened them and looked again, but still nothing. Tried again. Once more, I shut my eyes as tightly as I could and cleared the caches of my memory banks. Erased all thoughts of the last several centuries from my mind. Imagined myself in a long, flowing silk cloak, standing in a French art museum in 1503, and opened them again. This time, I saw what she was talking about. This time, I got it. Understood exactly what Chloé was talking about.

But I wasn't looking at the *Mona Lisa*. I was looking at Chloé. She was gazing at me, and I was gazing back at her, and she smiled. Just a little. And that was it. That was my *Mona Lisa* smile. It was sublime, mysterious, eerie, magnetic, far away and up close. For a few minutes we just stood there, staring at each other, in front of that crowd of hundreds of craning necks. And I got it. I knew what da Vinci had seen, understood what all the songs and poems had been about.

"Do you understand it now?" she asked.

"I do. I do. I was just—"

She cocked her head to one side and nodded. "So was I."

We didn't move. I had this crazy idea that she was going to kiss me. We stood, staring at each other, alone in our little bubble, until someone bumped my elbow.

"We should go," she said. "Is there anything else you'd like to see?"

"Yes! How about...the Impressionists?"

"Let's."

Ah. Finally. Here was a period I knew something about. My parents had a library of books about the Impressionists on display in the study. I had never seen them open one. I think they just liked the way they looked on the shelves, but during those long years of high school, I spent most of my free time reading them. It started as a way to kill time, to fight the loneliness and the boredom of my life, then it became a hobby that turned into an obsession. While everyone else was going to parties and football games and sneaking into bars, those books were my best friends.

There was a red leather chair in that room, and many evenings and weekends all I did was sit in that chair, feet up on the ottoman, reading about the lives and works of Cézanne, Matisse, Pissarro, Rodin, Cassatt, all of them, but especially Monet. I felt completely connected to him—this brilliant artist who considered himself a failure throughout his entire life, lost and rejected, who believed that he had been "born under an evil star." He was me.

Today that obsession was about to pay off in unexpected ways. Chloé and I walked up several flights of concrete stairs to the second floor. I was excited, looking forward to sharing my vast knowledge with Chloé, to showing her that Declan Tucker was a true intellectual. That we were on the same level, art history-wise, or at least in the same galaxy.

"Where are you from, Chloé?"

She didn't say anything for a few beats. Just kept walking ahead of me, head down.

"Are you from around here?"

Still walking. No answer.

"Does your father own lots of paintings?"

She didn't answer.

"What does your family do?"

She sped up, until she was almost a flight of stairs ahead of me.

"I like Joy Division, too," I called.

She kept walking, faster. Why? Was she trying to get away?

"I don't have any paradigms, you know."

She stopped. Turned around. Looked down at me. Eyes glazed.

"Do you have any paradigms?"

She kept looking at me for a few moments, holding tightly onto the rail. "You're strange, aren't you?" she said.

The shell cracked. I stood, looking at her, my lips moving but nothing coming out. Flashbacks to sitting alone in the high school cafeteria. To hearing kids make fun of me while I sat at the front of the class. To spending weekends alone in my parents' library. To my psychiatrist's office, trying to explain why I never talked to anyone. To everyone I had ever tried to be friends with, friendships that always ended with the same kind of question Chloé had just asked me, before they took off and never spoke to me again.

"No. Yes. I guess maybe, but I'm trying not to be," I managed to say.

A pause, a shake of the head. "Don't."

"But I thought—thought you were just—"

"No. I wasn't. I like you. Please don't try to be like everyone else. Normal people always make me feel like I'm the strange one. You don't. You make me feel like I'm...I don't know." She turned around and started back up the stairs. Before I could ask another question—I had so many I wanted to ask, and none of them were about art—we walked into a small room. Small for the Louvre, that is.

"The Louvre isn't known for its collection of Impressionists," she said. "But they have a few."

We stood in front of a painting of a cabin and trees beside a road covered in snow. She seemed to want to forget what just happened.

"Oh, yes," I said. I knew this painting. "*Snow near Honfleur*. Monet painted this in 1867. It was one of his first winter scenes. Did you know that when he painted this it was so cold he had to wear three coats?" Chloé nodded, so I assumed she was enraptured with what I was saying.

"See how the snow—painted the same in the foreground as it is in the back— interrupts our sense of pictorial space?" I pointed to the path that disappeared into the background. "By erasing the traditional visual markers that give us scale, such as people walking, it makes the background as immediate as the foreground." She seemed interested, so I kept going. "It was a motif Monet would come back to again and again throughout his entire life. He painted something like one hundred and forty snowscapes. If we consider a later work, say *The Magpie*, for example, we can see how he had evolved..."

I looked around and she was gone.

Five

You don't tell the muse when you're ready, the muse tells you. Mine had woken me just after seven in the morning and told me to get out of bed and get to work. I tried to explain how I was feeling, that I was depressed and anxious, and that I really needed time to myself right now to sort out some feelings. I told her how Chloé had abandoned me in the Louvre, and that I was feeling a lot of rejection, some anger, maybe depression, and that I was hungry, but the muse didn't care. Told me that if I wasn't in the mood, she could just go find someone who was. I detected sarcasm in her voice. I asked if there was any way I could grab an espresso and a bagel first but she said no and that was that. So I crawled out of bed, grabbed my pencil, and was sketching away before the muse got angry.

The muse was right. The muse is always right. I came here to become a famous artist, and Paris had gotten in the way. Never again. I had a blank canvas, pencils, paint, brushes, and inspiration. That was all I needed. Nothing could stop me now, even the fact that I hadn't eaten in, well, I couldn't remember how long. I had a concept, or at least an idea for the painting, or a theme. Maybe not quite a theme, call it more of a general notion of the subject. But I did have that. I even had a name for it: *Chloé Among the Ruins.* This painting was going to be my great masterwork, my *Mona Lisa, David, Last Supper,* and *Starry Night,* all wrapped up in one impassioned explosion of pure, unbridled love. It was going to be big. Huge. It was going to make me famous, get rave reviews, make me a pile of money, and most importantly, send Chloé running back to me and promising never, ever, ever to leave me standing alone in the Louvre wondering what the hell happened. So there was a lot of pressure.

A few sketches, a few lines, a long ponder, more sketches, quickly erased, more pondering, more sketches, soon replaced with other sketches and lines that were just as quickly erased. Sketch, erase, ponder, sketch, erase, ponder. A few hours later, I was still staring at a blank canvas (I thought I heard an exasperated sigh from the muse) but there were ever-larger waves of inspiration building inside me. Sketch, ponder, sketch, and—wait, stop, look again— there was something. Yes, definitely something there. Ponder, sketch, ponder, erase, ponder, sketch. Several hours later I had a few lines that felt right, that I thought were starting to give this work the shape I was searching for. I had a beginning. It was exciting. So far it was only a few lines on a blank page, but I could feel the brilliance building inside me. I knew exactly how Michelangelo must have felt when he made those first few brushstrokes on the ceiling of the Vatican. I couldn't wait to—

"What's that, Declan?"

What? No.

No, no, no, no, no and no.

My body went into a deep freeze, my pencil stuck in midstroke. This couldn't be happening. What was that? Where did that come from? I was afraid to look around. Deathly afraid. That voice—I knew that soft, high-pitched voice almost as well as my own mother's. It was Neil Beckwith's voice. But no, it wasn't, it couldn't be. It wasn't his voice because if it was his voice, Neil Beckwith would have to be there, sitting behind me, and he couldn't be, because he was dead. He had passed on, officially concluded his human journey, the final papers had been processed and filed, and he had made his eternal exit from the global stage. It was not him. It was just the old universe playing tricks on me, as it is wont to do, flexing its preternaturally malevolent muscles on my poor, young soul. Why did it hate me so much?

No. Neil couldn't be there. It was just my imagination. The Pudgy One was buried and forgotten by everyone but his closest friends, dearest relatives, and me. Yes, me. I had not forgotten, though I had tried. That well-rounded man had continued to haunt me in my dreams and crawl around my subconscious almost every night, like an eternal and infernal bug. Maybe I just had a guilty conscience, although I wasn't conscious of feeling guilty. I don't know, but somehow the Weeble that wobbled but didn't fall down had wheedled itself into my soul. Now my weakened mind had taken those subconscious musings into another realm, deceiving me for reasons I could not imagine. I pushed those thoughts away, forced myself to believe I was alone in this room, and tried to concentrate.

"Is that supposed to be a person?" the disembodied voice behind me said.

Focus, Declan. Do not be distracted.

"It doesn't even look like a person to me."

I felt the muse eyeing me suspiciously and redoubled my efforts.

"If it *is* a person you have to have arms and a head and stuff."

"It's not a person!" I said.

Shut up, Declan! Why did I answer? I must have been talking to myself, because there was no one behind me. Just a sign of early-onset insanity, nothing serious. I went back to work, keeping my eyes ahead of me and cursing myself for my lack of mental control. C'mon, Declan. You got this. Focus.

"So if it's not a person, what is it?"

I put both hands over my ears and squeezed my eyes shut.

"Do you ever paint trees? You should paint trees. People love trees."

That was it. I turned around, hoping against all hope to see nothing but my apartment, but no. I found myself staring at the worst excuse for a nightmare anyone had ever seen. Neil was there, looking as in the flesh as anyone can possibly look. He was on my couch, his feet on the coffee table and his hands behind his head, wearing a red-and-green T-shirt that stretched too tightly over his protruding belly and tucked into his pants. His cargo shorts had pockets large enough to hold a dozen jars of mayonnaise, and his blue knee-length socks were squeezed into brown sandals. He looked at me and smiled, like a long-forgotten in-law that had shown up at your door uninvited and was about to ask for money.

Neither one of us spoke. We just looked at each other, like we were having some kind of otherworldly eye fight. This staring match went on for a few minutes, his expression not changing one molecule, that dumb smile frozen in position. I suppose I was thinking that if I stared long enough, he would disappear, or evaporate, or turn into dust. But nothing. Eventually I gave up and turned around.

"People love trees," he repeated. "You should paint trees. And mountains and lakes. Who doesn't like lakes? And beaches. I like dolphins, too. Do you like dolphins?"

Only forty-eight-odd hours ago I thought the universe had finally decided to turn a kind eye in my direction. Since then, I had been abandoned by the love of my life, nearly arrested, and now I was being rudely accosted by a rumply ghost. I realized how wrong I had been, could see with perfect clarity how deep and far the universal forces lined up against me had stretched. They went far beyond our small planet, deep into the farthest galaxies in the cosmos, light-years farther than even the Hubble Space Telescope had yet to go. Why else would I be sitting here with this poorly dressed bogeyman, who was resting his feet on my coffee table and believed he was somehow qualified to educate me?

"For your edification, I'm not a landscape painter," I said. "But thank you so much for your sage advice. I can tell you're a man of highly sophisticated tastes." The sarcasm was laid on pretty thick, even for me, but I thought he might miss it otherwise. Did ghosts even get sarcasm?

"What's *edification* mean?" He took off his socks and sandals and put his white bare feet back on my coffee table. The stench wafted through the room. "And what's a *sage*? Is that like some kind of plant?"

Why? Why me? Why was this boorish poltergeist intruding on my artistic journey? Why was I being asked these questions? And also, shouldn't ghosts just know this stuff? "Mr. Beckwith." I spoke slowly, deliberately. "I know you're not here. I know you're a manifestation of something that...that is going wrong in my mind. So I hope you don't think I'm being rude if I just get back to my work."

"Sure. Go ahead." He waved his hands dismissively. "Whatever. Don't let me interrupt."

I turned around and tried. For those who have never experienced it, trying to work on a piece of epoch-defining art while someone is watching you from behind is difficult. If that someone happens to be a ghostly apparition, it's even more difficult. But I picked up my pencil and got back to work anyway. My muse was getting impatient, and I could tell she was going to walk out if I didn't settle down. Focus, focus, focus. The ghost lay down on my couch, and I could hear his fingers scratching his oversize belly, but I kept my focus. For about four minutes.

"Do you have anything to eat?"

The words cut through my consciousness like poisoned daggers. I understood then that I wouldn't be able to simply turn my back on this problem. Denial, my go-to resource for managing most of life's difficulties, wasn't going to work this time. "No." I turned around. "There is no food for you here." I was trying not to yell and only half succeeding. "Now go away. You can't stay here. You can't be here. You can't be in my head. I need to work, and I need you to dis-ap-pear." Since when did ghosts even eat? I went back to work, but it was impossible. I tried anyway.

He was quiet for about seven seconds. "Even a hot dog?"

"Shut the hell up!" I shouted. "Shut it!" I picked up a tube of paint—ochre red—and threw it at him. It went right through him and landed on the couch, leaving a small blotch. Damn. First a ghost, and now I was going to get hit with a cleaning bill. I went back to painting, more determined than ever, pushing through it. I wasn't going to let this *thing* stop me.

"I'm just hungry. Geez," he said. "You're killing me." A high-pitched giggle escaped from his too-large lips. "That's kind of funny, right? Because you actually did kill me."

"I did not!" Once again I had to stop and turn around. "That was an accident. Or something, I don't know, but it wasn't me. Why are you here?"

He took a deep breath. "I just thought I'd visit. You know. Old friends and all that."

"We're not old friends!"

"You should be nicer to me. I am dead, you know." A raised eyebrow and a meaningful pause. "No thanks to you."

"I didn't kill you," I mumbled.

"Oh, really?" He pursed his lips and raised his other eyebrow. "So what did?"

"I don't know! High blood pressure? Clogged arteries? Bad clams, for all I know. And if you're so dead, why are you here?" I threw my brush on the floor, leaving another blotch. "Clearly you're not dead enough."

Neil's eyes opened wide and his face twisted into a pathetic grimace, like a boy whose parents had just yelled at him for the first time. He turned around on my couch and curled into a ball. I thought he was crying. What the hell was this about? Bad enough to have a ghost in your room, but to have that ghost sulking and crying was so much worse. To be thinking that I was the cause of this emotional outburst stretched the already stretched bonds of my sense of reality.

Was it something I said? My understanding of the accepted protocols of speaking to dead people was nonexistent, but I supposed I had crossed some invisible line in the supernatural world. Was it insulting to tell a dead person he wasn't dead enough? How would I know? Are there rules for this kind of thing? I didn't know and wasn't sure I cared. This blobby specter, lying with his back to me on my couch, shoulders shaking and a loud whimper coming from his weepy mouth, had already taken up enough of my time.

"Why did you have to say that?" he said.

"You have to leave." I suppose I should have been more sensitive, what with him all weepy and dead and all, but I wasn't a sensitive kind of guy. In fact, I was getting increasingly angry—whatever inspiration I had found for my great masterwork had disappeared. My muse snorted in disgust and left.

"I'm not going anywhere," he said. "And you can't make me."

"You can't stay here. You have to go back to—wherever you are from."

"Where's that, Declan?" He rolled over and looked at me. His eyes were wide, red, and wet, and his lips trembled. "Georgetown? Go back to the *Herald* maybe? Well, I can't. I can't do that because I'm dead. Apparently, I was killed by an attack of bad clams."

That answered my question about ghosts and sarcasm. "I'm sorry, but..." I wasn't going to admit to anything. "I'm sorry about what happened. But you still have to leave. There must be someplace you could go. Don't you have family to visit?"

"No. I was a swinging bachelor before I died."

"So go swing!" Can't ghosts go anywhere they want? Why would he want to be here? If I were a swinging bachelor ghost, I'd be on a beach in California, in the dressing room of some Italian modeling agency, or checking out some other swinging planet in the universe. Why not? What was stopping him?

"I'm staying here. Good luck trying to make me leave." His lips were still trembling, but his wet eyes had taken on a steely, determined expression. "I'm going to have a nap." He turned over. There was a blanket hanging over the couch, and he grabbed that and pulled it on top of himself. A few minutes later, he was asleep. Turning around in my chair, I tried to get back to work, but the muse was gone for good, and when the round apparition started snoring I gave up. If I hadn't killed him already, I would have now. I put down my pencil, went outside, and slid the door shut.

My small balcony didn't offer much of a view—it faced the wrong way, so rather than the beauty of the Paris skyline all I saw was a gray ocean of small houses and apartments. The night had turned cold, the wind harsh, and a light rain fell from a dark and cloudy sky, but I was better off out here than in there. At least I couldn't hear him snoring. I pulled up my small plastic chair and sat down to figure this out. It took several minutes of deep breathing exercises, but the initial shock of what had happened wore off and I was able to think.

This was not the first time my grip on reality had loosened. The first time it happened I was about fifteen. It started slowly and then moved quickly. Things were slipping away and my head was racing around in places that didn't make sense and that I couldn't stop. It seemed like parts of my mind were dropping off in chunks and pieces, like rocks falling off a cliff. Friends kept canceling on me until I didn't have any left. I dropped out of activities until there weren't any activities left to drop out of. My parents asked me if I wanted to see a doctor. I said no, everything was fine, then I said yes.

We called him Uncle Sam. Soobramani, I think was his name. Nice guy with long gray hair. Every Thursday at 6:00 p.m. I would show up at Uncle Sam's door, and we would chat. "How has your week been so far?" He had an endless fascination with how my weeks had been. "Fine, thanks. How has yours been?" "It's been fine, thank you, Declan. Have you been working on anything interesting at school?" "No, nothing very interesting. How about you? Have you been working on anything interesting?" I was being a complete and utter jerk, at the hourly rate of $125.

He had me write some tests. Which I passed, if getting high marks on a psychiatrist's test is a pass for anything. There were "issues," he said. The wires in my brain didn't fuse, was the way he put it. I remember him telling me there seemed to be ADD, anxiety, depression, and bipolar disorder, and I can't remember what else. The term he used was *comorbid*, which meant there were two or more illnesses interacting together, which made the results unpredictable. I was on enough spectrums to create my own rainbow. He recommended medication, which I politely declined. "But this doesn't have to be a negative, Declan," he said, his head nodding as if he was trying to convince himself. "I don't want to glamorize it. This is a very serious issue—but you should know a lot of famous artists have neurological challenges. Mariah Carey, for example, has bipolar disorder."

If he was trying to make me feel better, he could have found a better example. But Uncle Sam didn't have to worry about me taking his diagnosis as a negative. For one thing, it helped explain a lot; I was relieved that there was a name for what I had. And besides, I did kind of find it inspiring. There were theories that Van Gogh was comorbid. If I was going to suffer from some neurological disease, at least I was in good company.

Uncle Sam meetings went on for almost a year, and the conversations never went much deeper or wider. I didn't give him much to work with. That was a mistake, I knew now. Standing outside on that balcony, trying to hold my shaking hands still on that cold banister, I wished I had put my time with Uncle Sam to better use. Because now it seemed like my wires had become completely untangled and that the falling rocks had turned into a landslide. Part of me wanted to look in the window to see if Neil was still there, but I was afraid I might jump off the balcony if he was. The reality of being alone in a city so far from home just hit me. So I stood there, taking deep breath after deep breath, trying to stop my hands from shaking. Finally, I calmed myself down enough to turn around. Looked back inside, quickly.

Saw nothing. Walked to the window, looked again. Still nothing. The room was clear. The couch was empty.

Neil wasn't there after all. It was just a weird dream, like the one I'd had in Montmartre. Scared the hell out of me though; but now it was okay. I swung open the thin metal door, walked back inside and was thinking about getting a glass of milk and some food—I hadn't eaten since yesterday—and going to bed. I was going to be okay, I just needed sleep. Maybe I should have taken the day off. That's when Neil walked around the corner of the kitchen holding a paper plate piled high with meatballs. He stopped and looked at me accusingly.

"Don't have any food, huh?" he said. "So what was this doing in the fridge?"

I held it together just long enough to get to the door, open it, run down the hall, and get outside. I had nowhere to go, but I couldn't stay here.

Six

When you're wandering alone on the streets, without money or hope, a cold and rainy night in Paris isn't much different from a cold and rainy night anywhere else. The clouds are just as cheerless, the winds just as bitter, your clothing gets just as soaked. I turned down one long street then another with no direction or plan. Groups of young and stylish Parisians passed by, telling each other little French secrets, making cute French jokes, laughing, happy in their skin. Not long ago, I had been like them. Now I was looking at life from the other side.

I walked with my head down and tried to think, paying no attention to where I was going. After an hour or so, the bookstores, grocers, and restaurants turned into dollar stores, check cashing services, and tattoo parlors. An emaciated woman sat on the sidewalk with a handwritten sign beside her that said *J'ai Faim.* Please Help Me. I tossed a euro on her blanket and walked for several more blocks, turned around to find my way back, took a wrong turn, then another, and became completely disoriented.

I had no idea where I was. There was nowhere to go, and no one to talk to. Making my way through the evening crowds, my feet got soaked and my hopes dimmed with every step. The rain fell harder and the wind blew colder. I was lost, shivering, and alone. My future as a world-famous artist seemed like a random dream from another lifetime. Now all I could think about was how I was going to survive the night on these streets. I hadn't eaten since I-don't-know-when, had abandoned my apartment with nothing to wear but this thin shirt on my back. This time, my misery had an air of permanency.

Hours passed. The night became darker and colder, my clothes soaked through, my fingers turned numb. Coming upon a small park, I sat down on a hard metal bench and considered my options. There were a few coins in my pocket, maybe enough for half a bagel, but not much more—I had left my credit card, cash, and passport in the apartment. The idea of going back to that apartment made me sick, even if I could find my way. I couldn't face that...that thing—whatever it was—right now. Was he real, I wondered? Or was it something in my head? Neither option offered comfort; both ended in madness. I considered calling my parents again (if I could talk someone into letting me use their phone) but that would mean admitting they were right. No, thanks.

C'mon, Declan, think! Come up with a plan! And I tried. Oh, I tried. Thought as hard as my shivering brain had ever thought. More hours passed. The lights of Paris dimmed, and my hope dimmed with them. Soon, the streets cleared, and the only sound was the rain beating on the sidewalk. Extreme hunger and cold took their toll. Thinking became impossible. I was too weak to even sit straight. I lay down and prepared for the worst.

Shivering in the cold, I felt my fingers turn from a sharp pain to a throbbing numbness, and my toes joined in for good measure. I felt like I had run out of options. Truly alone, thousands of miles from home, I had nowhere left to turn. I had no money, food, friends, or hope. My life was over. I don't know how long I lay there—another hour?

Three? But at some point, I simply gave up. Having realized there was no way out, nowhere to go, I was finally forced to accept that the end had come. My eyes shut, possibly for the last time. I decided to let fate have its way with me. If my life had to end, let it end here, while soaking up the Paris rain.

The metal arm of the bench pressed against the back of my head and the rain continued to pound around me while the consequences of my coming death reverberated in my mind. How my parents would suffer. How my few former friends would grieve and wish they had been nicer to me. How many girls would realize, with heartbreaking regret, that they should have given me a chance, that I really was the one for them—if only they had taken the time to understand me. What sadness! What sobbing and tears! What epic tragedy!

The death of young, brilliant artists like me has always been an epic tragedy. Keats and Shelley proved that over a century ago. But for me, the tragedy was even more epic—not that I want to get competitive about this, but I was younger than they were. Also, my artistic journey had ended with naught but a few random scratches on a canvas; no one would experience my genius in the flesh. There would be no rooms in the Louvre dedicated to my work, no coffee-table books with photographs of me on the cover. And—horrors piled upon horrors—my beautiful Chloé would have to live the rest of her life without me, tortured with guilt as she relived our sad, final scene together, possibly blaming herself for my untimely demise. Pity and sorrow! I shut my eyes and waited for the end. If there was any consolation, it was that my life would make a great movie one day.

I felt a cold hand resting on my forehead. The hand of God, I supposed. Interesting. Didn't expect that. So this is how it ends.

"Croquis? Is that you?"

I felt someone's fingers trying to pry my eyes open.

"Croquis?"

My eyes were wedged open and I saw Gaétan leaning over me. He was wearing nothing but a T-shirt, jeans, and a pair of worn leather sandals on his feet. He was also soaking wet, and must have been even colder than I was—and I was freezing to death. Quite literally, I thought.

"It is you! Hello, my good friend." He sat down beside me and threw his head back. "So nice to see you. Such a sweet night, yes?" He let the rain fall on his face while I tried to muster some enthusiasm for the weather. It was not possible. My lips were shaking too much.

Gaétan held out his arms and took a deep breath. "I love the smell of rain. It smells so fresh. Doesn't it?"

I remembered trying to respond, but there was nothing but a croaking sound.

Gaétan looked over at me. "What are you doing here? I assumed you lived on the ummm..." He nodded to the other side of the city. "In the ritzy section."

"Ahhh," I responded.

He looked closer at me. "Are you alright?"

"Great," I said, my yammering teeth making it sound like *gudda-rade.*

"You look a little—what is it? Queasy?"

"I fine, thanks," I managed to say. "Just code."

"Code? Oh—cold. But it's not *very* cold," he said. "Why are you here? Are you sick?"

All I could do was shake my head.

A flash of genuine concern crossed his face. "When did you last eat?"

I shook my head again.

"I see." He gazed at me for a minute, as if he was deciding whether to pick me up and carry me or call an ambulance. "Is it possible for you to stand?"

It took some time, but with his help I got up and stood, legs shaking and head floating. I hung onto the bench for support.

"Follow me." He stood and walked away, heading toward the city streets.

Standing was almost impossible, and walking seemed out of the question, but what choice did I have? I really wasn't ready to call my life over just yet. Through sheer force of will I hobbled along behind him, uncertain of where he was going, why I was supposed to follow him, and how long I would last. But I did. I had to. He walked slowly but with purpose, past stores and restaurants, down one block and then another. How I managed to keep up I don't know, but I was certain that if I lost sight of him I would die on these streets. So that provided motivation.

Then he stopped, turned around, and told me to walk on the other side of the street.

"Why?" I was already anxious, tired, and hungry. Now I was also confused.

"Just watch me."

We kept walking, him on one side of the street and me on the other. Morning had come to Paris, and the streets were coming alive again. The rain had stopped, the sun was coming up, and stores were opening. He was easy enough to see from a distance, walking slowly and against the tide of serious pedestrians hurrying to work. A few minutes later he stopped outside a small grocery store. The store was brightly lit inside and out, had shelves stacked high with fresh breads, fruits, and vegetables covering most of the sidewalk. Gaétan lingered in front, gazing at the colorful displays as if he were deciding what to have for breakfast. Then he picked up a few apples, a bunch of bananas, some oranges, three loaves of bread, and with his arms full of food, turned around and ran away.

A half second later, a man ran out of the store, chasing Gaétan and shouting obscenities you could hear for blocks. "*Arrêt!* Stop! Come back here!" Despite his broad girth and age—the store owner must have been over sixty and was built like a square block—he ran with skill, speed, and determination, like a retired champion who had never lost his competitive edge. Half a block later I thought he was going to catch Gaétan, who was slowed down by all the groceries he was carrying. The old grocer was no more than a few feet behind him and gaining. But Gaétan shifted into a higher gear and quickly got away. The grocer gave up and stopped, bending over on his knees and hands, gasping for air and covered in sweat, exhaling more obscenities.

Gaétan had left me far behind, but I just kept walking in the direction he had run. After a few more blocks, I found him in a dark alley between two small stores. He was sitting on the ground, eating one of the apples he had recently poached. He looked up, nodded for me to join him, and tossed me a loaf of bread. I caught it with both hands, sat down, and shoved it into my mouth. It was perfectly fresh, still warm, and smelled like butter. It was the best bread I had ever had, even in this heavenly land of the holy loaf. I ate in silence, nodding my appreciation while chewing and swallowing like a long-starved prisoner of war. Blood started circulating through my veins again, my body warmed up, and I regained a small portion of my senses. The excitement of the chase and the food working its way to my belly gave me new strength.

"You like?" he asked.

My mouth was too full to answer. I nodded my head so hard I banged my skull on the brick wall behind me.

"What were you doing back there? On that bench?" he asked. "You didn't look so good."

"Just out for a walk, got a little tired. Bit of a dizzy spell."

Gaétan nodded as if he understood, took another bite of his apple, and threw the core down the alley. "I suppose that happens."

"What were you doing there?" I asked.

"I live around here. This is where people like me live."

We sat in silence while I peeled an orange and jammed half of it in my mouth. A few minutes passed silently.

"Feeling better?"

I nodded.

"Do you have a place to stay?"

I shook my head.

He didn't say anything for a while after that, just ate another apple as I finished off the orange and started another.

"Would you like a place to stay?"

"Yes," I said, mouth full.

Gaétan bit into a loaf of bread and smiled. "This may be your lucky day. As it happens, there is a luxury suite available at the exclusive hotel I'm currently residing in. It is officially called The Most Magnificent Great Grand Royal Ambassador Palace Hotel, but we just call it The Grand. It is on Boulevard St. Jacques, in a prime downtown location. Close to the best shopping and entertainment in Paris. Would you be interested?"

That's how I got started in a life of crime.

———

It had housed a steel manufacturer, at one time, or a knitting factory, Gaétan wasn't sure which. The white brick front was three levels high and half a block long, and looked like it had been a serious building, a productive building, many years ago. Now it looked like an abandoned playhouse. It was covered from top to bottom in painted swirls of bright reds, blues, and greens that looked like waves, or fireworks, or the deep inner consciousness of a frothing psychopath, or all of those. Rows of deep-set windows with black frames looked out like the sunken eyes of a gang of drug-addicted teenagers.

Gaétan pushed open the front door and held it for me. The interior was mostly unfinished plywood walls covered in more random swirls of paint and an unfinished concrete floor. One wall was covered with a painting of an angry bald green man shaking his fist at the sky, his brown face half covered by an unruly orange beard. The floor was covered in dust, with cardboard boxes and garbage strewn about. There were piles of empty paint cans, used brushes, and canvases pushed against the walls. A six-foot cracked mirror with an elaborate yellow frame lay on the floor, looking up at the sky as if it had yet to give up hope that better days lay ahead.

"This is the main lobby," Gaétan said, bowing slightly. "Designed to reflect the elegance and sophistication of our treasured guests."

We walked through the lobby and into a long hallway. The far wall was covered with a manga-style painting of a young woman in mid-scream. She was wielding a can of spray paint like a gun and surrounded by whirling oranges and greens.

"The hotel lavatory and powder room are here," Gaétan said. We were standing in front of a dirty room with a sink covered in green mold. "I apologize for the lack of bidet. Also for the lack of a shower, toilet, and running water. And while I'm at it, I should also apologize for the lack of lighting, heating, air-conditioning, and electricity." He opened a door, and the knob came off in his hands. He pushed it back and smiled at me. "Maintenance has been notified."

"How long have you lived here?" I asked.

"Oh, I don't know. Since they kicked us out of our last hotel. About six months."

"Kicked out?"

"Yes. Evicted. Expelled. Kicked out. You see, we are not residents, in the legal definition of that word. We are squatters. Regular eviction is just part of the lifestyle."

He pronounced *legal* like it was some abstract and amusing concept. The smell of wet concrete, dust, paint, and leftover food fought its way through the thicker smell of mold and rot that filled the air. We continued down the hall, passed by a series of small rooms, every one littered with a random scattering of garbage, broken chairs and tables, empty food containers, and well-used art supplies. There were a few feral cats roaming around. A couple of the rooms had small, dirty mattresses lying on the floor. We stopped in front of one and looked inside. Someone had painted "Four legs good. Two legs bad." on the wall.

"Behold our one-of-a-kind executive suites. Where modern luxury transcends time itself."

Another door led us into a large, open room the size of a small gymnasium. It looked like an artists' workshop, storage warehouse, and circus tent all in one. Paintings, street signs, advertising posters, old couches, a small tricycle, a guitar without strings, mismatched chairs, a lot of garbage, three naked mannequins, a few installations-in-progress, and lots of half-finished canvases covered the floors and walls. Eight or nine people, most of them in my age bracket, stood scattered around the room, painting, sketching, building, or staring into space. No one looked at us, or at each other. The room was quiet, except for the hissing sound of a welding torch as one of the artists fused two steel beams together. She was wearing my shoes—the pair that had gone missing at the same time as my wallet.

Gaétan sat down on one of the couches. The springs squeaked, and a mouse ran out from under the cushion. He spoke quietly. "This is a very exclusive hotel. There is a long waiting list to get in. But for you, we may be able to make a room available."

"Who lives here?"

"Artists, philosophers, writers, musicians, criminals, revolutionaries, and renegades. And a priest."

The couch beside us had a body lying on it. It was dead still, wrapped under a thin, blue wool blanket. An unruly wave of dark purple and yellow hair was just visible from under the blanket at the far end of the couch. One dirt-covered bare foot was visible near us.

"This is our CEO, Director, and General Manager. Madelaine." He reached over and shook her ankle. "Madelaine, this young gentleman would like to apply for a suite in our hotel."

Madelaine crawled out from under the blanket and gazed at me, pulling her hair back. She looked like she had just awoken from a hundred-year sleep.

"Hi, Madelaine, what's up?" I said, a little forced-friendly. I was trying to figure out her age. She seemed older than Gaetan or me, by five or six years.

Madelaine stared at me for a long time, her brow furled in serious contemplation, her face puffy and streaked with makeup. Finally she looked over at Gaétan and nodded before crawling back under the blanket and pulling it over her head, as if shutting the door to her office.

"Congratulations. You have passed our background check," Gaétan said. "If you're still interested, we have one of our Royal Suites available."

What could I say? I loved it. Loved it, loved it, loved it. The Grand was every dream I ever had come true, alive and in the flesh. It was nirvana, Shangri-la, and eternal paradise, all packaged up and placed here for my personal benefit. Every particle of grime, every sandwich wrapper on the floor, every empty jar of paint and discarded brush seemed to have been placed by the Interior Designer of the Gods just for me. It was the opposite of everything I had ever experienced, the inverse of every room in which I had ever laid my weary head, and therefore perfect. This was the squalor I wished I had grown up in. It was a dream come true: my very own Le Bateau-Lavoir. Perhaps I had been born in the right century after all.

"I'll take it," I said. "How much?"

"The rent is twelve baguettes." He rubbed his finger against his chin, thinking. "Three pounds of salted butter. And a selection of cheese. Would that be acceptable?"

That sounded very reasonable to me. More than reasonable, there was no arguing. A mere pittance, as they used to say in England—or peanuts, in a more modern American parlance. A few bits of French food for the privilege of residing in this great, grimy palace was far less than I had anticipated, and I was grateful for the generous offer. Of course I would have jumped on said offer, wouldn't have hesitated for the slightest of seconds, under normal circumstances. Yet there was one minor hurdle that needed to be overcome. One tiny difficulty. Yet it was a tiny difficulty that was completely and irrevocably insurmountable. I had no money. Nothing. And with an uncivilized ghost guarding my cash and cards in the apartment, there was no way I was getting any. Gaétan may as well have asked for a million-dollar down payment with half the jewelry in the Hamptons thrown in for collateral.

"We are hosting a banquet here tomorrow," he added, perhaps noting a look of consternation on my face. "A grand celebration for an old and honored friend. Of course you know it is not possible to have a banquet without baguettes and cheese. A civilized society such as ours cannot exist without rules."

I wanted, more than anything in the world, to be accepted into this beautiful squalor, this dumpy castle of decrepit grandeur. So I agreed, accepting the terms of payment without the dimmest idea of how I would satisfy said terms. We signed the lease with an awkward fist bump, and I was shown to my Royal Suite. Turns out it was the room with "Four legs good. Two legs bad." painted on the wall. The mattress was a lumpy, damp, and worn-out stained mess on the floor. There was a thin blanket and no pillow. The room looked sad and smelled, there was mouse excrement on the floor, and water dripped from the cracked ceiling. It was beautiful.

Gaétan left and I lay down on the mattress. The crack in the ceiling bent like a crooked smile, and I smiled back. Sweetness and perfection, all here: soft, wet, and wonderful. It was late, I was tired, and I was in bed, happy and content with my place in this new world. I drifted off, thinking there was only one small defect in this otherwise heavenly bliss—I couldn't help thinking how nice it would be to have my old toothbrush. Otherwise, perfection.

I put my hands behind my head, stared at the ceiling, and began to think of where I was going to get the baguettes and cheese for tomorrow's banquet. If there was sufficient time and resources, I would have planned a proper baguette heist. Spent months on baguette burglary research, dug tunnels underground, arranged for getaway cars, hacked computers, bribed an inside man or two, created a team of heist specialists, and made a plan with lots of complicated moving parts that looked like they would never come together but somehow ended up working out just right. An Ocean's Eleven, but for baguettes and cheese. If only it were that simple. It wasn't.

With just slightly more than twenty-six hours to organize and execute the crime, I had to do the best I could with what I had. I had made my promises to Gaétan with a casual shrug and nod, as if I were some sort of experienced baguette criminal. Now, I had to deliver, and I would. There had to be a way. Gaétan's grab-and-run method wouldn't work for me; I couldn't run that fast. I needed a more sophisticated approach to stealing food. A few hours later, just when I was about to give up, I thought of something.

But first, I have another confession to make. I had earlier suggested that I had led a life of great innocence, that when I lived in Georgetown I had followed the rules of society as if they were universal commandments never to be questioned or crossed. I wasn't being completely honest.

So now the truth, pure and unvarnished. Long ago, when I was a mere eleven years old, I had fallen in with a gang of thieves—one of our teenage neighbors had lured me in with the promise of free chocolate bars. Our small group of criminals roamed the streets of Georgetown that summer, striking small corner shops and plundering grocery stores at will. We were mad, bad, and dangerous to know. Grabbing candy, soda, chips, ice-cream bars, cigarettes, whatever we could stuff into our pockets, then running to the schoolyard and eating and smoking until we were sick. So I was not unfamiliar with the workings of the criminal mind. That was how I came up with the perfect plan. I could see the entire scene play out in my mind.

Seven

The Great Baguette Heist
A Screenplay by Declan Tucker
Based on a True Story

Scene One

A friendly, honest-looking young man walks down an old Paris street, smiling pleasantly at passersby. He approaches a grocery store on St. Martin Boulevard named Les Halles Bosquet. Stops outside and looks inside, gazing at the fruits and vegetables on display. Glancing upward, he searches for something near the ceiling. His eyes land on a security camera. Then another. He watches them for a few moments, smiles knowingly, and walks inside. Light jazz music plays in the background.

Scene Two

The young gentleman is now wandering the aisles of the grocery store. He seems to be impressed by the rich selection of fruits, vegetables, dairy, and other fine products on the shelves. Stopping in front of the cheese display, he nods his head appreciably. Then he walks to the back of the store, picks up a cardboard box, and returns to the cheese. Choosing carefully, he drops several into the box: Camembert Extra-Fin. Brie de Meaux. Pont l'Évêque. E. Graindorge. Then he wanders over to the bakery section and places twelve baguettes in his box. On his way to the cashier, he picks up three pounds of salted butter.

Scene Three

The amiable young man is nearly at the checkout counter when he stops. He has forgotten something. Shaking his head, the man returns to the back of the store, where he looks up again at the security camera, waits until it swings in another direction, and picks up another cardboard box. This one is just slightly smaller than the one he's already holding. He puts the smaller box inside that box, expertly concealing everything lying inside, and walks back to the front of the store, coolly and confidently. The music picks up dramatically.

Scene Four

On his way back to the checkout counter, he throws a handful of penny candies into the box he is holding. At the cashier, he pulls the candies out of the box, pays for those, and explains to her that he needs the boxes because he is moving. Charmed by his charisma and good looks, she does not suspect there is anything else in the two boxes he is carrying. Then he walks toward the exit. His escape is certain. The music builds to a crescendo.

Scene Five

An older man wearing sunglasses and a tan jacket approaches him. *"Arrêtez!"* he shouts.

Scene Six

Dammit. That was not in the movie I wrote. The man gets closer.

Shit, shit, shit, shit, shit.

Scene Seven

Cut. Cut! This is not how the scene is supposed to play out. Cut!

A blind panic overtook me and I ran out of that store as fast as my skinny legs would take me. Half a block later I was already running out of breath: my life-long avoidance of anything resembling exercise was quickly catching up with me. I could hear the pounding of the store detective's feet on the sidewalk just a few feet behind me. He was getting closer and seemed to be picking up speed while I was losing mine. There was a moment when I was sure all he had to do was reach out and grab me. The box did not make running any easier. I was wishing I'd been asked to steal something smaller. Truffles, for example. Much easier to run with truffles. Then I felt his hand on my back, trying to get a grip on my shirt.

Have you ever heard those stories about seemingly impossible feats of strength, such as a mother lifting a car to save a child? Or a man fighting off an attacking bear? I can tell you now those stories are true. For when I felt that grip tightening on my shirt, I discovered the superhuman strength that adrenaline powered by pure fear can provide. At that moment, I had so much adrenaline pumping through my bloodstream I could have set a world record for the 100-meter dash with a tractor on my back. And so I ran, faster and faster, ran until the footsteps behind me slowed down and disappeared. Then kept running, because at that point I couldn't not run. It was twenty or thirty blocks before I could even slow down.

I have had my share of class-leading marks in school, made the Dean's List twice, earned glowing commendations from several teachers. I was elected secretary of the student committee in eighth grade, won art contests, earned compliments for my performance on the high school debate club, and even scored a game-winning goal in my soccer-playing childhood. But none of those achievements made me feel as good as I did when I laid that box of cheeses, butter, and still-warm baguettes in front of Gaétan.

Eight

Madelaine walked me down the long, dark hallways of the squat, stepping over holes in the floors and dodging water dripping from ceilings. She wore a short white T-shirt that kept riding up her belly and loose jeans that seemed in constant danger of falling. A jumble of big, colored bracelets on her left wrist jangled happily every time she moved. Her eyes were dark crevices: the kind of eyes that could see deep inside you and make you feel guilty about things you didn't think anyone knew about. We stopped in front of a cramped yellow room with a fridge, round metal table, and a toaster. "This is the kitchen. Help yourself. Everything here is for everyone here."

She had invited me for an official welcoming tour of the hotel, and as we walked I realized she was more than just the CEO, Director, and General Manager. The way she spoke to the people there, the way they listened, made it clear she was also their Pope, Imam, Rabbi, Elder, and Emperor. We stepped into the large artists' workshop/storage room. A few more people were there, painting, working, and thinking. One elderly man in a worn green tracksuit was doing tai chi. Different faces, different art, same vibe. No one spoke.

"Did Gaétan tell you what this place is about?" She stopped and turned toward me, her eyes burrowing into mine. "I hope you don't think we're some poshy bobo home."

"No, he... What's a bobo?"

"Bo-bo. It means we're not bourgeois bohemians. We're not just a bunch of spoiled, rich brats on a recess from civilization, acting out because our parents were too strict. We're not just shouting artsy-communist propaganda because it sounds rebellious. We are serious. We mean it."

"I don't know what you mean. What artsy-communist propaganda? What are you serious about?"

"So Gaétan didn't tell you." She shook her head and swore under her breath. "The Grand is not just an art squat. The Grand is a revolution. We are at war. We are fighting for our freedom as artists, and this is ground zero. We're here to bring about the end of the commercialization of art. This is where the end of days for agents, galleries, and auction houses starts. And that day is coming. Soon. It's coming soon."

"Oh, that." I nodded, as if I knew all about the revolution.

"Art has to be independent," she said. "It has to be free. It's too important to let itself be controlled by the corrupt palms of greasy capitalists. Artists shouldn't be forced to think about what some hedge fund investor thinks would look good in their living room, whether blues and reds sell better than browns to make a living. So—if that's what you really want to do, if you're just in this to make money"—hard notes of contempt creeping into that small, soft voice—"that's fine. That's up to you. But if that's what you want, you've checked into the wrong hotel. So..." She crossed her arms. "Which side are you on?"

My only goals in life were (a) becoming famous and (b) making millions selling my art, which didn't exactly qualify me for membership in this revolution. But I had fallen in love with this squat, these people, this makeshift Eden with its broken windows and smell of mold. So I nodded and said I was on their side.

"Pinky swear?" She smiled, holding up a finger.

"Pinky swear." We pinky swore, left the artists' workshop, and continued down the hall. "Who owns this place?"

"Some billionaire landlord from China, or America, or Russia, probably. Who knows, who cares. One day, they'll close us down and we'll be evicted, then we'll find another abandoned building to live and work in. Our revolution is bigger than any building."

The idea that this dilapidated paradise might be broken up one day struck me as a tragedy, but Madelaine just shrugged.

"There are all kinds of art supplies lying around here. Some donated. Some stolen. Some found. Some of it might even have been paid for. Take whatever you want." Madelaine led me into a large room, empty except for a scattering of old furniture, garbage, and a couple of oversize bean bag chairs. We sat down on them, and she rested her bare feet on my legs.

"What do you want, Declan?"

"I'm okay, thanks."

"No. I mean, what do you want?"

Oh, that.

The truth is, I wanted everyone on the planet to know my name, I wanted to have museums named after me and books dedicated to me, I wanted to be studied in university classrooms on all seven continents and have my name whispered by art students in dingy bars a hundred years from now. I wanted to be bigger than Coke and Pepsi, to have an entire room in the Louvre dedicated to my work, a statue of myself in Westminster Abbey, and my own hall in MoMA. I wanted middle-aged ladies in Brooklyn to read about me in the *New York Times* and to have fridge magnets with my work on them, and I wanted to make bags of money. But I couldn't tell her that because I had just pinky sworn. So, this is what I told her: "All I want is for artists to be free."

She was rubbing her feet on my lap, smiling that smile, the smile of happiness, freedom, and absolution. And before I knew what was going on, she had pulled her T-shirt and jeans off and I pulled mine off and she was sitting on my lap and suddenly everything was beautiful and for a few minutes I didn't feel like I was so alone. Then she lay on top of me, played with my hair, and fell asleep.

It was late, and I could hear a soft wave of sounds from outside our room. Music being played, people talking, work being done. There was no night in this squat, no daytime, no working weeks or lazy weekends, no deadlines, and no judgments. Life just flowed, followed a rhythm as natural and indecipherable as the tides. Every color in the rainbow was represented here: gay, straight, and everything in between and beyond, every culture, religion, and attitude, doing whatever they did. It was the perfect world writ small, a global paradise hiding out in an abandoned knitting factory. I wanted it to last forever.

When I woke up, everything felt different. The laconic vibe of yesterday had been transformed into a frantic energy as everyone helped prepare for the grand event that evening.

"This banquet is in honor of a great man. A poet of international repute and historical importance," Gaétan told me. I had found him in the dining hall, where he'd been working since early morning. "You chose a good time to join us." More and more people streamed into the room, dropping off an exotic assortment of decorations, lamps, chairs, utensils, plates, glasses, paintings, and musical instruments. Gaétan acted as master of the court, directing everything to its proper location, telling everyone what to do and how and when they should do it.

"Where did all this come from?" I asked.

"It's all donated. Contributions from unsuspecting benefactors." He must have noticed the confused look on my face. "We stole it."

Judging by the sheer volume of goods in the room, I imagined that half of Paris had been looted for contributions. The Grand Hotel was part art squat, part rebel enclave, and part den of thieves.

The walls were covered in all sorts of artwork, patio lanterns hung from the ceiling, and every inch of the table was covered in a wild mashup of antiques, art, and curiosities. There were voodoo dolls and Plasticine horses, exotic lamps and Chinese jigsaw puzzles, miniature African masks and antique candleholders. There was such a variety of plates, glasses, and cutlery that they seemed to have at least one piece from every continent in the world covering the last several hundred centuries. Almost everything looked old, chipped, or broken. It was as if they had been to an ancient garage sale put on by history's greatest empires but arrived late. The good stuff had already been taken, and they had to pick through the leftovers.

Eight o'clock. Everyone arrived right on time, as punctual as bankers, dressed up for the big night. They wore orange wigs and ostrich feathers, bowler hats and sparkling tuxes, sequins, and pounds of glitter. Gaétan wore a purple velvet coat that was so long it dragged on the floor, a fake fur collar, alligator boots with six-inch heels, and a silk top hat. He looked like a pirate in drag.

In Georgetown, I was always the weird kid. The one that was different. In a world where everyone fit in, I didn't. I tried, but the more I tried, the worse it got. There's a large price one pays for that, and I did. But here, it wasn't like that. No one fit in, no one tried, everyone's wires were disconnected. Here, it was normal to be weird and weird to be normal. Everyone was strange, like an island of broken toys that reveled in their brokenness. We all got to choose the colors that went in our rainbow.

There were thirty-two seats at the table, and only one was empty. That seat, at the exact center of the table, had been reserved for the guest of honor. I sat beside Gaétan, near the middle. At the end of the room was a stool surrounded by guitars, violins, ukuleles, and drums, like a miniature stage. Everyone at the table was talking, laughing, and singing. All these introverted caterpillars had transformed into social butterflies, energized in part by the vast amounts of alcohol and drugs that lay around the room as casually as Kool-Aid at a kid's party. One man, sitting at the end of the table, was reciting a long and rambling poem about a gay bear that fell in love with a straight farmer.

"That is Adalbert." Gaétan leaned over, shouting over the noise. "He's one of the guests of our hotel. An artist, poet, philosopher, and spiritual advisor." Gaétan poured wine into our glasses and nodded. "He was also a human smuggler, Carthusian monk, and world-class violin player."

"Is any of that true?" I asked.

Gaétan shrugged, as if the subject of truth was unworthy of serious consideration. "He plays the violin."

"By the way, Madelaine was telling me about our revolution."

"Oh yes." He nodded. "Our great revolution."

"Why didn't you tell me?"

"Because of what you told me at Le Bateau-Lavoir."

I supposed I should thank him for not telling everyone here about my plans for riches and fame, but I wondered why he hadn't at least warned me. Just as I was about to ask, the room went silent.

Everyone stopped and put their glasses down and became so still it seemed as if they had stopped breathing. Eyes went to the door at the end of the hall. It swung open, slowly, creaking on its broken hinges. On the other side of the door stood a small and slightly bent old man, leaning on a cane and staring at the crowd that was staring back at him. His eyes were small black circles, and a scowl suggested he wasn't impressed with what he saw. A dark blue suit, cut of fine silk but so big you could almost fit another person in there, hung off his hunched shoulders. The buttons were done up, but in the wrong places. A soft pastel green tie, loosely knotted, silk hat, and matching pocket-handkerchief pulled the entire ensemble together with eccentric style. He looked like a grumpy king, long since retired, who got dressed after too many drinks.

As he walked slowly toward the empty chair, the room stayed silent, as if in awe of the creature ambling toward his seat at the table. The only sound was the scratching of his shoes on the floor. There was not a movement other than his. It took a long while for him to get there, and I suspected he was dogging it a bit. Making a point, perhaps, that he could take as long as he wanted and everyone else could bloody well wait. Then he sat down, looked around, found Gaétan, and nodded.

Gaétan stood up, quietly clearing his throat.

"Tonight we honor one of the great poets of the world, and of history. For this is a man not of our time, but of all time." Gaétan waved his hands toward the man in the silk hat. "But he is more than a poet. He has influenced every great art movement of the last two hundred years, inspired the inspirers, guided some of the greatest artists in history throughout the creation of their most beautiful works. He is a lover and philosopher, student and soldier, sage and savant. Every word he speaks turns into a star; those are his words, not mine, but I borrow them for this special occasion. Ladies and gentlemen, and everyone in between, I give you Wilhelm Albert Wlodzimierz Apolinary Kostrowicki." He paused to take a few breaths and bowed slightly. "The Great Apollinaire!"

The room erupted in a cacophony of cheers, enough to lift the roof and shake the cutlery. Everyone stood and applauded with all the vigor they could muster. It went on for several minutes. But the old man didn't move. Didn't even smile. He sat, looking around, the scowl on his face still remaining, hard and stern. I did, however (it might just have been me), notice just the slightest whiff of a tear in a hardened eye. Perhaps, I thought, he wasn't quite as unmoved as he appeared to be.

There was just one little wrinkle. I had read about Apollinaire in my art history books, and I happened to know he had been dead for over one hundred years.

As soon as the cheering slackened, I whispered to Gaétan. "Who is he?"

"Weren't you listening? That is The Great Apollinaire."

"No, I mean who is he, really. Is he from around here?"

Gaétan furrowed his eyebrows and shook his head. "He is Apollinaire."

"I know, I know you're saying that's who he is, but *the* Apollinaire was a French poet. He died in 1918."

Gaétan looked at me, a hint of suspicion crossing his face. "For an artist, you have an unhealthy relationship with the truth. Of course he's dead. Then, as you can clearly see, he came back."

The old man picked up his glass, grudgingly accepted a toast from everyone, and the official party began. It was loud, so loud you had to shout to be heard over the laughter, cheers, speeches, and songs that filled the room. Soon, the table was filled with dozens of plates filled with all sorts of food, announced with great fanfare and received with greater enthusiasm. "Blanquette de veau! Cassoulet! Moules marinières! Boeuf Bourguignon!" More cheers erupted with every plate, and they kept on coming. I'd be impressed if this were a Michelin Star restaurant, but here, without as much as a working kitchen, electricity or plumbing, it was a culinary miracle. Had they liberated the city's top restaurants as well?

As the celebration went on, the old man they called Apollinaire sat by himself, occasionally shaking his head, drinking his wine, watching the revelry with a distant look on his face. I didn't hear him speak to anyone for at least an hour after the affair had started. Just sat and mumbled angry-sounding words to himself. Then Gaétan left his seat and I found myself sitting next to him.

He turned his head and leveled his eye accusingly in my direction. "Who are you?"

"I'm Declan. Nice to meet you, Apollinaire." He shook his head, as if to say I shouldn't expect him to return the courtesy.

"Where are you from?" he asked.

I almost blurted out *Georgetown,* before remembering the story I had told Gaétan. "San Francisco."

"That so?"

I didn't know what to say to that, so I just sat there. Could he tell the truth, just by looking at me? Was he really a sage and a savant?

"What do you do?"

"I'm an artist," I replied. "Painter. Oils."

"Ha!" He snorted. "That so?"

Once again, I didn't know what to say.

"I bet you love Renoir," he said.

I don't know why he said that. But I didn't. I didn't love Renoir. Renoir was quite possibly the artist that I disliked more than anyone. Long-dead poet or not, Apollinaire had insulted me and I was forced to defend myself. "You're wrong. I don't like Renoir."

He banged his glass on the table. "Ha!" he said again and shook his head. "I don't believe you."

"I don't. I don't like him." I started to launch into all the reasons I didn't like Renoir—his dull composition, treacly themes, white privilege subjects—but Apollinaire changed the subject before I could gain momentum.

"I knew Renoir. He was an idiot." Apollinaire banged his glass on the table again, harder this time.

"I believe it. I mean, actually, I don't believe it—how could you know Renoir? He died more than a hundred years ago."

"Why are you here?" he asked.

This was a better line of conversation. "I've come here to paint. I aim to—"

"Ha!" he said.

This would have been a good time to explain my philosophies on the noble art, but the minute I started talking he held his hand up to my face, palm just inches from my nose. I stopped talking. He kept staring at me, and all I could see was one of his eyes peeking out through his fingers.

Meanwhile, the party was getting louder, and more people were coming in all the time. A group of musicians had taken their place around the stool at the end of the room, playing songs while everybody danced and sang along.

"I'd like to propose a toast to the newest guest here at The Grand." I looked up and saw Gaétan standing on top of the table, glass of wine in hand, looking at me and shouting over the noise. "Everyone! Please. I would like to introduce our newest guest. Declan Tucker." The room went quiet. "This handsome young man, a brilliant and struggling young artist, born into poverty on the streets of San Francisco, has made his pilgrimage here to join our revolution! A toast!"

I felt a twinge in my gut as I smiled and accepted the cheers. One day I was going to pay for my lies, but for now I would just enjoy it. Why not? "We can also thank him for this fine cheese and bread." More cheers. Out of the corner of my eye, I could see the old man staring at me during the tribute. After the cheering died down, he spoke again.

"You look like Picasso."

"Really? I look like Picasso?"

"Oh yes," he said. "Spitting image."

I didn't look like Picasso. "Okay, well, thanks. No one has ever said that before."

"It's obvious to me."

"I never noticed."

"I didn't say you were smart."

"No, you didn't. That is very true."

"Maybe you are Picasso," he said. "Haven't you read the *Lotus Sutra*?"

"No, I haven't, I don't know what that is, and I'm not. I'm Declan, and I'm—"

He waved me off, eyes digging into mine. "You are. I'm sure of it."

"No. I'm Declan, and I'm from—"

"Yes, you are."

I wasn't Picasso, reincarnated, reborn, or otherwise. Wasn't a possibility. Couldn't be, obviously. I didn't believe in all that stuff, for one thing. Not a tiny bit. But even if I did, I'd be Monet, not Picasso.

"Thanks, but I'm—"

"Stop!" he said. "Please. Deny it if you will. But yes. Yes you are!"

"No."

"Ha!" he said, without explanation.

I just shook my head. "Thanks, I guess, but I'm—"

Apollinaire looked up. "Don't thank me. It's not a compliment. Picasso was an idiot."

A young man was dancing on a chair and fell onto the table, knocking it over. Everything fell on the floor with a loud crash. No one seemed to notice or care. Everyone was dancing, drunk-arguing, eating, or singing. I got away from Apollinaire as soon as I could, found a spot on an old couch near the back of the room, and settled in to enjoy the spectacle.

A young woman dressed like a dancer in a Toulouse-Lautrec painting was standing on the stool, kicking up her legs and warbling about some long-lost love. I was about to get up and find a drink when Chloé sat down on the other end of the couch.

She was wearing the same ripped jeans and Joy Division T-shirt she wore during our tour of the Louvre a few days ago. She had a sandwich in her hand and a plateful of food on her lap. Nodding her head to the ragged beat of the song, she seemed to have no idea I was there. My stomach turned into a tightly wound knot along with my tongue. I tried to think of something to say as I watched her with sideway eyes, while the warbling singer was replaced by a spoken word artist reciting something about a "supper, upper, and a rubber."

What do you say to the love of your life, the woman you prayed loved you, if she had run off and abandoned you without a word? What words could possibly fit this occasion? What makes that right? Should I confront her? Ask her what happened? Tell her how she made me feel? Or should I stand up, get her attention, give her a deep, meaningful stare, shake my head, and slowly but dramatically walk away?

But no. Walking away was out of the question. This was a chance for redemption, although I had no idea what I was redeeming myself for. The next few minutes were spent searching the deepest cavities of my mind for a simple, friendly, confident, maybe just slightly provocative, insightful-yet-amusing multilayered comment. Something that acknowledged the fact that she had abandoned me, left me to die alone, but that I was fine, really fine with everything, that I was strong and independent, yet not totally insensitive, but yeah, that I was totally over it, and life was great, full of joy and personal fulfillment. Also, something witty enough that she would fall in love with me again. Why was this so hard?

I was still searching when she glanced my way.

"Hi!"

"Oh, hi there!" I responded, opening my eyes wide in a pathetic attempt to pretend I just noticed her.

"I bet you never saw anything like this in San Francisco," she said.

So there it was. That was it. We were going to pretend nothing happened. Okay. Fine. If she could do it, so could I.

"Not where I came from," I said. She slid over on the couch toward me and smiled, sending a three-thousand-volt electric current coursing through my veins. Stay calm, Declan. Stay cool. You're fine. Totally fine. "The only banquets on our streets were in soup kitchens," I said. Dammit. That was not cool. I was such a liar. Such an idiot.

"Soup kitchens?" She laughed and shot me a curious look.

There was still time to change the subject, time for me to leap into a less incriminating conversation, something that wouldn't bury me in a sea of untruths. If only I had the will and inner strength to be honest. I had neither. Lacking another topic to latch onto, desperate to fill the air, I dug myself in deeper. "It was pretty tough, after my dad left us. We had lots of money, you know, when he was there, lived on yachts and stuff when I was little. But then he left, and it was just mom and me, and we didn't have anything. We lived in a trailer and, well, it got pretty bad, what with my mom's drinking and everything. Anyway, after a while I ran away and joined a traveling carnival. I was eleven. Got caught and had to go back home, but I ran away again and just rode the rails..." I laughed and shook my head, as if my imaginary decrepit youth was just an amusing anecdote I liked to tell at parties. "When I was growing up, I thought chicken noodle soup was a banquet."

"What is *riding the rails*?"

"You know, trains? Riding in trains?"

Chloé just shook her head. "That is all very different for me. But it does sound like you have had an interesting life."

There must be some psychological reason for why I would unleash these spasms of fabrication about my history. It was like I had some kind of Tourette's syndrome for personal fiction, a disorder of neurons that forced me to describe the unlikeliest, most fantastical stories about who I was. Why else would I invent this character, this sad and pitiful human being that grew up so poor on the streets of San Francisco? Why would I lie so habitually, so systematically? Was there some deep need buried in my unconscious that could only be treated through extended psychoanalysis?

No. There wasn't. It was simpler than that, and I knew it. Deep in places buried inside my own soul where I didn't want to look, I knew these lies were not created because of some cognitive disconnect in my personal wiring. This was not a problem Uncle Sam could solve. There was no psychological need being filled, no emotional wound being covered over, no need for Freud's red couch. I knew what it was. I lied because my true story was boring—no one wants to hear about straight white kids that came from well-to-do families. I wanted people to think I was interesting. I lied because I wanted people to like me. Even more, I wanted Chloé to like me.

Chloé looked at me as if she couldn't decide whether to hug me or run away. She said nothing, but tipped her head, just slightly, reached over and put her hand on my leg, just above the knee, and patted it three times. Three. It was as if

Mother Mary herself had come down from the heavens to bless my tortured soul. All was forgiven. She may as well have just granted me sainthood. The pain she had caused me when she had left me alone in the Louvre was forgotten. I loved her more than ever.

Then she turned away from me, looking around, surveying the room. For one terrifying second it looked like she might get up to leave. *Speak now, Declan. Speak! Engage this beautiful human beast! Show your empathy for the human condition! Impress her with your wit and charm! Say something dazzling! Don't let her get away again!*

"Does your family have a lot of money?" I blurted out.

"I'm sorry?"

"Does your family have massive amounts of money? Are they, like, royalty? Or anything?"

A glacier-thick sheet of ice formed in the air between us. She gave me a hard look, crossed her arms, and turned away. That was not the look I was going for. What was I thinking? I swallowed a panic attack and reached back desperately in my mind for another conversational gambit, something that would warm her heart and make her fall in love with me. "Why are you here?"

It took approximately one millionth of a second before I realized what a stupid thing I'd said—again. Chloé's eyes opened wide, her eyebrows raised, and she looked at me as if I had stabbed her. She slid a few inches away from me and looked away.

"I'm sorry. I just wondered...I didn't mean it that way. I'm glad you're here. I'm nervous, I guess."

She looked back at me, arms still firmly crossed. "Every artist in Paris is here. It's not exactly a secret."

I should have stopped there, should have left a little bit in the bottle, quit while the quitting was good. But I didn't. The neurons in my brain had shifted into overdrive, and my mouth didn't have the wisdom to stop them before they got out. "It's just that I've always had this idea that you're—that you had some kind of royal background, and that you live in a palace, or something like that, with chefs and butlers and everything." She looked away again, shaking her head. Why did I have to say that? If the universe had any feelings for me at all it would have sent a meteor hurtling toward my head at that very second. No such luck.

She looked at me, her face hard with anger. "I wonder why you are asking so many questions about who my family is."

"I don't mean to be, no, it's not that. I'm not being nosy. I'm just, I don't know..." I muttered and noticed her plate was empty. "I apologize. I shouldn't have..." Drowning in self-hate and confusion, I was desperate to change the subject to something less annoying. "Can I get you some more food? Or some wine?"

She lifted her chin and glared at me, voice bristling. "Maybe we do have royal blood, and maybe we are as rich as the Rothschilds. So what if my mother is the Queen of England? Maybe we live in a castle? My family is nobody's business."

I wanted to run away, disappear, bury myself in the couch, but instead I tried a different tactic. Denial. "I didn't mean it the way it sounded."

"Really? Then what did you mean?"

"I didn't mean anything, I was just making conversation."

"Why is your making conversation always about where we live or how much money we have? I'm sick of having my family, and who we are, being cross-examined. I don't know what you're trying to find out, but stop it. Just stop it."

A loud cheer went up in the room, and everyone started clapping.

"Are you one of those reporters that chases people like us everywhere? Do you work for one of those rag newspapers? You keep telling me how poor you are, but you are wearing, I can see, three-hundred-dollar jeans. I don't believe you. I don't believe you are who you say you are."

"No! No. I am. I'm an artist, like I said. I live here."

"I don't believe you." She turned away and slid down to the other end of the couch.

Her words cut into me like a thousand knives. I knew, by the look in her eyes, there was no redemption possible. I had been given a chance, a chance for a last at-bat-game-winning-home run, a Hail Mary touchdown in overtime, had it land right in my lap, and I had blown it by being stupid. I hated myself. I hated everything. I muttered a string of apologies, got up, and walked away.

Before I left the room I looked back and noticed that Gaétan had taken my seat on the couch. Ten minutes later, I worked up the nerve to look back in the room. The couch was empty and they were both gone. I looked around the rest of the squat, but they had disappeared.

Hours later, lying in my so-called bed, staring up at the cracks in the wall, I decided that I really did hate everything. I hated animate and inanimate objects, cold, rain, wind, clouds, sun, and heat. I hated small towns because they were boring and big cities because they were crowded, religious fanatics, atheists, and everyone that was in between. I hated the ceiling in this room. I hated TV because it was stupid and books because they thought they were smart. Hated people and pets—well, some dogs were okay, but mostly I hated pets. I hated every country in the world, but all for different reasons. I hated air, exclamation marks, colons and semicolons, the color cobalt and the chemical cobalt. I hated oceans and deserts equally, this room and this stinking mattress, the smells, and I hated myself and everyone I had ever known. I hated not having a glass of milk before bed and not having my old toothbrush. But the thing I hated more than anything was Gaétan.

How could he do that to me?

Nine

If you've ever been abandoned and left to die a miserable, lonely death, you know this sad truth: life goes on. My life disassembled. I stared into space a lot, felt tired all the time, didn't eat much, didn't care. Slept a lot. Avoided the other residents of The Grand. I mostly just sat in my room, watching mice scuttle around the floor and cockroaches crawling over the walls and ceiling. Occasionally I walked to the kitchen and back. If I saw anyone I would duck into another room until they passed by, then go back and hide in my room. And repeat. And repeat. And repeat. Day after day after day after day.

Only a few weeks ago, I was full of energy, inspiration, hope, and life. Those days seemed like a hundred thousand centuries ago. Now, I didn't want to get out of bed, didn't want to wake up. Didn't want to go outside, didn't want to be inside, didn't want to be anywhere. I didn't have enough energy to do anything and didn't think it mattered. Felt like I was stuck in a subterranean state of mind. I had turned into my own personal black hole, getting sucked deeper into an abyss with no way out.

I tried to paint once. Forced myself to pick up a paintbrush and stand in front of that canvas. I stood there, with my chin up and shoulders back, trying to force inspiration to happen. It didn't. I remained steadfast, holding onto that paintbrush and staring ever harder at the canvas, challenging it, willing it to give itself up to me. It didn't. Every now and then I would lift my hand, holding the paintbrush like a sword, as if daring the canvas to deny the force of my presence, but it showed no fear or mercy. That stretched fabric remained an insolent white, staring back, blank and foreboding. I detected a smirk. Even it knew there was nothing in me. The divine power that had guided my hand and fired my spirit had disappeared. I gave up and went back to bed.

One night, while I lay on my mattress trying to determine whether that stain on the ceiling was spreading quickly or slowly, a shadow appeared on my wall through fragments of moonlight. It shifted, as if a gloomy ghost were floating above me. A short and round ghost. No, I told myself. No. Clamped my eyes shut. It couldn't be. Please tell me Neil hadn't followed me here. Life had already crossed to the wrong side of unbearable: only Neil could make it worse. *Oh God, please tell me that evil poltergeist hadn't followed me here, and I promise to start going to church every Sunday.*

"*Merdi. Merdi. Merdi.*"

That didn't sound like Neil.

I opened my eyes and stared into the dark. All I saw was the shadow of a human outline in the door. My eyes adjusted and I could make out the general shape: short, thin, suit, tie. Top hat. Either Neil had had an afterdeath sartorial renaissance and learned to speak French, or it was someone else. Then the moonlight escaped from behind the clouds and I could make out Apollinaire standing in my doorway. I took a deep breath and sat up in bed.

"Apollinaire?"

"Who did you think it was?"

"Never mind."

He took a few steps into the room, sat down on the floor cross-legged, and stared at me for a few minutes. There wasn't much light, and the combination of the glow of the moon and the streetlamps threw waves of undulating shadows on this drooping, wrinkled invader.

"What are you doing, Tucker? Why have you locked yourself up in your room?"

How did he know I'd been locked in my room? "Thinking. I'm thinking about—"

He held up his palm. "Please."

"Please what?"

"When is your birthday, Tucker?"

"Why? What do you—okay, it's October twenty-fourth."

"I knew it. Scorpio. Ha! Same as Picasso." He punched a mottled fist in the air. "I knew it!"

Not that again. Please, I just wanted to be left alone in my misery. "I'm not Picasso, Apollinaire. I'm Declan." I really wasn't feeling very Picasso-like at that moment.

A derisive snort shot out of the dark. "Despite all the evidence to the contrary. You still believe that, do you?"

"What evidence? Tell me." I was getting angry, having had a good bout of self-pity interrupted. "What proof do you have?"

"It should be obvious, even to you. I'm sure it's crystal clear to everyone else on the planet, but no, Declan Tucker refuses to concede the point. Always has to be right. Typical." He shot me a stern look from under his hairy eyebrows.

I had no idea what was typical about it, but I didn't have the energy to argue about horoscopes, reincarnation, or anything else.

"Let me look at your palm." He removed his top hat and crawled toward me on his hands and knees. His head was close enough that I could see individual hairs on his spotty, balding skull. I smelled rotting teeth, cigarettes, and cheap brandy. I laid my hand in his. He pulled it close enough to his face to lick it and stared at it for a minute or two in silence.

"I knew it," he muttered, almost to himself. "Long Heart line. No Head line. Same, same."

I pulled my hand back and pushed myself against the wall, gaining as much personal space as I could. Thankfully, he slid back to the other side of the room.

"Same as what?" I asked.

"As if you don't know. You're also as dumb as Picasso."

"Okay, well, anyway," I said. "Listen, I don't need this—"

"Why aren't you painting?"

How did he know I wasn't painting? I didn't think anyone knew. "I'm taking a short break. Resting up. Germinating."

Another snort. "No, you're not. Why?"

I was about to ask him to leave me the hell alone. Why would I discuss this with him? But he seemed like he wanted to hear my story, and I had been alone for a long time. I supposed talking to someone might be helpful.

"You're right, you know. I'm not painting. Or doing anything. I don't know what it is, but I'm a bit depressed.

Extremely depressed, really. I can't explain it. It's almost like, like I don't care anymore about anything. I don't know what it is. I actually feel so horribly depressed, I don't want to get out of bed. Not to paint, or eat, or talk to anyone. Everything just feels so—black. Like nothing. But, you see, well, there was this girl, and I thought we really had something going on, you know, but then she—she left with my best friend. My only friend." I paused for a few breaths, so I could pull myself together before I started crying. "I've never had a lot of friends. My psychiatrist, he thought that maybe—"

"Boring," he said.

"What?"

"Boring," he repeated.

"But you asked me!"

"Yes! I asked a simple question and got an essay in return."

"Okay, fine, forget it. I'm going to go back to bed, then, so...."

He put his top hat back on. "Think you're the first one who's ever suffered?"

"No. I don't. And that doesn't help, really, so if you don't mind."

"Didn't you once say pain and anguish were like oxygen to an artist?"

"No."

"Yes, you did."

"I never said that."

"You did."

I hadn't said that—at least, not out loud. But I had thought it. Hundreds of times. Did he know that?

"Well, they are," he said. "And you know it." Apollinaire lay down on the floor, pulled a cigarette out of his pocket, and lit it. "Did I ever tell you about Picasso's best friend?"

"No. I didn't know he had a best friend."

"He certainly did. His name was Carles Antoni Casagemas."

He was born into a wealthy family of influence, of important politicians, composers, and writers. Carles Antoni Casagemas was good-looking, cultured, stylish, and one of the leading artists and poets of the modernist generation. He was everything the twenty-year-old Picasso wished he could be but wasn't. The two of them lived together in Montmartre, spent every day with each other, where they wrote and painted, frequented clubs and brothels, and drank a lot. Then Carles fell in love. Germaine was beautiful, with long, dark hair, full lips, and wild eyes, but she did not return his love. He loved her more. She mocked him in return. He became inconsolable, depressed, and soon, an alcoholic. One night, at the Café de l'Hippodrome, as she was walking out, he pulled a revolver from his pocket and shot her. He had only intended to frighten her, but she fell to the ground, and he believed she was dead. Thinking he had killed her, he put the gun to his right temple and shot himself. Germaine was unharmed. Carles died the next day. He was twenty years old.

"That's a horrible story," I said.

"It's a beautiful story."

"How is it beautiful? He shot himself when he was twenty."

"Yes, but it is inspiring," he said, filling the room with rancid smoke.

"He committed suicide! What exactly are you trying to inspire me to do?"

"You don't get it, do you?

"No. And this story isn't making me feel any better."

"The lesson isn't about Carles, idiot. Use your head. The lesson is about Picasso. He went into his own depression after his best friend died. But he painted his way out of it. Said it was the death of Carles Casagemas that started his Blue Period. Best work he's ever done, you ask me. You get it now? He painted himself out of it. Use it. Use it, you thickheaded fool! Use everything. Depression. Failure. Doubt. Tragedy. Lost love. That's where the inspiration is. That's what art is. The friction that makes the oyster."

I was about to ask where he got that line—I thought it was mine—but he just shook his head.

"You really are dense, you know that? If you had half a brain in your head, it would rattle." He stood up and stamped his cigarette out on the floor. "I have to go."

———

Once you've accepted that life is one endlessly recurring cycle of pain and suffering without any meaning, it doesn't seem so bad. It's the positivity that does you in. Better to relax and go with the misery; reconcile yourself to the fact that happiness is nothing but a fleeting delusion, existence will never amount to anything but futility and hopelessness, that death is the only escape, and—presto!—everything gets better. You've gone over the mental cliff and you've made it. You've gotten over the worst and you don't have to work so hard to be happy all the time. I had Apollinaire to thank for that. He was responsible for helping me see the light. The black light, I suppose, but the light nonetheless.

Since arriving here with the idea that I would soon be a famous artist, I hadn't managed to scratch out more than a few random lines on a canvas. Now I was ready to start again. The first thing I did the next morning was pick up my paintbrushes and start painting. My old muse had vanished, but another had come for me. This muse was a dark angel—a depressive, nihilistic type with too much pancake makeup, devil tattoos covering her arms and neck, and a dozen nose rings—but you can't choose your muse. She told me that I had spent more than enough days and nights staring at the ceiling and that I better get back to work. Trouble, depression, and turmoil had inspired many artists before me, she said, and she could see no reason why I couldn't put my own to good use. She was right.

My first canvas was covered entirely in black paint. Layers of black swooshes, black swirls, black rolls and twirls and whirls. So were my second, third, and fourth. I used carbon black, coal black, Vantablack, roseman black, charcoal, black olive, and café black. Every shade of black imaginable found itself on those canvases. If they didn't exist, I invented them. There was only one rule—I could use any color I wanted, as long as it was black.

This blackness was not a conscious choice on my part. I was merely a channel for an unseen force guiding my hand, choosing my colors, and putting paintbrush to canvas. In other words, I couldn't help myself. The paintings wanted to be black, and black they would be. My tenth, eleventh, twelfth, and twenty-first paintings also wanted to be black, and I was in no position to argue.

I felt like ten thousand miles of nerve endings. The ideas came to me like explosions going off in my head, so fast I had to work harder and harder just to keep up with them. I did three, four, sometimes five paintings a day, stopping only to buy more supplies. I painted in a mad fury, without thought given to composition, form, color, or time. My fingers were being guided by a power greater than my own, unable to stop or even slow down. I tried to sleep, would lie down and force my eyes shut, but visions of that empty couch where Chloé and Gaétan had sat would appear in my mind and I had to climb out of bed and pick up my paintbrushes again. This went on for days. Before long, every inch of wall space on the floor of my small room was holding up a finished canvas or three.

This dark muse was intense. I wondered if muses were just a bunch of messed up teenage girls who kept sneaking into their parents' liquor cabinet.

After nine or ten days of almost nonstop painting, I had worked myself into a semicomatose state. One morning, I lay down to rest for a minute and couldn't get up, couldn't even lift an arm. My body felt like it was nailed to the mattress. It was over. The obsession that had possessed me was finished. I felt empty, drained of whatever it was that had stoked the fire. But before I shut my eyes, I looked around at what I had done: dozens of black canvases filled every wall, every inch of floor space in my room. They weren't like anything I had done before, not like anything I had seen before. But they were as real and true as anything I had ever said or done in my life. Those paintings were me. I shut my eyes and slept.

A sense of renewal came over me. For the next few days, I walked around in a state that was both horrifically bleak and heavenly blissful. Although I was completely depressed, I was also full of energy and inspiration. Started getting up, going outside, talking to other people. I asked around and no one had seen Gaétan since the night of the banquet, which was fine, just fine. That just made it easier to move on with my life. One day I found some old books that had been left behind and read a few: Albert Camus's *The Plague* and *The Stranger.* Discovered that there is no salve for depression like the musings of a miserable, long-dead French philosopher who believed life was void of meaning. I wasn't the only one. There was a group of us that would get together on the roof of The Grand and discuss the finer points of universal desolation:

"As humans we want order, meaning, and purpose in our lives. But the universe is blank and indifferent. There is no meaning! Camus was right. Which is why we are such tragic, sad, and desperate creatures, always searching for hope where there is none."

"If that's true, then why don't we simply kill ourselves? What is the point of living?"

"Suicide is the coward's escape. We must accept that life's meaninglessness is truth, that meaninglessness is life. That life is better if it has no meaning."

"So to be hopeless is to be happy?"

"The point is to embrace the hopelessness of life. Only then we can be happy."

"You're wrong. You ignore the dualistic nature of man."

"Oh, here we go. Not the dualistic nature of man thing again!"

"Yes, here we go. And we'll keep going, until you understand that the opposition of metaphysical concepts represents a deconstruction that cannot limit itself to neutralization. It must embrace the binary hierarchical oppositions that dualism implies."

"You quote Derrida like he's some kind of god."

"Don't knock Derrida. He would be a god, if God existed."

What a great time.

I had spent most of my life trying to keep up with the mantra of positivity. Be the Change! Attitude Is a Choice! It was like air, always around but invisible and without substance. I had often wondered whether this rote optimism could be one of the causes of my own life-long battles with negativity and depression. I was expending so much effort trying to be happy, I was exhausted. It wasn't like that here. Everyone just accepted that you couldn't be happy all the time. You could walk around as depressed as a traffic victim and no one would ever say, "Someone's got a case of the Mondays!"

By now I had amassed a collection of fifty-two paintings, all of them sitting in my small room, resting on the floor. There were tidal waves of black, flowers of black, buildings of black, black skies and black dreams, swishing swirls of black, black hells and black heavens, and each one evoked a different dark rainbow of human emotions. No one, once they had laid eyes upon these works, would ever believe that black was not a color.

It was time to share my work with the world, time to let the gallery owners fight over who would win the right to hang these brilliant paintings on their walls.

Yet I couldn't. I had officially committed myself to the free-art movement, completely and without reservation. But as I lay on my mattress, looking at all the work I had done, I couldn't help questioning that decision. The price of that commitment grated away at my bones. On one hand, I got it, sort of. Free the artist! Free art! Yes, of course...but...on the other hand...maybe not this artist, and not this art. It killed me to see these beautiful works sitting on my floor, unseen and unappreciated by anyone but a few struggling artists from the squat. What if Van Gogh had kept his works hidden in his bedroom? Would the world be the same? Would humanity not be lessened if Monet had locked up his paintings in his attic? It wouldn't be fair to allow them to remain here. Not fair to me, not fair to the world. No, I couldn't do it. I could not be that selfish.

Digging through a closet full of abandoned art supplies, I found a worn portfolio that looked almost respectable. I packed as much of my work as I could squeeze inside that old bag, then set out to introduce myself and my work to the art galleries of Paris. I felt a sense of history. Monet had made the same trek as I was about to do, spending his days peddling his art to the local galleries, hoping to make a sale or two. So had Picasso, Van Gogh, and so many others. This was how it started, the first steps in the great artistic journey. I felt like James Cook setting off to discover a new world, or Alexander the Great setting off to conquer it. I was ready. There was only one minor complication.

Since the residents of The Grand believed that art galleries, dealers, agents, and anything to do with selling art was evil, I had to get out of here without being seen. If anyone saw me walking out with a portfolio of work, they'd send the hounds of hell baying for my blood. If anyone even got a whiff that I was planning on selling my art they'd have me hanged, disemboweled, beheaded, quartered, and burned, not to mention evicted. So I woke up early in the morning, grabbed my bag and snuck down the hall, quieter than the mice that ran ahead of me. Fortunately, the halls were empty. I escaped without being seen.

My first stop was in Galerie Kamel Perro. Pushing open the heavy glass door, walking in and looking around, I felt like I was shrinking. The gallery was big enough to park an airplane. There was a solemn hushing sound that shut out the world beyond. Everything felt important and expensive. Even the hum of the air conditioner seemed profound. A few canvases dotted the white walls, a few installation pieces were scattered on the floor. Far away, at the back of the store, was a large white desk. A thin, sharp-featured man was sitting there, staring intently at his computer. I looked around, stepped up to one of the first artworks hanging by the door and stared. It sparkled. I was still trying to figure out what it was when a whispered voice announced itself behind me.

"A most impressive work, yes? Over seventy-two thousand pieces of glass, each one individually hand-cut and polished by Stuki herself. Bold, beautiful, and brave, is it not?"

I turned around to see the gallerist standing right behind me. His big eyes looked down at me over half-moon glasses. The top half of his head was shiny-bald, the sides covered in long, straight hair that hung past his shoulders. He reminded me of one of those old college professors who couldn't believe how dumb kids were these days.

"It requires sedulous effort," he said. His voice was so quiet, it seemed as if he were whispering. I had to lean in to hear him. "Each canvas can take months, even years to complete, yes? But that is simply what must be, for that is how Stuki creates a singular experience that is so unique to each individual. An audacious work. What do you think?"

He hadn't taken his eyes off me, hadn't even blinked. Just stood there, waiting for a response. I tried to think of something intelligent to say. "It's sparkly."

"It is very, as you say, sparkly," he said, making a heroic effort at hiding his abhorrence at my boorish critique. "I suggest you act quickly. As you must know, a work of this stature will not remain available for very long."

It was not clear how he could mistake me for a potential customer. Since moving into the squat, I had adopted the street urchin look that Gaétan had perfected. My clothes were wrinkled and ragged, my shoes torn, and I smelled a bit. It should have been obvious that the price tag—€20,200—was €20,200 more than I could afford.

"It is also a great investment. Her work will soon be worth many times its current value. One need only follow the results at the most recent Sotheby's auction to—"

"I appreciate that," I interrupted. "I like Stuki, but—"

"It's very brave, yes?"

"Yes, it sure is brave. But anyway, the thing is, I'm an artist. I'm here to show you my work, not buy anything."

The gleam in his eyes turned opaque. "I see." He bent his head lower, saw my portfolio bag for the first time. "I see." A longer pause. "Mmm. Well. I thank you for your interest. Unfortunately, this cannot be. Our gallery represents a very select group of artists." His whispery, melodramatic voice changed to a bored drone. "Those artists are selected by a jury that meets but once a year. In July. The submission regulations are on our website. I suggest you read them carefully. Thank you once again for visiting us." He turned around and walked away.

July? That was months away. I planned on being an international success by then, and he wasn't even going to look at my portfolio? "Excuse me?" I said. He stopped but didn't look back. "It's just that, well, I was planning to be—" I took a deep breath, reminding myself that I was an extraordinarily supernaturally talented artist that would probably be at the center of an international bidding war soon. "I can't wait until July."

"Perhaps another gallery, then. Goodbye." He took a few steps, stopped again, turned around, and must have read the expression on my face and taken pity on me. Walking back, he rested a hand on my shoulder and sniffed. "Listen to me. I understand how you feel. I've worked here for thirty years, and I still can't get my work on these walls. Or any other walls, anywhere." He shook his head sadly and looked down at the floor. Was he crying? "Want my advice? Give up now. It's too late for me, but you—you still have your whole life in front of you. Quit while you're still happy." Watching him shuffle back to his desk, his head buried in his chest and shoulders slouched, I felt almost as sorry for him as I did for myself.

If I had known then that Galerie Kamel Perro would turn out to be one of the most positive and supportive galleries I visited, I might have given up and gone home. Packed up and moved back to Georgetown, gotten a job at Starbucks, or delivering pizza, or at the steel plant. But I didn't. Lucky for me, I had no idea how bad it could get.

Ten

My second stop was Aimée's Fine Art. It was a small and unassuming shop that couldn't have been more than thirty feet wide and held no more than twenty or so paintings on the wall. I had seen Aimée standing inside on a few occasions. She would be standing near the window looking out, and I would gaze in to see her lonely face gazing back at me. Occasionally, we traded smiles and small waves. I instinctively liked her. She was middle-aged and had a shock of bright orange hair on her head that resembled a motorcycle helmet.

I swung open the door and she glanced up from her phone, her face breaking into a big smile that held its position for exactly the amount of time it took to realize I was carrying a portfolio. Then it dropped and she went back to her phone while I hauled it in front of her and stood, waiting for her to look up again.

"What do you want?" she asked.

"Are you Aimée?"

"Yes. What can I do for you?"

I began at the beginning. My earliest memories, how art had been an inspiration all my life, my personal history (the San Francisco version), the lack of paradigms—the whole story. I was about fifteen seconds into my presentation when she held up her hand.

"Tsch." She crooked a long-nailed finger at my portfolio. "Let me look." I lay it on her desk, where it landed with a dull thump. "*Skurwysyn!* Are you selling by the pound?" she asked. That didn't sound French. Her accent had changed. It sounded Eastern European.

"I have over fifty works here. Let me give you the—"

"Tsch." That fingernail again. It could have been a lethal weapon on the wrong hand. She opened my portfolio and turned a page. *Study in Black #11.* Stared for a moment. Then turned the page. Far too quickly, in my mind, for there was no way she could have experienced the full range of emotions the work was intended to evoke in the short time she looked at it.

"Excuse me, but you kind of rushed that," I said. "Did you notice how the—"

"Tsch." She was already onto the next work.

"This is *Study in Black #3.* I used a different brushstroke here, to evoke a sense of the multiple levels of despair—"

Fingernail up. "Tsch." A few seconds later, she turned the page to another work. *Study in Black #16.* I wondered if I should have spent more time on the titles.

"You might appreciate this work better if I explained its evolution. It's interesting. The initial concept for this particular piece came to me one night after a cockroach—"

She looked up at me, stern and unsmiling—it seemed like a warning. The finger lifted again. "Tsch." Five seconds later, she turned the page. Why was she rushing? She couldn't possibly have understood the genius of the work in five seconds. I tried to help. "See that color black? I call that black *Arsenic Black.* I invented it."

Fingernail up. "Tsch. Shut." Page turn.

"The concept behind this is simple. I asked myself, what if everything was black? Have you ever thought about what life would be like if the air was black? It's a serious—"

Fingernail up. "Tsch!" Page turn. Stopping and resting her chin on her hand as she stared, sometimes sighing, sometimes smiling (but what kind of smile? This-is-sheer-genius smile? Or I'm-looking-forward-to-a-glass-of-frozen-vodka-after-work smile?).

"*Study in Black #27*. The idea is that you enter into this piece, immerse yourself in it, then when you come out, you've changed into a—"

"Tsch." I was getting tired of all the tschs. Tired of how quickly she was racing through my work. Also tired of standing up. Why don't galleries have chairs? Finally, after thirty minutes or more, she shut the portfolio and pushed it back to me.

"No." She picked up her phone and started scrolling through emails.

"No? Wait—I'm sorry? No?"

"We only take online submissions. Application criteria is on our website."

"What do you mean *only online*? Then why did you even look at them?"

She held her phone closer to her face. "Online only. Too many artists wishing for space in the gallery. I can't see all of them."

"But you already did. You just saw these."

"Tsch."

Tsch? After standing patiently, quietly for thirty minutes, I deserved more than a *tsch*. "I understand," I said.

"You want me to follow the rules of submission. You get lots and lots of applications for every space and can't look at every one. I get it. But you—you're right here. You've already looked through them. So you can at least tell me. Tell me what you think."

"No. Not here."

"Just tell me."

"Email your proposal."

"I can't. I don't have a computer! Or a proposal, or anything. I don't have anything. This," I said, pointing at my portfolio, "this is all I have." It struck me. This really was all I had. I had this one hope, and that was it. If that disappeared, then what was there? What would be left? I was leaning over a mental cliff and close to falling.

She looked through me then. Right through me, straight through to the street outside, where I guessed she wished I was standing right now. Put her hands behind her head, pressed against her hard, orange hair. "It would be better if you left. Just go. Forget you were ever here."

"No. No. I'm not leaving until you tell me. This"—I pointed at my portfolio—"is better than all that." I waved my arms around the gallery. "I know my work is good. So what's wrong with it? Why can't you tell me?"

"There is nothing wrong with your art."

"But you said *not here*. I need to know. What's going on?"

She lifted her eyes and looked at me again, her face softening the smallest of specks. That finger lifted and was put down again. "I should say nothing. Nothing good can come of it. But I will anyway. Here goes. Are you ready for the hard truth? It's very nice, yes? Your work is very nice, beautiful even. It speaks to me. It speaks to me in many, many ways. I like what it is speaking. The black is—is what? I don't know. It is speaking to me about my father, who is dead, who died a horrible tragic painful death, and this art speaks to me about that. The poor man was killed in a fire, burnt to a crisp. Now I have closure. For this I thank you. This work, it is brutal and elemental. Sticks sharp daggers into the core of my soul. Which I like.

"But you want to know, why not here? Because that is not enough. Not"—she waved both hands at the window, as if she were trying to push the world away—"in this gallery, not in this city, not in this country. Not today, not anymore. There is no true art in Paris anymore. One hundred years ago, yes. Today, no. Here, in this land of the la-la, there is nobody serious left. There are only the professional art buyers, investors, rich tourists, and people with stupid amounts of money; nothing but charlatans and whores who think that art means only happy things, bright colors, flowers, trees, patterns that fit over couches and match the furniture and go with the pillows and make money. They are cultural prostitutes, selling their empty souls for a hollow smile. You're better than that."

A thimbleful of hope in an ocean of negativity. "But—"

"But nothing. You think someone is going to pay good money to hang a black canvas over their two-hundred-thousand-euro Louis Vuitton couch? Stick to greens and blues if you want to sell anything today. Paint with ochre. Orange, red, yellow. Then more ochre. Or better yet, be a famous person. People love to brag about their art, like they bagged some exotic animal. Look at me, I've got a Balincourt! I've got a Panier! I've got a Warhol, Koons, Pollock, Kandinsky, Sherman, Kusama! That is art today. You know, I wish these people would crawl back under their sandalwood floorboards."

I couldn't help thinking about what Madelaine had said. About not putting a price on art. How art should be free, that it should exist in its own context. But that wasn't what I came here to accomplish. I would prove Aimée wrong. My chin went up, and I tried to project a tone of masterly confidence in my voice. "I will. You watch. My name is Declan Tucker and I will—"

"You won't. If you want to sell this work, go to my country. Poland is a serious place. We understand black, brutalism, and elementalism. We love a good despair. Go. Try a gallery in Warsaw. It is two thousand kilometers away, so you better start walking."

I had one more question before I left. "Are you really Aimée?"

"Of course not. I'm Gertruda. But no one in this cultural cesspool of a city would buy art from someone named Gertruda." She shook her head, jangling her earrings. Affecting a French accent, lifting her chin in a desultory French style, she said, "So I am Aimée. *Bonjour, les amis. Très bien, merci?*"

I kept going. In gallery after gallery, throughout that day and the day after and the day after that, I kept going. Heard nothing but muttered apologies, closing doors, and variations of the same speeches. If they spoke to me—and most didn't, other than telling me to apply online—they cried about their lives and the state of art today. Mostly they just rushed me out and sent me on to other galleries.

If I was miserable before, I'd at least found a way to be content in my miserableness. I had accepted my depression, even learned to think of it with a kind of warm affection, as a pathway to inspiration. But that was then, back when I still believed my art had divine power, that I had a uniquely supernatural talent and that it was only a matter of time before the world realized my genius. I had hope. Now, I was starting to lose even that. And I thought nothing could be worse than that.

I was wrong. There was a lot worse than that.

———

Sneaking out of The Grand was easy enough if I left early in the morning, because no one was awake. Sneaking in at night was more difficult, but I had found an open window near my room and all I had to do was wait until the hall was clear and I could crawl in without being caught. There was little chance of being seen on the street—the galleries I was visiting were in a part of town the squat dwellers didn't frequent.

So I spent the days walking all over the city, lugging my portfolio around, being turned down everywhere I went. I visited so many galleries that I lost count. My feet hurt, my legs cramped, my shoulders screamed, but I refused to listen. It wasn't the physical pain that hurt, anyway. Rejection was just part of the business, I told myself, although I never believed it would happen to me. But now that it was happening it hurt like hell. It seemed as if a six-foot-thick steel door had been shut in my face.

On some level I was still convinced of my own powers, otherwise I might have ended this quixotic search. But I was convinced, and I didn't stop. It didn't matter what they said, I repeated to myself a thousand times a day. Whatever, whatever, whatever. Imbeciles and ignoramuses! Uncultured idiotic morons! They didn't know what they were missing out on. Yet every *no* was like a hot poker stuck inside my tender artist's heart. It was a kind of psychic torture, this constant rejection, but I kept at it. There was no way I would allow these nattily dressed gallerists with their questionable hairstyles and clear enunciation to stop me.

My hopes faded to a barely perceptible sliver. After another day of confronting a wall of rejection I lay on my mattress, exhausted beyond reason, and stared at a cockroach crawling across my ceiling. Of the two of us, it seemed to lead the more charmed life. At least that insect had a reliable supply of food and water, no fear of being evicted, and lots of friends and family nearby. Also, it hadn't just spent the last few weeks having its artwork rejected by just about every gallery in Paris. I imagined that ugly bug had spent a leisurely day lounging around, talking with other cockroaches about their lives and loves, what everyone else in the nest was doing, and making plans for the next day. Leading a nice, relaxed cockroach life.

Or perhaps not. Perhaps that cockroach led that comfortable, happy life at one time, secure in its luxurious cockroach home—but decided it wasn't enough. Maybe that cockroach had somehow convinced itself it was better than all the other cockroaches and was meant for bigger things. Perhaps that ancient arthropod had convinced itself it was the most brilliant cockroach in the nest, and had quit its job and abandoned its home and family to search for international cockroach fame. Then, after a few weeks, that lousy stupid bug had found nothing but rejection and was beginning to think it had made a huge mistake and wished it could just go home. What a stupid cockroach move that would have been.

There was still one door that hadn't shut on me, and it was the most famous, powerful gallery door in all of Paris. The Baumhauer Gallery. My last chance. I woke up early the next morning, picked up my bag, snuck out, and started walking. This was it. All the chips were in the pot and every card was on the table. If I didn't make it here, I would have to—no, that was not an option. I had to make it here. There was no room for ifs anymore.

The gallery was on Rue des Déchargeurs, a gentrified street in the South Pigalle neighborhood of Paris. I saw the Baumhauer Gallery from a few blocks away, surrounded by trendy cocktail bars, a small bakery, and a new condo with a sign in front that read, in English and French, Live the Life YOU Deserve!!! Easy for them to say. Set far back from the street, the gallery was a large, flat, three-story red-brick building, one of those industrial warehouses from the 1900s that had been restored to retro-coolness. I walked up to the gallery door, pulled it open—it was a big door, and required two hands—and stepped inside.

Like every other gallery I had visited, it had a hushed quiet that seemed to have never felt the echoes of a raised voice. The main desk looked small from here, but only because it was so far away. I walked toward it, passing under a massive iron structure that looked like a giant spider, past a row of framed burned-out light bulbs on wax cubes, and almost stepped on a pile of white bricks lying on the floor, looking as if they had been dumped from a wheelbarrow. I thought it was an area under construction until I saw the plaque beside it.

The woman at the desk was busy with customers, so I wandered around the gallery, waiting for an opening. The works here weren't all landscapes and bright colors, not all blues, greens, ochres, and happiness. There was a pile of dirty laundry spread out on the wooden floor. The plaque beside it somberly announced its title: *A Pile of Dirty Laundry*. There was a jar of used toothbrushes under a glass case. Title: *Used Toothbrushes*. This was my kind of gallery. The canvases dotting the walls included shapes and swatches of darker colors and abstract intent, random pieces of no obvious context and haunted profiles with a primitive sensibility. This gave me hope. Maybe my black canvases had a chance here. I kept looking back but the woman at the desk remained busy, and more customers were lining up. It seemed like there would be a long wait before I could see her, so I went up the stairs.

The first room I found had four worn-looking duffel bags near a wall. I thought it was an installation, but a woman wearing an orange vest and hard hat picked one up and walked away with it, so I wasn't sure. A wall-sized screen in the next room played a video of a man lying on a beach. Watching the video for five minutes revealed nothing more than a seagull flying. The seagull must have been a symbol for something, but I couldn't guess what. It was probably something brilliant: one mustn't judge too quickly. Remember, I had a portfolio full of black canvases.

Then I saw him. Hans Abel Von Baumhauer. He was sitting behind an oversize wooden antique desk, staring intently at his computer screen. The man who had been pulling every string in the art world around here for decades. The man who owned many of the most successful galleries in France and beyond. Abel Von Baumhauer could start a rush on an artist with one purchase or destroy her with one deprecating remark. He was, to many, the final arbiter on what was good and what was bad. He was the King of the Galleries, the God of the Art World.

Standing near his door, I stared, watching him work while working up the nerve to make my approach. I was so close! This was it. I was just a scruffy unknown with a fading sliver of hope, but I knew this was my big chance. An audience with the great man himself! What luck! Finally, the kid from Georgetown was catching a break. This was, I thought, quite possibly the most exciting moment of my young life. I couldn't possibly screw this up.

"You will leave. Now." He didn't even look up when he spoke. His stiff German accent reverberated off the windows around his huge office. At first, I wasn't even sure if he was talking to me. But there wasn't anyone else around, so he must have been.

"Mr. Baumhauer. Please. I just need a minute. Sorry to interrupt, but I'd like to—I'd really like to show you my work."

He didn't look away from his computer. "You are unwelcome to do so. Go away. Do not invade my space again." Every word enunciated with military precision.

"I promise. It will only take a minute." I took a few tentative steps forward and stood inside his office. It was only after a long and uncomfortable pause that he turned around and looked at me. Thin lips with hard eyes, a dark black suit and blue tie. Back straight. There was a look of contained hysteria across his face.

"Go away. Shut the door and do not come back. I have no interest in your work."

"I can't. I just can't. I can't leave." I was trying to keep my voice deep and important sounding, but failing miserably. It sounded like I was singing falsetto. There was sweat forming on my back, forehead, and upper lip. "I've been to every other gallery. No one's giving me a chance."

"Leave. Or I will have you arrested."

No way. This was my chance, and I was taking it. I took another step forward.

He reached for his phone.

Walking toward his desk, chin down, determined to get my work in front of him, I passed by the one piece of art in his office: three basketballs in a fish tank, suspended in water. I recognized it from a book I had read. It was Jeff Koons's *Three Ball Total Equilibrium Tank*. It had been described as "one of the most influential works in the history of art," and I remembered that it was worth over $20 million. I'm pretty open to new art, but this—to me, anyway, and I'm trying really hard to be open-minded—this was just a few floating basketballs.

"Please." I stood beside his desk and laid the portfolio on it. Gently.

"There is a trespasser in my office." He spoke into the phone, his eyes warning me away, one manicured hand clenching into a fist. "Send the police now." He looked at my portfolio as if I had permanently soiled his antique walnut desk. "Get that shit away from me."

"No." I stood straight, chin up, felt my chest sticking out. "You can take one minute and look at my work." My lips trembled and my hands shook, but I wasn't backing down. Not now. It was too late for that. If this was going to be Declan's last stand, it was going to be one to remember. I wasn't giving up without a fight.

He stood up. We were less than a foot apart, staring at each other, breathing hard. Hostility flashed in his eyes. He put his chin down and wound both of his hands into tight fists, like he was getting ready to punch me. It seemed impossible. Was he really going to fight me? When I said I wouldn't give up without a fight, I didn't mean a *fight*. We were both such thin, bony creatures. I bet the weakest punch in the world would shatter us into a million pieces. You couldn't find two less likely fighters in the world; I doubt that either one of us could beat up a cat. But he still looked like he was going to wind up and clock me.

Then Baumhauer lifted his chin. "No one looks at your work because you are an ugly, odoriferous, short-browed punk with a bad haircut and the clothes of a street urchin. Why don't you go back to your little country hole and put your pictures back on your mother's wall?" He unclenched his hands, looked at me like I wasn't worth the trouble, and sat down at his desk.

It was too much. My last sliver of hope had closed, my dreams had officially died. It was all over, my life was finished, everything was done. I had failed. It was time to give up and accept the inevitable, pack my bags, and take the next flight back to Georgetown. So I turned around to leave and took a few steps toward the door. But on my way out I stopped and drove my fist through his fish tank.

I had only intended to give it a good punch, but my arm went right in, all the way to the elbow. There was a loud crash, the glass burst and cut into my hand and arm. The water spilled out and the basketballs dropped to the ground without a bounce and lay there. My hand was covered in blood, dark red from the nails to the wrist, the blood dripping all over the floor. There was a bone sticking out from my thumb. I don't remember feeling any pain. I do remember hearing a scream behind me, then two thin arms wrapped around me, and I was being pulled to the ground. Something sharp cut into the side of my head. Hans Abel Von Baumhauer was biting my ear.

I wiggled out of his grasp, somehow avoiding the glass on the floor. We both scrambled up, standing and staring at each other. The only sound in the room was our breathing. Von Baumhauer reached up and slapped me on the face, then slapped me again, and kept slapping me. Six or seven smacks echoed off the glass wall and I bent down, covering my head. Then he started kicking me. Hard. I tried to hold onto his waist so he would stop. He wouldn't. He was punching, kicking, screaming, and swearing at me, calling me names in French, English, and German, but I couldn't hear what he was saying because of all the blood flowing through my ears. He pulled my hair and stuck a finger in my eye.

I was trying to get away when some other hands grabbed me from behind and held me. When I looked up, there was a group of shocked and horrified people standing in a circle around me. Someone pushed me away from Von Baumhauer, who was now on his knees, covering his face with his arms. His head and shirt were covered in blood. My blood.

A few minutes later, I heard the wailing sirens of the Paris police force calling for me.

Eleven

At the police station I was dragged inside and locked in a cell. The door clanged shut: a menacing, echoing, end-of-life sound. The cell was a vision of hell itself—walls of white concrete covered in disgusting graffiti, a metal two-level bunk, a sink, and a small hole in the ground for a toilet. Thick iron bars blocked my escape, as if I was going to try to escape. Everything felt hard. The mattress was hard, the pillow hard, the walls concrete hard. Even the air felt hard.

There was no one in the cell but me and a small, elderly man who smelled like he'd been marinated in alcohol and stale body fluids. He was sleeping on the floor. I took the upper bunk, curled up in a ball, and tried not to think. But trying not to think only made me think more, and before fifteen minutes had passed I had imagined every prison nightmare anyone could imagine a hundred times. I swore I would never fall asleep, no matter how long I was in here.

A few hours later I felt like I had been locked up for ten years. Sitting in this small, cramped room had already started to make me crazy. How was I going to last another five or ten or fifty years? The drunk on the floor rolled over and looked like he was about to throw up. I redoubled my efforts not to fall asleep. Tried everything, including push-ups, meditation, math problems, remembering scenes from old movies. Eventually, I fell asleep anyway. The last thing I remember was wishing I had never watched *The Shawshank Redemption.*

A pounding of hard plastic on the steel bars of the cell woke me up. I opened my eyes to see one of the policemen standing outside, banging his baton back and forth on the bars of the cell. It took a few moments to focus, but when I did, I realized he wasn't alone. Gaétan was standing beside him, a big grin on his face.

"You are a lucky man," the policeman said. "Your friend has posted bail."

Gaétan posted bail? Impossible. This had to be a dream. He could not have posted bail. How could he? He was even poorer than me. My old friend (actually, my ex-friend, ever since *the incident*) never had enough money to buy a loaf of bread or a shred of clothes. How much was bail? I guessed somewhere between a few thousand and a few million euros. There was no way Gaétan could come up with that kind of money. This was a cruel joke, I guessed. Someone having a good laugh at Declan's expense.

"Croquis. So nice to see you again." He gave me a little half wave.

It had been weeks since I had last seen him, the night of the banquet, the evening of The Great Betrayal. He had vanished from the squat that night and no one had any idea where he had gone. Now he had returned and was standing outside my cell, bouncing on his feet, smiling, and nodding his head.

"Thanks," I said. The word didn't seem nearly big enough, but I was anxious and confused and still angry and nothing was making sense right now.

Gaétan rested his forehead on the bars of the cell and looked around. "Are you sure you want to leave? It's so nice here. Reminds me of the Tate Modern." The old man on the floor rolled over and threw up. Gaétan smiled. "See? It's exactly like the Tate Modern."

The policeman opened the cell door and walked me to the front desk, where I signed something that I didn't read and they didn't explain. "Do not disappear," he said, making sure I gave him his pen back. "Or your friend will not see his fifty thousand euros again." He put his elbows on the desk and gave me a tough policeman look. "And we'll hunt you down and lock you up for a very long time."

Gaétan and I walked out of the police station and down the street. For a few blocks, neither one of us spoke. I should have felt an overwhelming gratitude, but I didn't. There was some gratitude. After all, this homeless person who never had a penny to his name had just donated fifty thousand euros to get me out of jail. But the gratitude was mixed with great gobs of anger and resentment. That anger had sunk into my bones, and I couldn't let go of it just like that. Ever since the night Gaétan disappeared with Chloé, I had been hating him a little more every day she was gone. I guess I should have gotten over it, moved on, forgiven and forgotten and all that, but I couldn't do that. I couldn't. Part of me wanted to tell him to go to hell, to keep his fifty thousand euros, and I'd just go back to jail, but I couldn't do that either. I wanted to hug him and punch him in the face in equal measure.

"How'd you know I was in there?" I asked.

"Everybody knows. Your face is on the cover of every newspaper in Paris." We walked past a magazine stand, where I saw my bloodied face on the front page of *Le*

Monde over the headline "Man arrested in vicious assault on art gallery owner."

Not exactly the fame I had come here searching for.

I tried to explain how I ended up in jail and thanked him for getting me out and told him what I thought of him for stealing Chloé and how I hated him and loved him and asked him how he just happened to have €50,000 and how he was the only real friend I ever had and that he was my worst enemy, but the words came out in a jumble so confusing even I couldn't make sense of it.

"Perhaps you would join me for a glass of wine?" he asked.

Good idea. A few blocks later, we found a small outdoor café and grabbed a table.

"My friend just broke out of jail and wants to celebrate," Gaétan told the waitress. "A bottle of Château Latour, please and thank you." *Latour?* I knew that wine. My parents had one in the basement. It was in the never-come-anywhere-near-this section.

The waitress looked at him suspiciously and folded her arms across her chest. "That's like, twelve hundred euros," she said. "You have to pay for it first."

Gaétan pulled a thick handful of wrinkled bills from his pocket and handed them to her. There must have been €2,000 there. She grabbed the money, looked at it as if it were counterfeit, and disappeared into the kitchen.

We watched the city go by while we waited for our wine. The café was busy, as cafés in Paris always seem to be. A warm breeze was washing the jail smell out of my clothes. The waitress returned, and this time she gave Gaétan a big smile and poured our wine without taking her eyes off him. She tried to make small talk, but he ignored her and picked up his glass.

"Cheers," he said. "Congratulations on your escape." We clinked glasses, and he leaned back in his chair. "So. Do tell. How does a nice, polite young man like you find himself charged with aggravated assault and property damage over twenty million?"

I took a long drink. Then another. "I'm going to tell you everything," I said. "But first, tell me one thing. Where did you come up with fifty thousand euros?" I figured I'd save the why'd-you-steal-Chloé-from-me question for later, since we probably wouldn't be speaking after that.

He drank again, let the wine slowly seep into his throat, and looked at me. "Oh, that."

"Yes, that."

"You really want to know?"

"Oh, I do, I do."

"Well. I suppose I can tell you, but...between us only?

I nodded.

He paused and looked up into the sky, then exhaled dramatically before looking me hard in the eyes. "Did I ever tell you that I have a painting in the Museum of Modern Art?"

I waited for a smile that didn't come. "You didn't mention that."

"I suppose I may have forgotten."

"I suppose you did."

"Then, I may also have forgotten to mention I have work in the Tate Modern and the National Gallery. Did I—"

"Nope. Didn't mention that, either."

A pigeon landed on our table and looked at Gaétan as if he were a celebrity, then looked at me and flew away. "I suppose I didn't."

"Funny how that would slip your mind."

"I heard a story that apparently your Beyoncé bought one of my paintings. They told me she hung it in her bedroom."

"She's not *my* Beyoncé, but still—really? You're not kidding? And if you're not—what the hell? Beyoncé? MoMA? Tate? What did you do? How? When? What? If any of that is true, why are you living in a squat? Why are you stealing food? Why don't you ever have any money? How could this not come up in conversation?"

"It's a long story." He picked up his wine, emptied it, and refilled both our glasses. "I didn't want to bore you."

"You can tell me now. I'm not going anywhere." Except to jail, but that wasn't until later.

The bottle was almost empty. He waved at the waitress to bring another.

"One day you're stealing spray paint from Castorama, the next day you're in Beyoncé's bedroom. You can imagine what that must feel like, right?"

No. I couldn't imagine what it would feel like to be in Beyoncé's bedroom. "Congratulations, Gaétan. That's unbelievable, and, wow, incredible. Why didn't you tell me? I am impressed." This was a lie. I was not impressed. I was shocked and dumbstruck. But more than that, my lingering resentment was now mixed with a cold jolt of jealousy.

It is a truth universally acknowledged that artists, upon hearing of the success of one of their fellow artists, will express great joy, happiness, support, and congratulations with gushes of enthusiasm, often accompanied by hugs, tears, and kisses. And they will, at the same time and without hesitation, secretly wish fire, hell, and brimstone upon that same fellow artist's loathsome soul in a pique of red-eyed envy. There are no exceptions to this rule.

A second bottle of Château Latour was placed in front of us. Gaétan dropped a pile of bills on the table, filled our glasses, and raised his.

"But first. To my brother Robert," he said.

"Brother?" We clinked and drank.

He didn't say anything for a minute, just tasted the wine and stared into space. When his glass was empty, he stood up and said, "I have to show you something."

There was more than half a bottle of twelve-hundred-euro wine left, but Gaétan was already standing on the sidewalk, waiting for me. He walked ahead and didn't say anything for the first two blocks. Then he stopped, turned around, took a deep breath, and started talking.

"My family, we grew up outside of Oran. That's a city in Algeria. My parents, my brother, and me. We were twins. My father worked as a carpenter when he could find work, but there wasn't much of that. But it was fine. It was fine! We didn't have any real problems."

Gaétan had always been slow and certain while he spoke, but now he was talking rapidly, as if in a hurry to finish. He turned around again and started walking, quickly this time. I had to hurry to keep up.

"There was always enough. It wasn't like we went hungry every day or anything. Not every day. We were happy, even. Then on our sixteenth birthday, I remember it perfectly, my parents told Robert and I that they were sending us away. Just the two of us. Happy birthday! You're going away. They said that. Happy birthday. They had paid for our passage to France. I honestly think they thought we would be happy about it. We weren't. We cried, we wailed, we told them we wouldn't leave, but they didn't listen. They said there was nothing for us here, nothing would ever get better, you know, unless. Who does that to a sixteen-year-old? My dad just kept saying 'just go, it will get better, it will get better.' He brought us to a man who threw us in the back of his truck along with twenty other people. We crossed the sea in an old tin boat that I was certain was going to sink, were loaded into another truck, and three days later they dropped us off on some street in Paris. That was it. We were on our own.

"It was hell. We slept in parks, alleys, and abandoned buildings, stole food to eat, cried all the time. But, you know, I guess you can get used to anything. Eventually we figured it out. We survived. Every now and then one of us would find a job in a kitchen or construction. We'd save up enough money for beer and spend our nights painting graffiti on brick walls in alleys or abandoned buildings. That's what we did for fun. We weren't trying to be anything. We were children."

He paused and I felt like I should say something, but before I did he started again.

"We did that for almost a year. Then the weirdest thing happened. We started getting a reputation as artists. Which was crazy. We were just a couple of stupid, drunk kids. But graffiti was the new thing, you know? One day it was graffiti, the next day it was street art. Ha. I think some people found meaning in what we did, and there wasn't, but. At first it was mostly underground press, then *ARTnews* did a feature on us, and boom! Just like that we had been discovered. It was— wow. Nice. Ha! So weird, surreal, ridiculous, stupid even, but also, for us, nice." He laughed. A high-pitched laugh I had never heard from him before.

We turned off the main street and walked down a small side alley, vacant except for a few run-down looking apartments. "Everyone was looking for the next famous street artist. They found Robert and me. Who knew? Not us. There were interviews on TV, radio. All the galleries, private collectors, auction houses, they were all fighting for their slice of the street art pie. We went from sleeping in tents to living in expensive hotels in a few months. Everybody was suddenly so nice to us. Fame, money, and more money. It was exciting, yes. But of course, you know what happens. We were dumb kids with money, and no one watching over us. Drugs were everywhere, and we didn't know any better, so guess what? We were doing ecstasy, heroin, whatever we could find. Most nights, we'd get so messed up we couldn't find the way back to our hotel."

Turning another corner, we walked into an abandoned lot, where one of the brick walls was covered with a painting of a gentle-looking monster and a giant in a blue suit. The blue giant was choking the monster. "I woke up one morning and heard some gurgling sounds behind me. I turned over and Robert was shaking, cold, and almost blue. A few minutes later he was dead." Gaétan pointed to a spot near the corner. "Right there. My brother was dead. Overdose."

We stood in silence.

All I could do was mumble *sorry*, but it seemed so stupid and inadequate I felt embarrassed. It was easier for me to look at the work on the wall. The words *I gave her my heart* were coming from the monster's mouth.

"That's his?"

"Yes, that's his."

"Beautiful."

"Yes, beautiful."

"So what did you do? After—"

"Robert was more famous dead than alive. They kept buying his work, and mine, and they kept putting more and more money in my bank account—I think the last time I looked there was something like two million euros there. Three million? I don't know. The agents took most of it, but I didn't care. I didn't want it. I wanted my brother back."

For a few minutes, we just stood in silence.

"What about your parents?"

"Died two months after we arrived. They were on their way here, to join us, traveling in the same boat we were in. Only this time, it capsized. Everybody died."

The horrors that Géricault had captured in *The Raft of the Medusa* flashed in my mind.

"I told you it was a long story," Gaétan said.

"Honestly, I really am sorry. I can't even—"

"Don't. It's okay. You don't have to."

"Gaétan, I don't know what to say. I'm sorry. I'm so sorry, and I know that's not enough, but...I can't...and also, I want to thank you for helping me out, and everything—"

"It's okay. Today was the first time all that money did anybody any good. I'm glad I could finally put it to use." He sat down, and leaned against the side of the building. "Now I've told you my sad tale. Mind telling me how you got into a fight with Hans Abel Von Baumhauer?"

My personal story had seemed like such an epically tragic tale ten minutes ago. Now, it seemed like a trivial footnote. All this time I had been feeling so sorry for myself, and Gaétan had lived through trials and tribulations I couldn't imagine. "Look. What happened to me doesn't matter." I had wanted to ask him where Chloé was, and now...now I couldn't.

"But I paid fifty thousand euros to hear this," he said. "For that, I think you can tell me."

Fair enough. So I went through the story, from sneaking out of the squat to the gallery visits to walking into Hans Abel Von Baumhauer's office and smashing the basketball art to confessing everything and going to jail. Gaétan just listened, nodding occasionally.

After I was finished, Gaétan smiled a grim smile. "I have heard about Baumhauer. He's not a nice man. You're going to need a good lawyer."

———

My court-appointed lawyer came well recommended from the court clerks paid to recommend him. We met in his office, a little square-shaped box with just enough room for two chairs and his desk. He was a gentle-looking man with a big, round jaw and a few strands of thin, gray hair combed over his head. Introduced himself as Bernard, and explained that he was the only English-speaking lawyer available today. His voice was so soft I had to lean in to hear.

"Tell me what happened, Declan."

To be honest, I wasn't that interested in talking about it, but he was my lawyer and my last chance at avoiding jail, so I told him. Missed nothing. Then he asked me to repeat it again and again, and asked me a hundred questions, and I answered them and told him the whole story again until I was sure I would die of repetition.

"So you punched the fish tank? With the basketballs?"

"Yes, like I said. I just hit it. It was the stupidest thing I've ever done. Don't know what I was thinking. But I hated it, and him, and I wasn't feeling very empathetic at the time."

"And your fist just went through the glass?"

"Just like that." He typed away, making notes on his computer. At least I thought he was making notes. He didn't seem to be paying much attention, so he might have been playing *Super Mario Bros.* "I didn't think I hit it that hard, and I didn't think it would break or anything. Thought I'd hurt my hand, maybe, but that's about it."

He typed away for a few minutes before he looked up. "That fish tank is worth a lot of money. I'm in the wrong business!"

———

The trial felt surreal, like watching a movie from the inside out. Bernard was sitting on my side of the courtroom, picking wax out of his ear. On the other side of the room, Hans Abel Von Baumhauer sat with four lawyers in black suits who looked like professional killers. They called me to the stand, asked me a million questions and I tried to look like I was sorry while I answered them because Bernard told me to look like I sorry. Bernard asked me a few quick questions and sat down. He seemed like he was in a hurry to get home. Then the lawyers announced they were finished with me and I climbed down and sat beside Bernard.

"Wow, those guys are brutal!" Bernard whispered. He was sweating. "Let's just plead guilty and hope for clemency. You probably won't get more than a couple years."

"No! I can't do that!"

"Well, I can't do this! Those guys are very aggressive!"

Just shoot me now, I thought.

It wasn't clear to me why Bernard was so afraid—I was the one going to jail. But as I watched him, sweating and shaking in his chair, I realized I wasn't the only one on trial here. There were a lot of reporters in the courtroom. This was a high-profile case, and everything Bernard did was being reported in the papers. His career was also on trial, and he was way out of his league. I wasn't the only one drowning in despair and self-pity.

As I looked around at the lineup of smirking lawyers on the other side, with a jail sentence staring me in the face, I thought of something I should have thought of a long time ago. "Ask the judge for a recess," I whispered to Bernard.

"What? Why?" he whispered back.

"Because! Just ask him. Get as much time as you can."

My mother often told me how much she loved arguing cases against lawyers who thought they couldn't lose. They were big-city litigators (always male) who billed a thousand dollars an hour and never imagined a small-town female lawyer had a chance against them. They never did their research and relied on grandstanding and bullying to win their arguments. She always did her research and she almost never lost. I knew those were the kind of lawyers we were up against. We just had to do our research.

Growing up as the son of a litigation lawyer, I had been exposed to as much legal discourse as a judge. I had been on the other side of many of my mother's questionings, had heard her debate the finer points of her cases on the phone, had even been able to watch her in court a few times. She had discussed the merits of her cases and her trial preparations at countless dinners, had celebrated her wins and mourned her (few) losses in voluminous detail. All that legal talk had seeped into my bones. I knew what we had to do.

An hour later, we were in Bernard's office. We were both sitting at our computers, doing research, asking questions, making notes, and doing more research. It was quite possible there has never been a more unlikely team in the history of jurisprudence, but he was surprisingly good about the technical side of law and I knew enough about developing legal strategies. Bernard had only secured a two-day recess, so we had less than forty-eight hours to pull our case together. It was after three the following morning before we had our first breakthrough.

"How thick was the glass on that fish tank?" he asked.

"I don't know. I didn't measure it."

"How thick do you think it was?"

I thought for a minute. "Just...very thin. My hand went right through it."

"According to this article, Koons's fish tank used glass that was two inches thick."

I thought about that. "There's no way I could punch a hole in glass that thick. I can barely open a can of spaghetti."

We worked through the rest of the night and had to run all the way to the courthouse to make sure we got there in time the next morning. Von Baumhauer was first in the witness stand and Bernard was in front of him, holding the list of questions and notes we had prepared.

"Mr. Hans Abel Von Baumhauer," Bernard asked. "Would you mind telling me about your *Three Ball Total Equilibrium*?"

"Of course. It is one of Jeff Koons's most renowned works. Quite possibly one of the most important pieces of artwork in the world. What is it, exactly, you would like to know?"

"I don't know much about contemporary art, Mr. Baumhauer. Can you tell me what it is? What it means? Why it's so important?"

Baumhauer smirked broadly, as if he were discussing quantum physics with a four-year-old. "The work operates on several levels," he began, his voice taking on new levels of self-importance. "It references socioeconomics, the power of mass media, and creation itself. It's about human aspiration in different levels of society, while reflecting the history of modern art."

Bernard looked over at me and I gave him a thumbs-up.

"Does that history include Duchamp's *Fountain*?" he asked.

"Yes, in fact, it does. How did you know?"

"It's often referred to as 'the urinal,' I believe, and everybody knows about the urinal, Mr. Baumhauer. But I'll ask the questions, thank you. Can you tell me how many of those urinals—*Fountains*—were made?"

"Twelve. Thirteen. The numbers are not conclusive."

Bernard checked his notes. "There are seventeen," he said. "That's pretty conclusive."

Baumhauer lost a little of his smirk. "That's one opinion. Why I said—"

"How many *Three Ball Total Equilibriums* were made?"

"Of this particular version, there is only one."

"Of course. Just one. After all, if there were seventeen, it wouldn't be worth twenty million. Is that correct?"

Hans Abel Von Baumhauer didn't say anything. Just twitched a little.

"I'm not clear on how the art business works. But I have to ask, when you buy art worth twenty million euros, do you get a receipt? Do you have a receipt for *Three Ball*?"

He sighed. Loudly. "I assume you mean a Certificate of Authenticity?"

"Yes, Mr. Baumhauer. The COA. The provenance. Proof that it's the original. That it is what you say it is. I think you know what I mean."

"I'm not responsible for filing certificates."

"I'm so sorry to hear that."

"Why do you ask?"

"Again, I'll ask the questions, thank you. The original *Three Ball* was created with glass two inches, or about five centimetres, thick. I'm not certain any human being could punch a hole in glass that thick. Yet this young man broke a hole in it as if it were as thin as a Riedel glass."

The courtroom got quiet.

"It would be helpful to all of us if you could find the receipt. Or something to prove yours is the original. Because, according to our research, the original is owned by a private collector in Switzerland. She asked us to keep her name confidential, but we do have a copy of her Certificate of Authenticity." Bernard pulled a certificate out of a file and handed it to the judge. "Can you prove otherwise, Mr. Von Baumhauer?"

Baumhauer looked like he wanted to crawl back inside himself. Bernard sat down and let that reverberate. He was trying hard to hide a smile.

One of Bauhmauer's team of lawyers stood up. "Your honor, we—"

"I'm not finished, counsel." Bernard stood up again. "Let's say, for the moment, that the *Three Ball* in your office isn't the original." He paused, waiting for an objection, but there was only a hostile silence. "At any rate, if it were fake, that would make it worth, I'm guessing, somewhere under a couple of hundred euros, depending on the market for scrap metal, glass, and a few wet basketballs. As you know, I'm no art expert. But now I'd like to move onto the charge of assault. Can you tell me what happened after the defendant walked into your office?"

Baumhauer leaned forward. Happy to change the subject, his eyes came back into furious focus. His speech was ready. "I was working on our financial projections when this—this odoriferous punk broke into my office and—." He went on and on. At one point, he said I tried to kill him. He actually said I tried to kill him. We were just two scrawny artsy types having a sad little wrestle, but he acted like I'd shot him five hundred times.

He told the story, and my lawyer nodded and asked the questions I had prepared for him. Like if I was the one that attacked first, why was my ear the one with bite marks on it? And why was it that I had the cuts, bruises, and a chipped tooth, and Hans had nothing but a stained shirt and a bruised ego? Hans tried to stick to his story but Bernard was on a roll. Those questions kept coming hard and fast and Von Baumhauer got flustered and his story became less credible the more times he told it.

Nothing that Hans claimed in his police report could possibly be true, as Bernard pointed out. What was true was that (a) Hans had attacked me first, and therefore I was acting in self defense, and (b) since his famous Jeff Koons wasn't, as it turned out, actually a Jeff Koons, I hadn't even caused substantial property damage. Under two hundred euros isn't very substantial.

Hans and his lawyers kept trying to bully their way back onto the pulpit, but nothing stuck. We had done our homework, and they hadn't. Bernard had, by now, quit trying to hide his smile. He couldn't help it. He knew he had just obliterated their case in front of their eyes. So he just kept smiling and going over the facts and eventually it wore them down and they ran out of arguments. When the judge ended the proceedings and called it a day, Hans and his lawyers looked like they'd been caught in the wrong weight class of a UFC cage match.

There was a crowd of people outside the courtroom with cameras and microphones, shouting questions and circling around us. We ignored them, walked down the street, celebrated with a glass of wine and a croissant, and went our separate ways. Bernard kept thanking me for what I'd done, but it wasn't just me. He had discovered something inside himself he hadn't known was there.

Twelve

Later, as I walked happily down the streets of Paris, it felt like my own personal Bastille Day. I was free. A celebration was in order! But who would I celebrate with? I didn't think I'd be welcomed at The Grand. They would know by now I had broken the freedom code and joined the evil empire. But I decided to go back anyway, because I had nowhere else to go. I bought a bottle of champagne and snuck into my room, where I quietly celebrated by myself. It felt great to be back, even if I had to hide. After a few hours, I fell asleep.

At some point in the night, I opened my eyes and felt a presence in my room. It freaked me out at first, but then I made out a green top hat, a huge red scarf, and a cane, and I figured it was Apollinaire. Standing in my doorway, looking down at me.

"How long have you been standing there?" I asked.

"How long has anyone been anywhere?" he said. "Since the time of Montezuma. Alexander. Caesar."

"That's a long time."

He just looked at me, shaking his head. "So you don't know."

"Know what, Apollinaire? What is it I'm supposed to know?"

Another long pause. "Maybe not knowing is knowing."

"Okay, well that's good, I guess." Apollinaire's verbal gymnastics never failed to leave me confused.

"Picasso got arrested once, you know."

"I didn't know. For what?"

"Stealing the *Mona Lisa*."

I could imagine Picasso would steal a painting. It seemed like the kind of thing he would do. But not that one. Not the *Mona Lisa.* "Why would he do that?"

"He didn't. But I told the police it was him."

Silly me. I had forgotten Apollinaire was over one hundred and twenty years old. "You told the police he stole it? Why would you do that?"

"Because I knew getting arrested would be a good career move for him. And it was. The dummy got a lot of publicity out of that. He should have thanked me. But of course he never did."

"Okay, I guess. Well, anyway, thanks for dropping by...and, hey, so, I have to get some sleep—"

"It's all in the stars," he said. "You should take the time to look at them now and then." He turned around and left. I still didn't know what he meant, so I just lay down, pulled the blanket over me, and shut my eyes.

I fell asleep a nobody and woke up famous.

Thirteen

That was not exactly how it happened.

The truth was that I woke up to this: "Get the fuck out."

I opened my eyes. Madelaine was standing at my door, arms crossed and lips tightly curled.

"Go. Just go. Now," she said.

"What?"

"You piece of shit. Get out."

"Why?" I swallowed deeply and stared at the floor. It was a stupid question, and I knew it. It's not like I didn't know the rules. Everyone here would know by now that I had been sneaking out and trying to peddle my art: my little dustup with Hans had been in all the media. I knew the risk I had been taking and now I was about to pay the ultimate price for my capitalist transgressions. I was being evicted, excommunicated, kicked out for good. Even though I knew it was my fault, part of me felt like I was being unfairly persecuted. I mean, c'mon. I was in a fight with the hated Hans Abel Von Baumhauer! The Emperor of the Evil Empire! Didn't that earn me a one-time pass? Couldn't we just forgive and forget this one time?

I looked at Madelaine. She sneered back. Apparently not.

My hands were shaking as I picked up my portfolio and scant personal belongings. The fact that I always knew this could happen didn't make it any easier. I had survived on my ability to deny reality for years, had always believed avoiding life's truths was a highly effective coping mechanism. And now that I knew it wasn't, it sucked. It just sucked. I didn't want to leave. I loved this place, loved everybody here, and I had thrown it away for nothing. I felt like crying.

One day you're a hero, the next day you're a bum.

One day you're the windshield, the next day you're the bug.

One day—it didn't matter. It was the next day.

"There's someone downstairs who wants to talk to you. He's wearing a *suit*." She said this with such a broad sneer you'd think he was wearing screaming baby minks still in their traps. "The conspiracy is here."

"Who?"

"An agent."

Why would an agent be here to see me? I didn't have an answer to that, but now I knew why I was being evicted. That's what sent me over the proverbial moral cliff. It wasn't just getting busted for trying to sell my art to a gallery. That would have been bad, but maybe, possibly, forgivable. They might have let me off with a warning. But not this. For whatever reason, there was an agent here to see me. The enemy was at the gates, and I had brought them here.

"What does he want?"

"Fuck would I know? You."

"Okay." I pulled on a pair of pants. "I'll get rid of him. Back in a few minutes."

"Doubt that," she said.

She stared at me all the way down the hall. It seemed like she couldn't wait to see me leave. I reached the door, twisted the handle and pulled it open. Before I walked out, I stopped and turned around.

"I'm not like that, you know."

"Bullshit."

"I'm not just about money."

"Yes, you are."

"How do you know?"

"Because you're a cheating, money-grubbing dickhead."

"Why do you hate me all of a sudden?" I asked.

"I always hated you."

"Really?"

"Fuck off," she said. "You've been lying since you got here. You never cared about anything we did. You don't care about art. Or me, or any of us. All you care about is Declan."

After being rejected by every gallery in Paris, I was now being rejected by what I thought was my home. I'd done it to myself, but it still felt so bitter there was bile rising up in my throat. I opened the door.

"Declan?"

She hiked up her pants and crossed her arms again. In those hard eyes, I detected a little splotch of softness. She took a few deep breaths before she spoke.

"They'll tell you it's all about the art. That the money doesn't mean anything. That all they really care about is you. And you'll believe it because you want to believe it." She picked up a broken doorknob and threw it at my head, just missing. "But just so you know? It's all bullshit. They don't care about you, you jerk. All they care about is money. And they take the beautiful work you do—like they take everything we do—and give you a few dollars and they'll sell it, turn it into collateral, and they get rich and no one will see your work again. We're nothing but cattle to them."

I shut the door and left.

Walking down the hall, saying goodbye to the cracks, mold, and mice for the last time, felt like the end of the world. It seemed impossible to process. Maybe she was right. Maybe I had sold out. Maybe it wasn't too late—if I went down there and told the agent to go away, like I said I would, maybe I could come back. But no, she was right: *doubt that,* she said. If that agent was really here to see me, I knew I wouldn't be back. This was what I came here for.

The man in the suit was waiting outside. He was standing alone on the sidewalk out front, looking lost and out of place among the motley sorts walking by. She was right. He did look like he was part of the conspiracy. Except that it was a kinder, gentler conspiracy than I expected. This man looked like someone my parents would have over for dinner and drink half a beer and try to talk everyone into playing Scrabble. His shoulders were slouched, feet bent slightly inwards, eyes that peered out from thick glasses, a face that seemed devoid of a chin; there was a straight line of loose flesh descending from his lips to his collarbone.

"Hello. Are you Declan?"

"Yes."

"Hi. I'm Alan. With Coles and Finch. This is a genuine honor." He stuck out his hand and we shook. "I hope I'm not interrupting anything. Would you be interested in grabbing a coffee?"

His accent sounded more small-town Midwest than art house Paris. "Sure. There's a place down the street." We made weather-talk and where-are-you-from-talk on the way. I told him that I was from San Francisco, of course. By now, that lie had been repeated so many times, the imagined facts repeated in my head so often, that it had come to feel more real to me than my actual life. "Where are you from?"

"I grew up outside Chicago, in a small town in the north called Glencoe. One of those, you know, one-gas-station kind of places. But since I became involved in the art business, I've lived here, in Paris, in Saint-Germain-des-Prés. Which I love. Over ten years now."

We grabbed a seat outside a café, ordered two café crèmes and waited, a little awkwardly.

"Thanks for seeing me, Declan. I assume you know who we are? You've heard of Coles and Finch, right?"

I nodded with a knowing shrug. Of course I knew Coles & Finch. I knew all the agents and galleries in Paris because I was a very worldly artist.

"We're all in love with your paintings." He shut his eyes and shook his head. "Crazy in love. They are brilliant. It's some of the best work we've seen in decades."

Well, well, well.

Well, well, well, well.

Well, well, well.

It was about time.

The café crèmes landed on our table, and while Alan was dumping spoonfuls of sugar in his, I leaned back in the chair and lifted my face to the heavens. The sun was shining down on me, the sky clear except for one harmless cloud hurrying to get out of the way. Everything felt so sweet. I had made it. The universe had finally come around to Declan's corner. I had made it. Congratulations to me. Not for the first time, I wished that I was a smoker. This would have been a good time to put my feet up on a chair, run my hands through my hair, and light up a cigarette to celebrate the fact that I had made it. Blow a circle of smoke in the air to demonstrate my cool and casual approach to the global fame that was about to come. Instead, I shrugged. A relaxed, I-knew-this-was-coming kind of shrug.

"Of course, we're interested in working with you."

"Great," I said. Cool. Calm. Slight nod. Well-modulated voice. I knew right away I was going to be very good at being famous. "How did you hear about me?"

"Aimée. From Aimeé's. You showed her your work, she recommended we call you. Sent us some photographs, and, well, that was it. And of course," he said, shrugging, "all the stories in the media about you and Hans."

"Yes, of course...and...Aimée?" Funny—I didn't remember her taking photographs.

"You know Aimée—she has this big head of bright orange hair and nails like Buck Knives. Thick Parisian accent. Owns a small gallery downtown. Would you mind if I had a look at your paintings?"

I laid my portfolio full of black canvases on the table and he went through it, saying very, very, very nice things. "That's wonderful. Breathtaking. Powerful. Original." He glanced up. "How would you describe your work, Declan?"

"Existential universality." Long pause, to give those words more meaning, even if I didn't know what they meant. "It's mostly about existential universality."

"Yes, yes, yes! I can see that. Very existential! That's good!" He was getting animated now, waving his arms and calling for another café crème. "Also…it's like a quixotic abstraction, or, no…it's a meditation on the vicissitudes of life. Yes, that's better." He wrote that down in a booklet he was carrying. "A meditation on the vicissitudes of life," he mumbled to himself. Then he looked up at me, over his glasses. "Does that sound right?"

I didn't know what that meant either. "Yes, it does. It certainly does. You've got a good eye, Alan, if you don't mind my saying so."

He nodded emphatically, like he had just received a compliment from the pope. Alan was nodding so much his chin was shaking and his glasses kept slipping down on his face. "We're going to make a great team! How many have you got?"

"Forty, fifty, I think."

"Good. That's okay. For now." He held out his hand and we shook again. "You've made quite a name for yourself. Good move there. You're already a brand."

"I'm a brand?"

"Sure are. The photographs of you walking out of Baumhauer's gallery, police cars everywhere, wearing handcuffs, with your face covered in blood? That's good stuff. You can't buy that kind of promotion. You were on TV, in the newspapers, everywhere. You're the new bad boy of art. The *enfant terrible.*"

Really? Declan Tucker was the bad boy? I was the *enfant terrible?* Before I came here, the worst thing I ever did was steal a few groceries. Truthfully, I was probably one of the world's most devout rule followers. I felt guilty when I used the wrong spoon for soup.

"Those photographs made you a brand. Indelible and undeniable. The antiestablishment dangerous rebel who isn't afraid of anything, even someone like Hans. The no-shit guy, shoot first, full of piss and vinegar. Never back down from a fight. You're like a modern-day Caravaggio. That's you!"

Caravaggio? The guy who walked around with a sword and killed someone? Okay. I guess that's what I was. Sure. Why not? "That's me. I am a no-shit guy," I said. That sad little wrestling match with Hans had turned me into some kind of Jedi-fighting-the-evil-Empire artist. This must have been what Apollinaire referred to as a "good career move."

Alan nodded at the waiter, who brought us two more café crèmes. He pulled a contract out of his pocket, told me I was going to make a lot of money, then mumbled some things about a percentage of this and agent fees for that, plus gallery commissions and salaries and charges for marketing and promotional events and stuff. Pointed out a few other items he thought I might be interested in. But after the words *contract* and *money* I didn't hear a single thing he said. My mother would have been shocked and appalled, but I signed without reading a word other than *signature*. We stood up, shook hands again, and he told me there would be a press conference in a few days, and we would have to start getting ready for it.

———

I left the café and walked down the street. Just like a regular, ordinary human being. Like the one I used to be, just a few hours ago, before I became famous and everything.

They say it can be lonely at the top, and now I understood what they meant. It would have been nice to celebrate, but the only friends I had in this city lived at the squat and they hated me. Except Gaétan, but he had gone missing again. And I still kind of resented him anyway, even if he had saved my life twice.

So I just walked along and smiled at strangers. It was too bad Monet wasn't around to talk to right now. Or Picasso. Gauguin, even. Someone like that. Someone to have a beer with, talk about what it was like to be such a huge art legend. Share a few lessons on how to deal with all the fame and the popularity. Maybe they could give me a few pointers on what to do when people ask me for autographs while I'm trying to have a quiet dinner, that kind of thing. Being new to this whole legendary-artist-famous-person thing, I could really use their advice.

The first thing I wanted to do was tell Chloé. She'd be all happy and excited for me, and she would hug me and we would have a big celebration. We'd go to the most expensive restaurant in Paris and drink Veuve Clicquot champagne while we stared into each other's eyes and laughed about the old days, back before I was internationally famous and everything. Then, well, you never really knew how these things would turn out. I was just guessing here, but I bet that when she saw how talented I was and how loved I was by people everywhere, and how I was the *enfant terrible* of the art world and still such a nice guy, still just good ol' Declan, I guess I wouldn't be too surprised if she dropped Gaétan and came back to me, because, well, I can really see her falling in love with someone like that. We'd probably be flying to her father's to see his Géricault paintings before the week was out.

The second thing I wanted was a shower. It was weird, but now that I was going to be rich and famous, I didn't want to sleep on a wet, moldy mattress. I wanted to squeeze shampoo in my hair and brush my teeth with my own toothbrush, put on clean track pants, and sit on a couch with springs that didn't stick out and stab me in the ass. I wanted to drink cold milk from a fridge and eat warm toast with jam, maybe heat up a frozen dinner in the microwave and watch TV. I loved life at the squat, but I missed this stuff. So the second thing I was going to do was book myself a room in a nice hotel. But first I had to find Chloé.

Which brought up the question: How do you go about finding a missing person in Paris? I couldn't just go knocking on doors. Besides, for all I knew, she wasn't even in Paris anymore, or even France. Who could I talk to? Asking Gaétan was not possible. I didn't know where he was, and I suspected he was hiding her from me. I didn't have any friends left. Who would know? Who could I ask? The only person in the city that was still talking to me, other than my agent (I loved saying that, even if it was just to myself: My agent. My agent. My agent.), was Neil, and he wasn't even an actual, real live person.

But then. Maybe—Neil? How about Neil? Would he know where she was? He might. After all, he was a celestial body, wasn't he? Aren't celestials omnipresent? Aren't they supposed to be everywhere, all the time? Don't they know everything? Of course I could ask Neil. He was dead, so he should be able to help.

It was over a month ago that Neil had appeared in my apartment and invoked the fear of madness in me, had left me certain I had lost my already shaky grip on reality. But I didn't feel that way anymore. Maybe he had just freaked me out because I was nervous, alone in a new city. Maybe I hadn't eaten enough, which makes me dizzy sometimes. Or maybe becoming famous had changed me on a molecular level, created a chemical reaction in my body so that I didn't feel fear. That might be it—I did feel kind of invincible. Either way, I was over it. Neil didn't frighten me now. And if he could help me find Chloé, well, I'd be happy to have him around. Maybe we could even be friends. Not every day or anything, but we could hang out now and then. I turned around and headed back to my apartment, feeling very good about the future of Declan Tucker.

The first thing I noticed when I opened the door to my apartment was a painting hanging behind the couch. Actually, not a painting. A print. The kind of print you'd find in the home-decorating section of a hardware store, or a sidewalk sale at a strip mall in Toledo. Giant oversize green palm trees gazing down on a bubbly blue-green-white ocean looking up at bright white puffy clouds in front of a neon yellow sunset. A happy dolphin family, frolicking in the waves.

The visual onslaught of that print blinded me momentarily, but it was only the beginning. As my eyes came back into focus, I realized the entire apartment had been redecorated. Wait. *Redecorated* was the wrong word. It had been undecorated and turned into an interior designer's nightmare. There were two other posters taped to the wall. One was a picture of a 1978 Trans Am. I knew that's what it was because big type underneath the picture shouted 1978 TRANS AM. The other was a little kitten hanging on a rope, with the caption When Life Leaves You Hanging, Don't Quit. There was a lampshade made out of an empty bucket of KFC. There's a KFC in Paris? There were half-finished meals and dirty cutlery and empty McDonald's packages lying on every available surface.

Neil walked into the room. He was wearing underwear and a too-small T-shirt. It was a sight that would be seared into my memory bank for life, and I regretted it immediately. For one thing, it was my underwear. His hands were wrapped around a grilled cheese sandwich and a bottle of Heinz Tomato Ketchup. We stood and looked at each other warily for a few moments.

"Oh, hi, Declan."

"Hi, Neil." Another moment or two, staring uncertainly at each other.

"I see you've redecorated," I said.

He walked over to the couch and plopped himself down. "Thought the place needed a little sprucing up." He took a bite of his sandwich. "You leb da plade ina mef." His mouth was full of grilled cheese sandwich, but I think he just told me that I left the place in a mess.

Keep it cool, Declan. Accept it. You are here for a reason, and you're going to be friends with Neil. "You're right. I did leave, and it was a mess. That's on me. No argument," I said, trying hard to keep the vibe light and casual. "I love the KFC lamp shade."

Neil picked up the remote, turned the TV on, and started watching a French version of *The Price Is Right*. Unbelievable! Not here, please God, not here! Couldn't American culture just leave one small corner of the earth alone? I recovered enough to remind myself that I really wanted to tell Chloé my big news, and I had no idea where she was, and right now Neil was the only shot I had at finding her. Stay positive, Declan. Smile. Make friends and influence people. Neil was shaking ketchup out of the bottle, spilling it on the couch, and ignoring it as it sank into the fabric.

"No, really, I like it. I like what you've done," I lied.

"You boo?" He swallowed. "No you don't. Do you?"

"Yes. Yes, I sure do."

"Did you get it? When life leaves you hanging?" he said.

"Not really."

"The poster over there. The pussycat on the rope."

"I see it, and I sure do like it a lot, but I don't get it."

"It's ghost humor. Like you're dead but not really."

Was that a friendly conversation starter or an accusation? It sounded like an accusation. I was about to remind him who was paying the rent for this place when I remembered that I had just signed a huge contract with an international art dealer, and that I was almost famous, and everything was beautiful, and I relaxed. Took a deep breath. I was bigger than this.

"I like it." Trying to sound encouraging. "It's funny."

We settled into a friendly-ish conversation. Neil told me what he had been up to since I left (which didn't sound like much but eating and watching television) and I told Neil about the squat and Alan and the contract I signed and I slowly, casually circled around to Chloé and how I lost her and needed to find her because I had something I had to tell her. "Hey. Just wondering. Do you think you could help me? Would you know how to find out where she is? I mean, being a ghost and everything?"

"How would I do that? Heaven only knows where she is."

"Because you're a celestial body, aren't you? Heaven only knows, so you should know, right? Because you're like, in heaven, right?"

"I said *heaven only knows* because it's a simile." Neil smiled, like a man tired of always having to explain what similes are. "It means that no one really knows."

"No, I know what *heaven only knows* means. But if you think about it literally, that's why I'm asking you. Don't you see? Because if heaven only knows, then you should know where Chloé is. Speaking celestially. Didn't you just say you were dead, or almost dead? Also, it's not a simile."

"Yes, it is. It is a simile," he replied, slowing down his voice and enunciating carefully. "Don't tell me you don't know what a simile is."

"I don't think you know what it is." Shouldn't he, as a former newspaper editor, know the definition of *simile*? Don't ghosts understand grammar? "A simile compares two unlike things. For example, say, my heart is like a...runaway train. That's a simile. *Heaven only knows* is, I don't know what. Something else. Maybe an idiom?"

Neil leaned back on the couch and put his hands behind his head. He pursed his lips, which I suspected he thought made him look deep and intellectual, but he looked more like a cross-eyed toadfish. There was a red stain on his shirt, a piece of green leaf in his teeth, and his thinning hair had a thick, oily sheen. My hopes for a supernal solution to finding Chloé were dimming by the second. Very disappointing. I had been brought up to believe that supernatural beings had supernatural intelligence, but this rumply bumpkin didn't even know what a simile was.

"Anywayyys," he said. "I don't know where she is. If she really is royalty, you should ask a prince or someone."

"What prince? Do I look like I know any princes? C'mon. Don't you have any connections in the netherworld? You should know *someone* in heaven, what with being dead and all. I thought we were friends. I was counting on you to help me."

"Oh, I get it. All of a sudden, I'm your friend."

"Well. Maybe. We could be friends."

He smirked. "If I find your girlfriend, you mean."

"No, not exactly." (But yes, exactly.)

"Why is your heart like a runaway train?" he asked.

"It's not like a train," I answered. "That was just an example of a simile."

"It's a bad example. Hearts aren't anything like trains."

"But that's exactly...look, are you going to help me or what?"

After explaining my Chloé dilemma to Neil, I thought he seemed somewhat sympathetic. Thought that he would be willing to use his otherworldly powers to help us come together. Now I was starting to believe he was just looking for a way to stay in my apartment and eat food without paying rent. What a crappy ghost.

"We're not in the missing persons business, you know. You seem to think heaven is just a big cloud where everyone just hangs out and looks down on earth and sees everything that's going on."

"Okay, fill me in. Save me from a lifetime of misunderstanding. Tell me what heaven is like. I'm listening."

Neil lay back on the couch and pursed his lips again. "Why should I?"

He was, without a doubt, the worst celestial being that had ever appeared on this planet. "Look. I don't know what you're doing here, but if you don't want to help me, fine. You don't have to. But if you don't, you have to leave. You can't stay here."

He stared at the ceiling, looking as if he was lost in thought. I guessed it wouldn't take a lot of thought for him to get lost in it. "You want me to help you, but you're not even going to say you're sorry," he said.

"Sorry for what?"

"You don't remember?"

"Remember what?

"Duh. Are you dumb *and* dumber?"

"What? What did I do?"

"For saying I'm not dead enough."

Then I remembered the look on his face when I had told him that he wasn't dead enough. Remembered wondering if I had crossed some kind of dead-person insult line. Now I knew I had, and he wanted me to apologize for it. Even if I didn't know there was a line to begin with. Fair enough. I had sort of killed him, in an accidental-not-my-fault kind of way, and it wouldn't kill me to say sorry. Besides, it was clear he wasn't going to look for Chloé without my apologizing.

"Okay. I'm sorry. Very sorry. My mistake. Shouldn't have said that. You're dead. You're good and dead, officially expired, wholly deceased. You're as dead as dead can be. Please accept my apology."

He rubbed his eyes and smiled. "Thanks, Declan. I'm not really that dead, but it's nice of you to say so."

We sat quietly for a few minutes. Neil kept smiling at me, his eyes wet, and I kept smiling back, uncertain how to proceed. It didn't seem quite right to ask him to get to work on finding Chloé, as we were now officially on friendly terms and friends don't tell friends to get to work. Not right away, anyway.

"So, what else have you been up to?" I asked.

We sat and chatted about stuff. The kind of cheeses we liked, why they called soccer *football* here, how the McDonald's in Paris weren't as good as the McDonald's in Georgetown. After a few promises to hang out soon and extracting a vague commitment from Neil to try and find Chloé, I had a long hot shower, and got an early night's sleep. I had to rest up for my press conference tomorrow.

Fourteen

I met Alan a few hours before the press conference started. The restaurant was Au Bon Pavilion Maurice. We were surrounded by heavy white curtains and eight chandeliers the size of compact SUVs hanging over our heads. Alan ordered the blue lobster with chestnuts from Piedmont. I ordered the Kobe beef with white truffles. It was an educational experience in many ways for me. I didn't know there was such a thing as white truffles or that Kobe beef was made by massaging the cows and raising them on a diet of beer. Must have been happy cows.

"Have you thought about what you wanted to say at the conference?" he asked.

I had thought about little else. My presentation would begin with a journey through my artistic past, followed by an enlightening discourse of my personal influences and vision, then a piece-by-piece analysis of my current work, *The Black Series.* I would explain the different colors of black I had used and what each one had been intended to communicate. It would be best to review them in alphabetical order, but if Alan had a different idea I would certainly be willing to listen. Alan listened patiently for about thirty-five seconds before interrupting.

"That sounds great!" he said. "But, I wonder, mmm, maybe it's better if I do the talking." He explained that it would be best for me to stick to one- or two-word answers at maximum. This would develop an aura of mystery around my personage, and make me even more enigmatic. I was already the bad boy *enfant terrible* of the art world—adding mysterious enigma would be good for my brand, he insisted. I understood that. Alan was right. You shouldn't talk too much when you're a mysterious, enigmatic *enfant terrible* like me. I promised to keep my answers as short as possible.

The press conference was in Alan's gallery on a back street near Canal Saint-Martin. I had somehow missed it when I was knocking on gallery doors. It was small, and unlike other galleries, jammed full of work from all sorts of artists I had never heard of. Alan and I sat in his office at the back while the gallery filled with people. Copious amounts of food and wine were being served while everyone was waiting. I wondered if he was trying to get everyone drunk before they started writing. Once the crowd reached almost thirty people—an impressive gathering of elite journalists, critics, agents, and influencers, according to Alan—he nodded and we walked through the crowd and took a seat at a table at the front. Alan stood up and asked everyone for their attention. They ignored him, remaining focused on the food and wine. He pulled a piece of paper out of his pocket and read.

"Good evening and thank you for coming tonight. You are about to lay witness to a phenomenal debut from an extraordinary young man, a man who grew up poor and alone on the streets of San Francisco. Declan Tucker is a rebel, radical, true visionary, and fearless artist. These are brave works"—he pointed at my canvases—"and you can feel the raw emotional power emanating from every canvas. Declan explores the very nature of human existence, the ways we see and think, our fears and our passions. Not only has this young man"—Alan paused and looked over at me with an admiring glance—"challenged our preexisting assumptions about art, but about life." He stopped and let that sink in. "Every brushstroke creates its own paradigm of expression. They are"—he paused for dramatic effect, and glanced up at the crowd—"a meditation on the vicissitudes of life."

I thought he was laying it on a bit thick, even for me, but I nodded knowingly while Alan sat down.

A journalist with tattoos over her face and neck put up her hand. "I have a question for Declan. Would you say your art speaks to the alienation people feel in society today?"

Alan said, "The power of his art is that it not only speaks to the alienation that people have always—"

"I asked Declan," she interrupted.

I leaned back in my chair. On the way to the conference I had purchased a package of cigarettes, thinking they would add to my *enfant terrible* image. I wouldn't smoke them, of course, but they looked good. I'd also purchased a Burberry trench coat to wear over my ragged squat clothes and some Spiker Styling Glue for my hair. Overall, I was pretty happy with my new look. I brushed back my hair, pulled up the collar on my trench coat, held my unlit cigarette to my mouth, and nodded. Just a little. A very enigmatic nod. "Yes," I said.

She smiled and nodded back, wrote something down and raised her hand again. "The layers of blackness give me feelings of isolation and fear, as if I were locked inside a fiery nightmare apocalypse with my own mother standing guard at the gate watching me burn. Is that what you intended?"

Alan interjected again.   "Yes, that's one of the vicissitudes of—"

"Declan?" She smiled at me.

"Yes," I repeated, speaking in a slow, purposeful, enigmatic voice. Straight line in the lower octaves. I put the cigarette back in my mouth and crossed my hands behind my head. For my first press conference, I was doing amazingly well. Absolutely brilliantly.

Another journalist put his hand up. "This is also for Declan. What is it about black that you find so inspiring?"

"Yes."

"I'm sorry," he followed up. "But that doesn't answer the question. I asked why black inspires you?

He was right. That question required more than a one-word answer. Alan looked at me a little nervously, but I laughed inside. I knew he had nothing to worry about. "You see, every individual who looks at this work will forge their own unique personal relationship with the painting. That's why black is so powerful—it forces one to ask questions. Such as, what is black? Why isn't it a color? Should it be? And what is a color? These are the essential questions—" I was just getting warmed up when Alan kicked me hard in the shin. "As I was about to say, yes."

A few more questions, then Alan thanked everyone and they went back to eating and drinking. As soon as the food and wine were gone, they disappeared.

"You were brilliant, Declan. They loved you," Alan said.

He was right. They did love me. I was very lovable.

"There's an after-party tonight at La Cordonnaire," Alan told me. "We've booked the entire restaurant. It would be great if you could make it. After all, the party is for you." He gave me a playful punch in the shoulder. "And Renée will be there."

A party for me? A party for Declan Tucker? Nice. "Who's Renée?"

"Renée Coles. You know Renée. She's the Coles of Coles and Finch."

"Oh, that Renée! Yes, of course, of course I know her."

If I was going to a party in honor of my own rebel self, and Renée Coles of Coles & Finch was going to be there, I had shopping to do. It was time to up my fashion game. After all, I couldn't just wear the same trench coat to every event held in my honor, and there were obviously going to be a lot of them. Having grabbed my credit card when I was back at the apartment, I was ready to spend money again. And I could, because I had lots of money coming in, piles of it, and soon. Very soon. As soon as Alan started selling my paintings, which wouldn't be long at all.

My shopping trip started on Avenue Montaigne, where I tried on Hermès, Louis Vuitton, and Burberry. They all seemed tailor-made to suit my new persona, so I bought one of each. Then I filled a few bags with Versace sweaters, an Armani cashmere trench coat, three Givenchy jackets, a pair of Arpenteur trousers, and two pairs of J. M. Weston shoes.

On my way back to the apartment, I passed by a watch store and stopped in. One in particular caught my eye: a Rolex. It seemed a little extravagant, at first, but only because it cost €27,995. So I did my research, studying the package label and discussing the features of the watch with the expert Time Representative behind the counter. He informed me that this particular Rolex comes with an oyster bracelet and self-winding caliber that actually enhances its reserve power. Not many watches do that. Plus, it had a sophisticated, minimalist look of understated elegance, which you don't find on your everyday Timex. And at under €30,000, it was modestly priced, all things considered. So, I wasn't being extravagant at all. More practical than anything. After all, I needed to know what time it was.

Lucky for me my credit card didn't have limits.

———

A few hours after the press conference, I was leaning on the bar at La Cordonnaire with an unlit cigarette in my hand. The sleeve on my Givenchy jacket had slid down, so anyone who was paying attention might catch a glimpse of my new watch. A fresh martini was in my hand, and I was aiming for a mysteriously enigmatic expression on my face. Everything was perfect, except for the techno music playing on the restaurant's sound system. I have no beef with techno music, but it was so loud everyone had to lean into one another's faces and shout to be heard.

"How long have you been with Coles and Finch?"

She was standing beside me, leaning over and shouting into my ear. Her name was Jasmine, or Jennifer, and she had introduced herself as a performance artist. I think. Older than me, by a few years. A tall woman with a large, aggressive jaw, jutting hip bones, and a tight-fitting green jacket that looked like it had been hand-painted onto her flesh. "I'm sorry, what?"

Jasmine or Jennifer leaned in closer. "How long have you been with Coles and Finch?"

"I just got here a few minutes ago," I shouted back, and waved at the bartender for another martini.

Fifty or sixty people were spread out around the room, split around the middle between the artist types and the business types. The artist types wore eccentric-casual, the business types business-casual, except for Alan who was wearing business-business. Several tables were jammed with wine and food and were constantly being refilled by the bored-looking staff.

"What do you do?" she asked.

"The Bay Area," I answered.

She nodded, as if she agreed with the point of view I had advanced and was seriously thinking about the larger repercussions of such a profound statement.

Around the room, the crowd hugged, kissed, shouted at each other, waved their arms all over the place, and drank a lot. It felt pretty surreal to me, like I was in the middle of a Salvador Dali painting. There was a bar that served nothing but mashed potatoes. There was more wine and more champagne. I had another martini while the techno music was replaced with dance music. People spoke to me, but the music was so loud all I could hear was "Urspojwzgd man auxmwt vmtya yaeptyx my new osbeazalweo!" Which I assumed were personal compliments on my press conference earlier, so I just kept saying "thank you!" Alan looked over, a big smile across his face, as if his own son had just won a national spelling bee. I congratulated myself again and had another martini.

At some point, someone pushed a line of cocaine in front of me. Although I had sworn to myself I would never touch the stuff, I realized things had changed. I was rich and famous now, or would be soon, and I was a young and enigmatic rebel artist who would be expected to engage in risky behaviour. It was part of my brand. Picasso and Basquiat and thousands of rebellious artists before me had taken opium, and I felt like I was responsible for keeping up the tradition. Also, I was drunk. I leaned over, sniffed, and ten minutes later felt like I was floating in midair.

The front door opened and a short, elderly, exotic-looking woman walked inside. Her large sunglasses obscured most of her face but didn't hide a strong, square jawline and bright red lipstick. She took about fifteen steps in and stopped. Renée.

"May I have a glass of champagne?" she asked.

It was the funniest thing I had ever heard. I laughed out loud, my head rolling back and hands covering my shaking belly. I was laughing so hard I was certain I was going to fall down, before realizing I was already on the floor. I was the only one laughing, and everyone was staring at me. Didn't anyone else get the joke? With superhuman effort I stopped laughing, stood up, and tried to get back to being enigmatic.

The rest of the night was star-crossed wonderful, every moment pure joy and happiness. There were celebrities there, I think, but I don't remember any of their names. I met Renée Coles. Alan introduced us. I told her I was the new Picasso, and he gave me a look and told her no, actually

I was the new Caravaggio. She hugged me, I remember that. I hugged her back, a few times. Told her I loved her. In fact, I told a lot of people I loved them. I remember dancing by myself. I remember Alan gently pushing me out of the room and into a cab. I remember telling Alan how beautiful everyone was, and that he was beautiful, and I told him that I loved him more than anyone in the world.

———

The biggest problem with cocaine is that there isn't any problem with cocaine. At least, not right away. You believe you are the ultimate embodiment of human perfection, that you can do anything and every word you say is brilliant, then it's over and you're a blubbering mess. That's one of the million reasons why, after I woke up, I swore I would never, ever, never touch it again.

Later that morning I met Alan at a restaurant. He smiled. "Have fun last night?" he asked.

"I don't remember. Just kind of hoping I didn't do anything too stupid."

He waved the waiter over and I ordered a few café crèmes, baguettes with extra butter, and crepes with salted caramel. I thought my blood needed thickening up.

"Never mind. Nothing Jackson Pollock didn't do. Or Rothko, Mitchell, and hundreds of other artists. Comes with the territory, I guess. I hope you got some sleep. We have a full schedule for you," Alan said. "Your paintings are already up in a few galleries. Press releases are out. There is another press conference tomorrow, and you're booked for a few interviews and meet and greets with potential buyers."

The idea of facing human beings didn't have a lot of appeal at that moment, but at least he hadn't fired me. I sucked in a breath of relief.

Alan slathered a stick of butter on his crepes. "Also, we should start planning your next showing," he said. "How long would it take to get another thirty or forty paintings? Would a few weeks be possible?"

I almost choked on my salted caramel. Another thirty or forty? I couldn't do that again in a month, not a year. *The Black Series* was a miracle, a once-in-a-lifetime confluence of inspiring disasters. "I thought maybe I'd take three or four weeks to fill up the old creative well again. You know. Get inspired."

Alan put down his baguette and stared at me. "But there's another exhibition planned next month."

I just shook my head and tried to keep my caramel down.

"That's okay." He took a deep breath. "We can use your back works."

"Back works?"

"Whatever you've got ready to go. Your old work. I'd prefer new works, but we'll make do."

"I don't have any back works."

His eyebrows lifted three inches over his forehead. "You don't have any...really? Really? But everybody...wow. Okay. So how long?"

"Eight weeks?" I was lying. Eight months, more like it. Honestly, I thought I was going to be able to live off the riches of *The Black Series* for at least a few years. I wasn't nearly ready to go back to the canvas.

Alan stared at me over his glasses, creases lining his forehead. "You seriously don't have any back works?"

"No. Not really. A few sketches. Not very good ones."

He stared at his empty plate and shook his head. "That's not going to work. We can't wait that long. I was, honestly, thinking three weeks, tops. You're hot right now. Did you see the reviews? There's demand now. But that's now. This business doesn't have a long attention span."

"Reviews? I didn't see any reviews."

He reached into his bag and pulled out his iPad. Scrolled around and read. "Evokes subconscious feelings that go beyond our current perception of the subconscious." Scroll. "Tucker's works put new perspectives on our sense of time, love, and the individual." Scroll. "Rebel Tucker has redefined what it means to be an artist in today's fragmented universe." He smiled and shook his head. "It's all cut-and-paste from the press releases I sent out, but still. The rebel Declan! The mad artist! They love you. You're the latest star."

Until then, I hadn't even realized I was putting new perspectives on time and redefining today's fragmented universe. "Okay. Wow. So. Two or three weeks?" I asked.

"Yes. You're hot now." Alan ordered a baguette. "In three months, you could be forgotten."

"What about *The Black Series*? Has anything sold yet?"

"Not yet, but very close. Some solid leads. So, can you do it?"

"Sure, I guess."

"I know you can. What's his name, Basquiat, he used to do five in a day. Picasso did two or three a day, usually a lot more. Modigliani could finish a hundred drawings in a day."

True, but they did more opium than I did.

"You had a good gallery showing yesterday, but that's just a one-off. If you're going to go anywhere, you have to feed the beast." He picked up his baguette and spread it thick with jam and butter. "Keep it up and you could be in Art Basel next year."

Art Basel was the biggest art event of the year. It attracted almost one hundred thousand dealers and collectors from all over the world. Over four thousand of the world's best, hottest, most respected artists would be there. If I was going to get where I wanted to go, that's where I needed to be. That's why I had come to Paris. That's what I had wanted, dreamed of, all those long nights sitting in my parents' library. And I was close now. So close. All I had to do was produce forty or more epoch-making, earth-shatteringly brilliant paintings over the next two or three weeks.

"We can do this, Declan," Alan reassured me with a vigorous nod.

We? What we?

After Alan left I walked back to the apartment. Thinking hard.

This sucked. I couldn't do this. No, it didn't suck. I was brilliant, I could do this, no problem. Remember the press conference! They loved me. No, I couldn't do this, I was an idiot, I had just gotten lucky last time. There was no way I could do anything like that ever again. Actually, that wasn't true, I was so hugely talented. I could do this, I would! These paintings would be a thousand times better than *The Black Series*. I'd probably create some of the best work ever done in all of history. This was not going to be a problem. Except it was, because I had no idea what I was doing. Wait, Declan, what are you talking about? You're easily the most incredible artist alive today. You are going to kill this! No, you're dead.

Three weeks. Twenty-one days. Impossible. No, don't think that. Think about ideas! I tried. Walking, thinking, desperately searching in every dark corner of my mind and every face I saw, everything I saw and heard, for artistic inspiration. If I could have willed divine power I would have done that now, even if it was cheating. I needed a muse, but there was no muse to be found.

While I walked, I thought. Looked back on my life for inspiration. Went back to the beginning. Kindergarten. Piano lessons. Soccer practice. Running for school president in eighth grade, and coming in eleventh out of eleven. Sitting by myself during school lunches. Birthdays. Playing Risk. Family trips. Disneyland. Disney World. Nothing.

What was left? It seemed to me that everything that could be done in art had been done. Blobs, points, swirls and stripes and every geometric shape imaginable, shapes and objects, the depressed and poor, rich and famous, traditional, contemporary and futurist, modern, postmodern, post-postmodern, stuff you knew and didn't know, the high and the low, conceptual and ironic, conscious and the subconscious. Dreams inside dreams, horizontal and vertical stripes, a series of vacuum cleaners. If vacuum cleaners had been done, what could possibly be left?

Neil wasn't home when I got back. Good thing—I needed absolute quiet. Complete solitude. I set up the easel, got my paints out, held my paintbrush tightly in my hands, and waited for creative lightning to strike. Cartoons? No. Lichtenstein and Warhol had already hauled the gold out of that mineshaft. Installations with dead animals? No. Too Hirst. Also, gross. An hour later, I was still waiting for the lightning when the front door opened.

"Hey, Dec. Howya doing?"

Neil. He was here. And he was walking around in my underwear again. So, apparently the great universal conspiracy against Declan Tucker was still going strong.

"Did you go outside like that?" I asked.

He laughed like we were old buddies. "I'm a ghost? Remember? No one can see me. Except you." As he lay down on the couch, his belly shook along with the cushions. "Whatcha been up to?"

"Neil. Listen. I have a massively huge pile of work to do. I'm really going to have to focus. So, I'm sorry, but if you don't mind—"

"Got it. Quiet. Zipped." He put his arms behind his head and shut his eyes.

I turned back to the canvas and tried to concentrate. Painting with a large, plump ghost lying on your couch was something I was going to have to get used to. I stared at that canvas. And kept staring. Thirty minutes. Sixty minutes. Two hours. Eventually, Neil started snoring. This should have bothered me, but by then it didn't really matter. There was no focus for him to interrupt, no channeling for him to break. I was calling for my muse, but my muse wasn't answering. I guessed my muse must be at an all-expenses-paid resort in Mexico drinking piña coladas because she wasn't anywhere near here. It got so bad I was staring at Neil's cat poster and his paint-by-number ocean scene for inspiration. I thought about just leaving the canvas white, a pale follow-up to my black period, but the white canvas thing had also been done.

I had been told by my friends at The Grand "you will use everything you know." So I thought back, tried to think of everything I knew, searching for a glimmer of a spark. Hours went by, and I tried harder, only to sink deeper into despair. High school teachers. Middle school recess. Posters on the wall at work. Girls I knew. Guys I knew. Games we played. Every moment of my spoiled and complacent childhood, every second of my teenage years, Uncle Sam. I scanned through every cell in my increasingly anxious brain, searching for something that meant something. My time in school, my miniature newspaper career, my trip to Paris. The croissants. Le Bateau-Lavoir. Wandering hopelessly and happily in the Louvre. Getting lost in Mesopotamia.

Mesopotamia. Mesopotamia. I thought about all the time I had spent in that cavernous hall. The spear-holding warriors, headless rulers, and winged bulls, the man's head on the horse's body. The images rolled into my head like a four-thousand-year-old highlight reel. Violence, mayhem, religion, invention, human sacrifice, and culture. It was perfect! Yes! That could be it. It was it! This was great stuff. I felt my blood start to circulate again. One image stuck in my mind. It was a sculpture of a smiling, peaceful-looking bald man in prayer, with a long beard and oversize blue eyes lit up with eyeliner. He was holding a spear and wearing a dress. Those Mesopotamians had everything.

Hahaha. That's how divine power works! I knew it. I was a genius. Picked up my pencil and started sketching. The big eyes. Bald head. Long beard. Big nose. Buddha smile. This was going to be—

"Is that supposed to be a guy?"

Breathe, Declan. Slowly, in and out.

"Why is he wearing makeup?"

Remain calm. Don't scream. Find your inner peace. Ommm. Don't throw anything. Calm down. Om, dammit, om! Focus on the art. We are friends, he is going to help me find Chloé, we are friends, he is going to help me find Chloé. Focus on the art. "Sorry, Neil. Would you mind? I'm really trying to focus."

"Sorry, sorry. Sure. Absolutely. Quiet."

It took time, but I refocused, got tuned in again. This was something. No one I knew had done Mesopotamia before—except, of course, the Mesopotamians.

"He looks like a guy in a dress!" A high-pitched giggle burrowed into my ear. "And guys don't wear makeup!"

I looked around. Neil was standing on the coffee table, looking over my shoulder.

"Oops! I can't help it. Okay, sorry. I'll stop. Promise." He jumped back onto the couch.

I couldn't do it. I couldn't. Not here. Not with that thing behind me. Outwardly calm, maintaining a friendly disposition—reminding myself a dozen times that I still needed him to find Chloé—I made a string of insincere apologies, thinking about nothing but all the precious time I had already wasted, packed up my supplies, and got ready to leave. Neil kept apologizing back, and I repeated my apologies, but what I really wanted to do was truss him up like an oversize turkey and stick him in a four-hundred-and-fifty-degree oven until he was done for good.

"I'll be back. I just have to—" Holding the door, I watched him put his feet up on the table and point the remote at the television. I had to ask. "By the way, you haven't gotten around to checking into the Chloé thing yet, have you?"

"Still working on it." He found *The Price Is Right* and turned the sound up. *Marg Bowman, come on down!* "You can't rush it. This stuff takes time."

Om! Om! I shut the door, walked down the hall, and headed back to the Louvre. It would be better there. Painting in the middle of all that inspiration (without Neil's running commentary) was just what I needed. Waited in line, paid my entrance fee, bought a map, and went straight to the Mesopotamia gallery. Walked past all the small mother-goddess statues, the five-thousand-year-old tablets, and stood in front of my strange, balding, and bearded inspiration. This was more like it. Now I was right in front of the real thing. The quiet, nearly abandoned room was perfect. I could focus here. My smiling statue sat peacefully in front of me. His name was Ebih-il, the Superintendent of Mari. He was from the twenty-fifth century BC. Fascinating stuff. I took a seat in front of him, unpacked my art supplies, and waited for the rush of inspiration that I felt in my apartment.

And then...nothing. I stared, waited, put my hand up to the canvas, and tried to channel the same emotions that had galvanized me just a few hours ago. But now it just looked like a strange guy insanely happy over some random event that took place thousands of years ago. The Mesopotamians had invented just about everything, and he looked to me like he had just invented beer. It didn't matter. I knew only that my muse hadn't returned after all. After an hour, I gave up and left. Nothing was working. I had lost a day, and the anxiety was making my hands sweat. There was nothing to do but get some sleep and try again tomorrow.

But tomorrow came, and the next tomorrow, and the next tomorrow, and there was still nothing.

Fifteen

Even Alaskan King Crab with Persian Cucumbers and Hudson Valley Peking Duck with Compressed Mission Fig gets boring after a while. The thrill of the perfect restaurant dulls quickly. Champagne is just wine with bubbles, *amuse-bouche* is just a small appetizer, and oversize chandeliers are just big lights. It's just another dinner, rich enough to make your blood coagulate midmeal, and you've had enough "culinary experiences" to last a few lifetimes. At least it did for me. All I really wanted was a hamburger with cheese and medium fries.

"How many paintings have you got, Declan?" Alan asked as he studied the menu with a jeweler's eye for detail. "The Moulard Duck Foie Gras looks delicious, by the way. It's slowly poached, which is the only way anyone should cook duck. And the Chanterelle Mushrooms will provide a nice balance, you know. Round it out."

"Twenty-eight. I'll have another ten or more in a week or two."

"Yes. That's good. Excellent." Alan took a long drink of champagne. "We'll get photographs for the brochure, first. Let's start with an email campaign to a few auction houses. That will get word of mouth going." Alan pulled a small notebook and pen from his pocket. "I have to write all this down, or I'll forget it in a second." He made a few notes. "I'll get the press release out tomorrow."

"Do you want to see them? The paintings?" I asked.

"Yeah, I guess." He shrugged. "No rush. I can wait until you're done. I'm sure they're brilliant. I have absolute faith.

And good for you." He glanced up from the menu. "You did it!"

He was wrong. I was lying. I hadn't done it at all. There wasn't a single splotch of paint on a canvas, not even the solitary scratch of a pencil. There weren't twenty-eight paintings. There weren't any. I had tried, tried harder than I had tried anything in my life, but nothing came and I just couldn't do it anymore. I didn't know if I ever would.

"I was worried about you," he said, turning his attention back to the menu. "Want a suggestion? I'd try the Crepinette. It's made with black Australian truffles, which I've never had before, but I've heard so many good things. And I love the Sauce Bordelaise here. We should celebrate, by the way. More champagne?"

I was worried about me, too. I still was. "Sure."

He filled both our glasses, emptying the bottle and ordering another.

"What are you having?"

"Do they have anything that tastes like a hamburger?"

Alan laughed. "Funny guy! I guess the Wagyu beef might be the closest thing they have."

"By the way, have you sold any of my paintings?"

"Really, really close on a few deals. Quite a few." The next bottle arrived and he filled our glasses. "Here's to art," he said.

"To art."

"The greatest business on earth!" He sipped his champagne, peering at me over the glass. "Something wrong?" he asked.

"Not at all. Everything's great."

He shook his head, a concerned look on his face. "Something is bothering you."

"Not at all. Every dream I ever had is coming true."

"You're happy with everything?"

"Absolutely. Over the top. One hundred percent."

"Okay then, good." Alan poured himself another glass. "I want you to be happy. I care about you, you know."

But something was wrong. It had been twelve days since Alan had given me two or three weeks to come up with thirty or forty new works, and I hadn't finished one. While we sipped champagne and made small talk about art, I was trying to figure out why I couldn't paint. While we chatted politely about the hottest markets, recent sales, and a new gallery that had just opened, I was wondering why I felt like the rocks were starting to fall off my mental cliff again. Something was wrong, but I didn't know what.

Somewhere in the middle of the second bottle of champagne and before the entrées arrived, Alan said something about how the business of art was so different from standard economic models.

"It's what?" I asked.

"It's a totally different model, financially, than any other. In a standard model, increasing the availability of a product decreases its value. But in art, it's the inverse."

"What do you mean?"

"It's like, the more you make, the more you make!" Alan's eyes lit up, as if he were revealing the secrets of the universe. "Look at Andy Warhol. Why do you think he called his studio The Factory? He pumped work out like an assembly line. Andy once said, 'the reason I paint like this is that I want to be a machine.' He produced over ten thousand works, and they just keep going up in price!" Alan emptied his glass. "That guy had it all figured out."

I remembered what was bothering me.

Basquiat used to do five in a day. Picasso did two or three a day.

The first question Alan had asked me today was how many paintings I had. Not the subject, the inspiration, or whatever it was I was trying to express. Not the brushstrokes or the brushes. He didn't even want to see them. He wanted to know how many. Then there was that comment about Basquiat, and Picasso, and Modigliani—about how many they produced. He was impressed with their production capabilities. Their manufacturing rates. I put the glass of champagne down. I'd had enough.

"I know what you're thinking," Alan said.

"You can't. I don't know what I'm thinking."

"You're thinking I'm too business. Too much about the money, not enough about the art."

"No. Not that. I get the business. And the money. I do. It's just that—" Maybe it was. Maybe he was right. But no, that wasn't it either. But it was something. What was it Madelaine had said?

The waiter filled Alan's glass and he picked it up. "You're not all wrong, you know. I do care about your work. I do. Just not the same way. It's just that—you see, we are two different people. I look at paintings the way you would look at a business forecast on an Excel spreadsheet. Just long enough to pretend you care. You like art. I like numbers. I love math. Does that make me the bad guy? Someone has to do it, you know. Someone has to do the business stuff. Or there wouldn't be an art business." The waiter placed an *amuse-bouche* on our table, and Alan ordered another bottle of champagne. "I used to work in the investment business. Stocks, bonds, futures. I was good at it. But, you know, we'd kill for an eight percent return. Eight percent! If we hit ten percent, we'd celebrate like we'd won the lottery." He emptied his glass and spun it around in his fingers. It was kind of mesmerizing, the way he did it. Perfect control.

"Why did you leave?"

"One day I read about some painting that had sold for over two million. Forget who it was. Doesn't matter. But I remember looking into it and found out that it had been purchased for under half that price four months before. That's one hundred percent return in sixteen weeks. Sixteen! It sounded extraordinary, but it wasn't. I started tracking down other sales, found out it wasn't even that unusual. Not in the art business. It was happening all the time. Prices doubling, tripling in months, sometimes weeks. They were making more money in a few months than I made in three or four years. And the penny dropped."

He hit his fingernail against the side of the glass, the crystal issuing a high, clear ringing sound that spread around the room. "We're talking returns in the hundreds of percent here. Maybe thousands. You see? That's what's so great about this business. I mean, I—well, you, you know, the artist—buy some paint and a canvas for what? Hundred bucks, two hundred? You do your little paintings, then I put those paintings up on the market, we spend a bit on PR, buy some food, wine, champagne for a gallery showing—a few months later, if things go right, we're selling those paintings for fifty thousand euros each. That's just the start.

"The secondary market is where the real money is. Resell. They go for triple, quadruple that, depending. Get you into a showing like Art Basel, get into the day auctions, then the night auctions—and those paintings are going for hundreds of thousands, then millions. Chinese money, Russian money—it's coming from everywhere. It's stupid money. Not for everybody, of course. Lots of people are trying to feed from this trough. But you get it right and you get it really right. Want more champagne?"

"No thanks. How do you know what will happen? Who will pay what? For how much?"

"We don't. Not always. We've all been hung out to dry a few times. But mostly, they're extremely predictable. We win far more than we lose. The secret is not letting the art get in the way. Don't let it cloud your judgment. People are buying brands, names, stories, bragging rights, and pretty pictures that make them feel good about themselves. This isn't voodoo. We make projections based on market research, qualify the key buying triggers, control the press with insider stories and little bribes. Manage prices by bidding up the pieces we want to go up, taking down the ones we don't. We have an algorithm, and it's pretty good—it can predict futures within eight or nine percent. At these returns, we can afford to miss one or two. And our basic up-front costs, like your press releases, promotional events, our time, dinners like this one, etc, are paid by the artists, like you, so even if we miss we still make money."

"So I'm an algorithm."

"Ha! That's right!" He slapped his knee. "You're a great algorithm! You came with a ready-made story. The minute you got in the fight with Hans, your marketing plan had already been prepared. The math was easy from there. Bad boy artist, kicking against the pricks. Violent, essential, primitive, angry. It was perfect. The backstory about growing up on the streets of San Francisco was a nice touch." He emptied his glass of champagne. "There's another event tonight. It's at Aria's studio. Also, there are three gallery visits tomorrow. A press conference. And we must get ready for Art Basel. Busy, busy! Cheers!"

I suddenly felt very tired. Beyond bone-tired, more like bottom-of-my-soul tired. I wanted to lie down on the floor, curl up in a ball, and go to sleep. Alan paid the bill, we shook hands a few more times, he told me how much Coles & Finch loved me. He handed me an envelope and I stuffed it in my pocket and went back to the apartment and straight to bed. There were chicken bones on the blanket, but they didn't bother me that night.

They'll tell you they really care about you. And you'll believe it, because you want to believe it.

Madelaine was right. I did want to believe it. I just wasn't sure if I could anymore.

It wasn't until the next morning, while I was hanging up the pants I had slept in, that I found that envelope in the pocket. I uncrumpled it, ripped it open, and pulled out a piece of paper. It had a nice logo on the top that read "Alan Gerrard, Artists Agent." The rest of the print was in simple, twelve-point Helvetica. It read "To Declan Tucker, Invoice for Services Rendered," followed by a list of items that included: Press Conference. Provisions. After Party. Champagne. Rental of La Cordonnaire Restaurant. Provisions. Ongoing Services (Press Releases, Phone Calls, Promotions). There was a list of every restaurant Alan had I had been to beside the cost of that meal. The bottom of the invoice read: Total Owing: €37,340.00. Terms: Thirty days.

I should have read the contract.

———

Neil was asleep on the couch when I woke up. I wanted to ask him about Chloé, but his eyes were shut and his mouth was open, he was snoring, and there was an empty tub of potato salad on the floor. I wanted to shake him and wake him up, but he looked so happy. I wondered about something he had said, that he "really wasn't that dead." Maybe that's why he hadn't looked. Maybe he couldn't help me yet because he wasn't actually dead? In a way, it didn't matter. Looking at him lying there, I figured I'd just have to find her for myself anyway.

My search started with a visit to the restaurant where I first met Chloé, but that garnered little but a vaguely worded acknowledgement that she may have worked here at one time, or perhaps not, but certainly not now, and excuse us but we are very busy. The stern guardians at the École nationale supérieure des Beaux-Arts were even less helpful: my questions were answered with stony faces and shaking heads, my request to look around the school and through their student records flatly denied. My efforts to do so anyway resulted in a fury of shouting, shoving, and threats of police action. What next? I broke down and bought a

MacBook Pro. If I couldn't find her, maybe Google could. While I was at it, I bought a phone. Since I was rejoining the digital age, I might as well go all the way.

The only thing I really knew about her—and I did know this, absolutely and positively, without a billionth of a centimeter of a doubt—was that Chloé had French noble blood coursing through her veins. So as soon as I got home and set up I typed "French nobility" into Google's search bar.

The first thing I found out was that French nobility hasn't officially existed since January 21, 1793. That was the day the last king of France, Louis XVI, marched down the planks to meet his fate under the guillotine's blade. His wife, Marie Antoinette, followed him nine months later. That was it. The end of the line for French nobility. Yet, perhaps not, for the lack of official recognition over the past two hundred years hadn't dimmed the convictions of the many stubborn French citizens who continued to claim a royal heritage. There were over one hundred thousand people who still called themselves French nobles, whether the republic agreed with them or not. So there it was. With a little online research, I had already narrowed down my search for Chloé to roughly one hundred thousand people. Progress had been made.

Now all I had to do was track down these one hundred thousand "royals" and ask them. One of them must know who, and where, Chloé was. It seemed straightforward enough, but a few hours later I realized it wasn't. I found lots of royals: Louis Alphonse, Duke of Anjou; Henry, Count of Paris; Charles, Prince Napoleon to name a few. But whether or not they were genuine royalty or just pretenders was highly questionable. And even if they were genuine, it wasn't like I could just pick up a phone and call them. Their home addresses weren't listed on Google, they didn't post their real names on social media. Where else could I look? I tried searching under castles. After all, if they were royals they must live in castles, or their ancestors had, at one time or another. Maybe I could find them there.

Google's bots found more than 6,500 castles in France in 0.54 seconds. The castle on the top of my Google search was *Château Saint-Michel*, a five-hour train ride away. According to their website, royals had lived in the castle for four hundred years. It was once a medieval dungeon, had been attacked by the pirate Bluebeard, and was now one of France's most magnificent *Châteaus*. What excited me the most was that a Count and Countess Louis-Jean de Nicolay still lived there. True royals. Maybe they would know Chloé, or be able to give me some idea how to find her. There were two castle tours a day, Tuesday through Saturday. I was on a train at six-forty the next morning, and by early afternoon was standing in the middle of a small group of tourists at the castle doors.

Our tour guide had the wide shoulders and thick neck of a low-rent bodyguard, but he was dressed like an eighteenth-century butler. He hustled us through the main hall and its double-helical staircase and into a large room lined with bookshelves. "The library dates back to the seventeenth century," he told us in a clipped voice. "There are over two thousand books here. Some of them date back to the sixteenth century, including an original Montaigne."

He eyed our tightly huddled crew with a look of suspicion, and, seeing us staring back in silent incomprehension, set his jaw slightly tighter and continued walking. "Through this door we find the grand ballroom." The group, all eight of us, followed dutifully. "The portraits you see on the south wall represent the Regent of France, Duke d'Orleans, and his wife, the daughter of Louis XIV. The writing desk belonged to Count Roy."

One of the members of our tour group, a lady in a frilly dress with a heavy British accent, piped up. "Who was Count Roy?"

"I don't know," he responded.

"I have a cousin named Roy," she added, perhaps hoping for some kind of human response. There was none.

"What's a Regent do?" a senior member of our group asked.

"If the king or queen are unable to execute their duties," the guide answered, "the regent exercised ruling authority."

"Why would they be unable to execute their duties?"

"Because someone chopped their heads off. For example."

The group looked around the room in a state of—if not exactly awe, at least reduced boredom. A massive elaborately carved marble fireplace dominated the room, and eight grand chandeliers looked down over gold-and-red patterns that spread across the walls and onto the floor. It smelled musty but looked impressive.

"This where they did all those big banquets and stuff?" another man, this one with an American Midwestern accent, asked.

"That is a definite possibility," our guide answered, and kept walking. "This is"—he pointed at another portrait on the wall—"the Count and Countess Louis-Jean de Nicolay. Current owners and residents of the castle."

"Where do they live?" the lady with the frilly dress asked.

"They are residents of the castle." He raised an eyebrow. "That means they live here."

She shook her head, her whole body shimmying along. "No, I know that, but I mean where? Can we see where they live in the castle?"

"No," he said with a stiff smile. Our host then executed a perfect pirouette on his heels and walked away. His interrogator stared after him, a flash of hostility crossing her face. She had paid nine euros for this tour and had so far discovered exactly nothing she could tell her neighbors about back home.

But I had discovered exactly what I wanted. When my fellow tour member asked where the Count and Countess lived, I saw the tour guide's eyes flicker toward the end of the long hall at the west side of the ballroom. Ah-bloody-hah. Dead giveaway.

"Alright if we see the dungeon?" the Midwestern man asked.

Our tour guide released a loud sigh. "Of course."

As they headed toward the dungeon, I made my getaway. The Count and Countess were in this castle, likely hiding from the hordes of curious tourists wandering around their home. I knew the general direction, but that still left a lot of ground to cover. With five levels, over two hundred rooms, and five secret passageways, there were a lot of places they could be hiding. I walked down the hall, following the flickering of the guide's eyes.

The first door made a noisy squeal when I opened it but otherwise gave no resistance. On the other side of the door was another long hall, much like the one I had just walked down, but this one was empty and unfinished. The floors were bare concrete, the walls unpainted plywood, and there were piles of sawdust everywhere. The first room I came to looked like an oversize garage, full of wood planks, tools, a band saw, old couches covered in plastic, and bits and pieces of broken statues. The next room sat empty, other than a thick layer of dust on the floor. I wondered—was that four-hundred-year-old dust? Had kings and queens, maybe Bluebeard himself, walked on that dust? Had revolutionaries stormed the castle on that dust?

Then I heard voices coming from inside a room further down the hall. Tiptoeing over, I jammed my ear against the door and listened. A man and woman were chatting earnestly in French. It had to be them. As I leaned on the door ever so slightly, it silently inched open, the smallest of cracks. I heard a few more words, louder this time. He sounded upset and angry, she sounded happy and drunk. Was it them? All I had to do was inch it open just a little more so I could see inside. I pushed gently, another half inch, and another. Then two large hands grabbed my shoulders from behind, squeezed tight, spun me around, and I was looking into the face of the tour guide.

"I wondered where you'd got off to," he said. He didn't sound like a butler anymore. He sounded like a bouncer. A lip-curled smile revealed a mouthful of gold-capped teeth. How did he get here? Did he lock the tour group in the dungeon? He shoved me into the room and I fell, landing hard on my back, head slamming on the concrete floor. The door shut.

From my floor-to-ceiling point of view, I could see an elderly man and woman in two large wooden chairs looking down on me. He wore a great white wig with curly hair that hung below his shoulders, a long purple silk robe and oversize white tassel, like a giant lace collar, around his neck. A king. She wore an even larger hat with feathers—they must have reached two feet over her head—and a gold and white dress that seemed as if it were cut from several miles of silk, velvet, and lace. A queen.

"Do not move," the Man-Who-Would-Be-King said, his wet, steely eyes staring at me and purple-veined hand squeezing a large, white cane. "We've been watching you on our security cameras. Tell us why you have been skulking around our halls."

I looked back at the door. The tour guide was standing there, blocking my escape, jaw aggressively jutting and fisted hands on his hips.

The king harrumphed. "I do hope you have an explanation."

"It's so nice of you to visit," added the queen, her big, toothy smile neatly juxtaposed with her husband's frown.

She stood up and bent over in a kind of grand royal curtsey, revealing a large fragment of royal skin. "Would you join us for tea and cake?"

"Cake?" The king snorted, banging his cane on the floor and shaking his head. "He's not here for cake. What's wrong with you? He's come for our heads." He looked back at me, holding my eyes as if he were willing me to confess my crimes. "If you've come to start a revolution," the king stated crisply, "you're about two hundred years too late."

"I'm not." I tried to think of a good excuse for why I was here, but I was afraid and confused and sharp pains were bouncing around inside my skull. Also, I wasn't used to speaking to people dressed like fifteenth-century monarchs while lying on my back, and they—or at least, he—seemed to be convinced that I had something to do with the storming of the Palace of Versailles.

"My name is Declan Tucker. I wasn't skulking, and I'm not a revolutionary. I'm an artist, and I'm trying to find someone. Her name is Chloé." The king's hand squeezed even more tightly around his cane, and the tour guide locked the door. There was a long silence, and I felt the tension in the room climbing rapidly.

"Not skulking, eh? Not here for our country? We will see." The king nodded to the chair. "Stand up, so-called Declan Tucker."

I wanted to make my escape, but the tour guide looked like he would hang, draw, and quarter me if I tried anything. Slowly, I got up and stood in front of them.

"If you really are an artist, and not a treacherous villain with bloody murder in his black heart, tell me. What kind of artist are you? What work have you done? And don't lie. If you lie, we will sniff you out and punish you like the bastard scoundrel I suspect you are." He stared at me, chin down like an attacking dog, and sniffed. Three long, loud sniffs in a row, as if he really was trying to sniff me out. "I'll have you know the dungeon is in perfect working order."

"But first, tell us about your friend Chloé!" the queen piped in, ignoring her husband's interrogation. "What is her name? What does she look like?"

There was little to do but answer. Starting with the queen, who, I allow, seemed less likely than the king to sentence me to life in the dungeon. "I don't know her last name. Or anything about her, really. I think she was born into a royal..."

"You better hope she's not with the House of Burgundy. The Burgundys are not royals," the king sternly weighed in. "They are mere pretenders, low-life bastards, criminals, and prostitutes."

"I don't know," I said. "I just thought that maybe because you were royals you might know her, or someone who knows her. I've been looking all over."

"We detest the Burgundys," the king said.

"It is a little complicated," the queen added. "You see, we haven't spoken to them in three hundred years."

"I didn't say anything about the Burgundys," I protested.

"Three hundred and eight! And we're not starting now. Nothing but rogues and scum!" He was shaking and pointing his cane at me like it was a weapon.

"But I don't suppose there's much harm in speaking to them now," the queen suggested. "They haven't attacked us in centuries."

"I'll tell you something, young man." The king was nodding excitedly now, banging his cane on the floor and shouting. "The French Monarchy is coming back. This First Republic crap with their liberal democratic ideals has run out of ideas, their pathetic egalitarianism exposed for the facile populist propaganda that it is. We will be back! We will triumph! And they will pay for their crimes. By God, they'll pay. I'll hang them all!" Then he leaned back in his chair and turned his eyes toward me again, staring at me as if sizing me up for a trip to the guillotine.

"You'll have to excuse the king, my dear." The queen cut a piece of cake and offered me a slice. "He's tired from all the renovations."

"A queen should not be serving a common radical cake," he said. "It's beneath you."

"We will do everything we can to find your dear friend Chloé," she promised. "But it won't be easy. Heaven only knows where she could be. There are a lot of people claiming to be royals galloping around France right now."

Heaven only knows. She was right. This was hopeless. I could already tell my investigations into royal families and castle-owners weren't going anywhere. I had wasted two days already. At this rate, it would take several years to visit all the other castles in France. If anyone was going to help me, it had to be Neil. He was the only one with contacts in the celestial universe, if he even had that—either way, he was my only hope. If I could just figure out a way to get him off that couch.

The king had fallen asleep, his head drooping lifelessly forward. The queen walked over and stood beside me. "Would you like to go for a walk in the gardens?" she asked, leaning over until she was exposing more flesh than permitted by the laws of the Republic. Her lips were only inches from mine when she whispered, "You can see the mountains of France from there."

Sixteen

Recent calls.

Alan G. (4) Yesterday

I didn't get back to the apartment until after midnight. Neil was lying on the couch watching television, in pretty much the same position he was in when I left him here. The only difference I could see was that there were more clothes on the floor and more unwashed dishes on the furniture. I sat down and started to tell him about what had happened with Alan, and he snorted.

"Why would anybody pay for your art?" he asked.

"I don't know if they will. I thought they would, but now…"

"It's not that good. I saw it, and I didn't even get it." Neil got up and walked to the kitchen. I heard the fridge door open. "It's just a bunch of black paint and squiggly lines. Honestly? A nine-year-old could do it."

"When did you see it?"

"Duh. Ghost?" he called out. "Remember?"

"Just because you're dead doesn't mean you're an expert on contemporary art." He ignored that and came back with a family-size bucket of KFC coleslaw. I suddenly had a hunger for something that tasted like regular, ordinary food. "Can I have some of that?"

"No. I only have a little bit."

"Is there anything I can have?"

"Buy your own food. I'm not your mother."

"C'mon man. I'm letting you stay in my place."

"Ixnay on the KFCfay."

He turned the television up and lay down on the couch.

"Did you find out anything about Chloé?" I asked.

"No." He shoved a fork in his mouth. "I've been busy."

"Doing what? I thought you were dead?"

"Not exactly dead." He got up, picked up an old chicken leg from a side table, and took a bite. "You don't get it, do you?"

"Get what? No, I don't. Please, enlighten me. Also, how long has that been there?"

He put the chicken leg back on the table. "See, I'm stuck in the bardo."

"What's the bardo?"

"It's like some stage in between life and death, and I'm somewhere in the middle. Not dead, not alive. Did not know about any of this bardo stuff when I was alive, but now? Ugh. Oh, and just FYI? It sucks. It really sucks."

"I did not know that. And what—or why, I guess—does it suck?"

Neil reached between the cushions and pulled out another piece of chicken. He took a deep bite and gnawed on it, silently. That had to be bad for you. If he wasn't completely dead yet, I figured he would be soon.

"There are supposed to be six stages of the bardo. The bardo of life and death, the dream state, meditation, moment of death, luminosity of true nature—whatever the effin'-H that is—and transmigration. Not sure what that is either. Anyway, I'm having trouble getting past the first stage. The whole thing is supposed to last forty-nine days, and it's been, like, sixty or something already and I'm still in the first stage!"

"What's the problem?"

"I don't know. Getting an answer out of these people is impossible. Apparently, I'm not very integrated or something. No idea. But I better figure it out soon because I don't want to be here for eternity. Not in this apartment."

"Integrated? You mean enlightened?"

"That's it. I'm not very enlightened. I don't even know what that is."

This sounded like a problem. I didn't want Neil here for eternity either. "Who are these people?"

"I can't even pronounce it. The Mahi-sak-sa or something. I'm telling you, it's not like anything we got taught in church. Spent my life being told there was a God, and Jesus and all that, and I fell for it, hook, line, and sinker. Then it turns out these Maki-saks or whatever are in charge." He rolled his eyes. "I'm trying to get a refund on my church donations."

This was getting too deep for me. I wanted to ask if they—the Mahisaka or whoever they were—could help find Chloé, but Neil was getting kind of emotional and I suddenly felt sorry for him. "Okay, well, that does suck. I'm sorry to hear all that."

It surprised me. Not that he wasn't enlightened enough to get past the first stage of the bardo—that didn't surprise me one little bit. It surprised me that I felt sorry for him. But I did. Even though he had moved into my place uninvited, refused to leave, left a mess everywhere he went, told me a nine-year-old could paint better than I did, hadn't lifted a finger looking for Chloé, and wouldn't even share his coleslaw with me, I wanted to help him. He seemed so lost. "Neil. What if I could help you get out of the bardo?"

He stuck his tongue out at me and made a farting sound. "Like you could get me out of the bardo."

"Not me. I can't. But I think I know someone who could."

"No, you don't."

"I do. I'm pretty sure."

"Ha. Doubt it. I don't believe you."

I got up, walked to the door and opened it. "Look, I'd like to help. But if you don't want me to, that's fine."

Neil shut off the TV. "Wait, wait. Okay already, don't leave," he called. I held the door. "Okay, okay. Yes, if you can. Help me. Please. I hate this."

"Okay, I'll do it. But if I do, will you please, please, please, at least try to help me find Chloé?"

He nodded. "Deal."

"Deal." I shut the door and hurried down the hall.

———

Recent calls

Alan G. (9) 11:38pm

Alan G. (7) Yesterday

It was midnight by the time I got there. The streets were dark, quiet, and empty, except for a few scurrying rats and a lost, mangy-looking dog. A thick fog had curled around the city, and by the time I made it to The Grand Hotel I couldn't see more than a few feet in front of me. So I didn't notice anything different until I pulled on the front door. It wouldn't open. I kept pulling, but it refused to budge. It took a moment before I realized the door was being held shut by a heavy lock. Looking around, I saw all the windows were boarded up with sheets of plywood. I ran around to the back of the building and all those doors and windows were also locked, chained, and boarded. Ran back to the front, where I discovered a yellow sign taped to the wall. It read "DANGER. DO NOT ENTER. KEEP OUT FOR YOUR OWN SAFETY. THIS IS A CONDEMNED BUILDING. UNSAFE. DO NOT ENTER. NO TRESPASSING. BY THE AUTHORITY OF THE POLICE DEPARTMENT."

No! No, no, no. There was a scrap piece of metal lying in the back alley, and it provided me with enough leverage to pull the boards off a ground-level window. The frame and sash were rotten so all it took was one good kick to open it up. I crawled in and waited for my eyes to adjust. Everything was dark, except for a sliver of light shining through the open window. There was nothing there. The Grand Hotel was empty.

I walked through the lobby, up the stairs, and down the hall. Saw nothing and nobody. Walked through the workshop, which was also empty. Almost everything was gone, except for leftover scraps of half-finished pieces of art, a few motley-looking couches, broken chairs, and empty food containers. Even the mice seemed to have abandoned the place.

They had told me this could happen. Madelaine, Gaétan, and all the others had said we could be evicted. But I only believed that on a theoretical level, like the earth *could* get sucked into a giant black hole, but it never did—I honestly never believed it would really happen. How could they? What purpose could this serve? This was our home, our sanctuary, our lives, our everything. It belonged to us. Whatever happened to squatter's rights? I ran up to Gaétan's room. It was empty. I ran down the hall, past the kitchen. There was nothing anywhere. Every room, every floor, every closet and cupboard were empty. After running around for twenty minutes, the only place I hadn't looked was the roof. I found the ladder, climbed up, pushed open the metal door, and climbed on top of the building. That's where I found them.

There was a small group of people standing near the middle of the roof in a tight circle. Their heads were bowed and their hands joined. It looked like a secret cabal meeting to plot a government takeover. I heard a few muffled voices, came closer, and saw a model of a building in the middle of their circle. It was built of cardboard and sitting on a large pile of bricks, like a funeral pyre. I realized it was a model of The Grand. It stood about four feet high and had the same windows, doors, and walls. They had even matched the graffiti. As I got closer I made out a few faces in the crowd. Apollinaire. Gaétan. The others looked familiar, fellow friends from our now-shuttered hotel.

"Oh supreme light, lead us from the untruth to the truth, from darkness to light, from death to immortality." It was Apollinaire, standing closest to the cardboard building. He was dressed in long, black flowing robes, a loose hood covering his head. "We welcome the death of The Most Magnificent Great Grand Royal Ambassador Palace Hotel as we would welcome a long-expected guest."

We welcome the what? No. No we didn't. We did not welcome that. Moving toward the edge of the circle, I caught Gaétan's eye. He nodded and moved sideways, giving me enough room to join in. I grabbed his hand.

"What's happening here?" I whispered.

"Final rites," he whispered back.

"Why? What final rites?"

"We have been evicted." A small shrug.

"They can't do this."

"But of course they can."

"Death is not feared here," Apollinaire continued. "Death is holy and auspicious. It is—"

"No, they can't!" I almost yelled.

Apollinaire paused, looking at me with an evil eye. "It is the first step on the path to enlightenment."

"Is he a priest?" I whispered to Gaétan.

"He was, twelve hundred years ago."

Apollinaire finished the rites, lit a match, and threw it in one of the cardboard model's empty windows. The model caught fire, and within a minute or two the flames were taller than any of us.

"The Grand Hotel is passing onto the next stage of its eternal journey." Apollinaire reached his arms to the sky and shut his eyes. Everyone joined him. For a few moments, all we could hear was music from the area clubs and the crackling of flames in front of us.

We watched in silence while the flames burned. A few minutes later, with the cardboard model of our old home reduced to a pile of embers and ashes, what sounded like a hundred police sirens and fire trucks wailed from the street below. Red strobe lights circled around the surrounding streets, tires screeched and stopped in front of our building. Car doors slammed. A helicopter flew over us, search beams lighting us up in the dark night. "The Grand has moved onto the next life," Apollinaire called out. "And so should we."

Everyone ran.

They were faster than I was. By the time I got to the ladder, most of them had already vanished down the exit—I was certain I was going to be the last one out. But as my feet dropped and searched for the first rail, I looked back and saw two others behind me: Gaétan was helping Apollinaire make his escape. At the speed they were moving, they wouldn't get out of the building until next Tuesday.

There was a moment that I was tempted to pretend I hadn't seen them and keep running. I had already been to jail once and didn't want to go back. Getting caught this time would mean charges of breaking and entering, property damage, and possibly arson. But I couldn't. I watched them hobbling along and knew I couldn't leave. There was no way I was going anywhere without those two. I went back, grabbed Apollinaire's other arm, and helped Gaétan get him to the ladder.

Apollinaire was having difficulty getting his footing, and Gaétan had to climb down first and set his feet on the rungs while I kept the old man steady from above. We moved one rung at a time, Gaétan holding his feet while I crawled down beside him, holding onto him with one arm. We were halfway down the ladder when we heard the front door smash open. The police were here: there was no more time. We all let go at once and fell to the ground, landing one on top of the other. Apollinaire was swearing under his breath as a man with a megaphone shouted at everyone to lie face down on the ground.

The back door was only a few feet away. We untangled our arms and legs, picked ourselves up, got Apollinaire on his feet, and the three of us staggered to the back door. I swung it open and we stepped onto an outdoor fire escape. We heard more doors slamming and men on megaphones shouting. They were getting closer. Gaétan pushed the door shut as quietly as possible and we made our way down the stairs and into the alley.

Holding onto Apollinaire, we stumbled along, gaining distance foot by painfully slow foot. It seemed like an hour before the sound of sirens finally faded, and a few dark alleys later we stepped onto the sidewalk and lost ourselves in the anonymity of the street. We walked for a few more blocks, just to put an extra-safe distance between us and the police, before we even spoke.

Ten minutes later, we found a small café and went inside. Parisians still have respect for men and women of the cloth, and Apollinaire's priestly robe got us a fast table and fawning service. For a few minutes all we did was breathe. After we settled down, Apollinaire waved at the waitress and ordered a bottle of wine. "I haven't had that much fun in a long time," he said. "Although I believe I've broken my hip."

"Were you really staging a funeral for a building?" I asked.

"More like a return to earth," Apollinaire told me. "The universe is like an eternal hotel—"

"Yes," Gaétan interrupted. "It's being turned into condos."

"The fire was out before they even got there. Did they think we were going to burn it down?" Apollinaire said.

Neither one of them seemed even slightly troubled by the fact that our hotel had been shut down, but I was shocked and heartbroken. This was my spiritual home. It was the only place other than my own home I ever felt like I belonged. The best friends I ever had lived there, maybe the only friends I ever had. For a minute, I thought I was going to cry. The best times of my life had been at The Grand and they had barely started. I couldn't believe they were already over. What would happen to everyone? Where would they go? Where would I go? And what about Madelaine? What happened to her?

"She left a few weeks ago. Moved back to Winnipeg. Mentioned something about getting into real estate," Gaétan said. "We had a funeral for her last week."

The wine was delivered and poured. I sat stunned. The Grand couldn't be gone. My miniature model of the perfect world couldn't be turned into condos. My friends couldn't just vanish.

"You disappeared, Croquis," Gaétan said.

"I guess we both disappeared," I said.

"I did. I was restless. It's hard to stay in one place, for me."

Had he been restless? Was that why he had left? Or was it something else? Or maybe...someone else? Someone with blond hair and almond eyes, perhaps? "I thought maybe you'd met someone..." I remarked, trying to sound casual.

Hoping to pry a confession out of him, maybe a clue as to where Chloé was.

He just looked confused for a moment. "No, not me."

"Oh? I thought I heard you had left with someone...named, oh, who was it? Stephanie? Carol? No, it was someone named Chloé, I think."

"Who? Chloé? No."

What a liar. Still, it was hard to totally hate a guy who had saved your life and bailed you out of prison.

"But you came back," he said. "After defeating the evil empire, you have returned, like some kind of conquering hero."

"More like an escaped convict returning to the scene." I went through everything that had happened since I had last seen him, starting at my first coffee with Alan through to the last press conference. Confessed everything. I told them about the galleries, the parties, Neil, and my so-called agent. Apologized for breaking the squat code, and for not being a free art revolutionary.

Gaétan waved a hand in the air. "That was really Madelaine's thing," he said. "We just went along because it meant so much to her."

"We should get more wine." Apollinaire cocked an eye at me. "A really nice wine, since we are now so rich and famous."

I was very far from being rich and famous, but I ordered a nice Bordeaux anyway. There was so much owing on my credit card now it didn't feel like it mattered.

"Make that a Château Margaux," he said, multiplying the price tag tenfold. I checked my pocket to make sure the credit card was there.

The wine was delivered, dutifully consumed, and another ordered. As we drank, we talked about life, loves, old friends, and enemies. Like any proper wake, we had soon forgotten why we were there. Rather, we were commiserating over the long list of conspirators and con men who we believed were scheming against us.

"Gallerists."

"Dealers."

"Thieves and cheats, every one of them!"

"Auction houses."

"Accountants."

"Corporations."

"Scum and vermin, all!"

"Business."

"Capitalism."

"Democracy."

"Condo owners."

"This is an acceptable wine," Apollinaire said, finishing his glass and waving at the waitress for another.

"So, The Grand is really gone." I shook my head. "Where will you go?" I asked Gaétan.

"Don't know. You?"

I told him that I had been thinking about life after art. That maybe it was time to do something else. Invent something, maybe. I always wanted to invent something. I didn't know what, though. I guess I hadn't really put much thought into it. Honestly, I had no idea what I was going to do. All I really knew was that I didn't want to lose everything I had found here. I wanted that life back—the squat, the merry band of art-rebels, exactly the way it had been—except, I explained, this time with Chloé. It was the third time I'd mentioned her name, given him a chance to come clean, and once again, there wasn't even a blink of recognition. How obvious did I have to get? Or was he just really good at pretending?

"Did I ever tell you about my friend Manet?" Apollinaire asked, like an old soldier about to tell a war story he'd told a hundred times before.

"I didn't know you knew Manet," Gaétan said.

"Of course I did!" He banged his glass on the table and shook his head. "You still don't get it, do you?"

Gaétan agreed that he probably didn't get it. At least I wasn't the only one.

"I was there when the Paris Salon rejected his great masterwork, *Le Déjeuner sur l'herbe*. They were fools! They didn't understand it. The Academy of Fine Arts was nothing but a bunch of thick-headed pompous government hacks and swindlers then, as it is now. But I did. I understood it completely. Even then, I knew it was the bravest painting in the history of art." Apollinaire's mouth tightened and he shook his head. "You know what I told him? I said, Who needs 'em, Édouard? Who? Not us. Screw 'em. Let the art establishment burn, burn to the ground. And we, we will break down the walls, you and me. We'll start the world anew." He banged his glass on the table again, earning a few stares from tables nearby. "And we did."

His mother was the daughter of a diplomat and goddaughter of a crown prince, his father a respected judge. They wanted Édouard to pursue a career in law. He tried. He failed. After that, his father wanted him to be an officer in the Navy. That also failed. Twice. He tried to drown himself in the Seine River. That failed as well. As an artist, he was also a failure. His work was dismissed by critics, criticized by fellow artists, called offensive, vulgar, and "full of errors." But he knew better. After his Le Déjeuner sur l'herbe *was rejected by the official jury of the Paris Salon in 1863, he rejected the official jury. Exhibited his work in a separate salon: the Salon des Refusés, along with the other works the jury had rejected. Seventy years later,* Le Déjeuner sur l'herbe *would hang in the Louvre, one of the most celebrated works in the history of art. Manet would be remembered forever, not just as one of the Fathers of Impressionism, but as a hero to the avant-garde and risk-takers everywhere.*

"You did what?" I asked Apollinaire.

"We stuck a finger in the eye of the establishment. Manet and I. We set out on our own, set art free from their iron grip. And it stayed free."

"Until now," Gaétan added.

"We should get more wine." Apollinaire said, gazing at me.

I waved down the waiter and ordered a bottle of Château Latour. It was the wine my parents opened for their most important occasions, and I suddenly felt like celebrating. A real celebration, this time. Apollinaire had just given me an idea. A big idea. It was still only a half-formed thought in my head, but I felt a rush of excitement. I had just thought of a way to get everything and everyone back together. I was just starting to figure out how it would work when the wine landed on the table, and I remembered the reason I was here. The big idea would have to wait. I had to ask Apollinaire for a favor.

"Could you get someone I know out of the bardo?" I asked.

He looked at me for a long time without speaking. It was a little frightening, to be honest. His eyes, large and black, were boring into me like a couple of pile drivers.

"What did you say?"

"I have an, umm, a kind of friend. He's stuck in the bardo, apparently, so he says—I'm not even sure what that is, but I promised I'd do what I could to get him out. Thought you could help."

More wine was poured in his glass and he emptied it immediately. Then he stared into space. Then at me. He poured another glass, emptied that one, and stared into space some more. Two thousand euros had disappeared down his throat in about three minutes.

"That is a very large request. A gargantuan request. To help someone out of the bardo is—almost impossible. Only a few people in the world are capable of such a thing. This isn't the Catholic Church, you know. You can't just buy an indulgence for him and off he goes. Who is this person?"

I told him about Neil. How I had (sort of) killed him, how he had ended up living in my apartment and how he said he could find Chloé if I got him out of the bardo. (Once again, not a blink of recognition at the mention of Chloé's name from Gaétan. What an actor.)

"I don't think he can be helped." Apollinaire leaned back in his chair. "It can't be done. He's too far gone."

"You can't help?"

"Absolutely not."

"Would it make any difference if I ordered another Chateau Latour?"

"I prefer Lafite."

We worked it out. The three of us finished the wine and stumbled back to the apartment.

There was no rational reason to believe that Apollinaire could help Neil get out of the bardo. But there was also no rational reason to believe that Neil was in the bardo either. So in a strange, twisted way, it felt like the universe was unfolding as it should—that Apollinaire really was a reincarnation of a several-hundred-year-old priest, and that Neil really did have connections in the otherworld and that all of these things were about to come together and help me find Chloé. Or else I was just drunk.

We got to the apartment, opened the door, and found Neil asleep on the couch. A rerun of *The Golden Girls* was playing in French on the television. We woke him up, made our introductions, and sat down.

Neil couldn't stop staring at Apollinaire. Admittedly, he did look impressive. It wasn't just the black robes—he also had that grave, priestly expression and was speaking in a lower timber that sounded like the voice of God. We told Neil about Apollinaire's twelve hundred years of experience as a priest, and that he knew all about getting people out of bardos. Neil believed every bit of it.

"Sit in a circle on the floor," Apollinaire commanded. We did. "Cross your legs. Shut your eyes. Hold hands." We did that too, except Neil couldn't get his legs crossed and kept falling over onto his back so we all had to help him up. After a few attempts, he sat with his legs straight out in front of him and Apollinaire nodded.

"We must all think positive thoughts about our dear brother, Neil."

This was going to be harder than I expected.

"Think about how much we love Neil. About how much happiness he has brought to our lives. About his beautiful soul, and his eternal compassion."

I tried to think about all the good things Neil had done for me. Kept trying to think about them, trying as hard as I had tried to think about anything in my life. Every time I thought I found one, something else would come up in my mind. Like the palm tree print he taped on my wall, the ketchup stain on my couch, or that he never washed the dishes once, not even once.

"Who is not thinking positive thoughts here?" Apollinaire sounded annoyed. "Who is not believing?"

Opening my eyes, I saw everyone looking at me. I refocused, with everything I had, doubled and tripled my efforts to channel all the positivity and love I could muster.

"That is a *little* better." I could feel Apollinaire's eyes on me, but he finally turned away and started chanting. "*Om ah hum vajra guru padma siddhi hum. Om ah hum vajra guru padma siddhi hum. Om ah hum vajra guru padma siddhi hum.*" This went on for ten minutes or more.

"Neil, my brother. How do you feel?" Apollinaire asked.

"Lighter?" he answered.

"Yes. You feel lighter. Do you also feel love?"

"Yes! I feel love. A lot of love."

"Acceptance?"

"Yes, I feel that too," Neil said. "I feel so much acceptance!"

I opened my eyes just a slit to peek at Neil. His face was all scrunched up and orange-red, like an overripe heritage tomato.

"You are entering the luminosity of true nature," Apollinaire said. "This is all you need to become enlightened. This is what you need to gain acceptance into the next stage of your life's journey."

Neil was nodding so emphatically I thought he was going to break his neck. "It's working! I'm really feeling it. I feel myself being transported."

"Of course it's working!" Apollinaire added, sounding even more annoyed.

"I'm lightening! I'm leaving the bardo!"

"*En*lightening," Apollinaire mumbled.

What? It was working? Really? It was? No, it wasn't. Wait. But if it really was, it couldn't—not yet. He couldn't leave yet. This was impossible, it couldn't happen, but if it were possible, and it was happening, he had to live up to his end of our bargain before he moved on. We had a deal. "You can't go yet!" I shouted at him. "Where's Chloé?"

"I'm moving into the second phase!"

"Wait. Wait, Neil. Stop." I was starting to panic. "Apollinaire, stop him. We had a deal. He can't leave until he's told me where to find Chloé." I got up and stood in front of Neil. "Tell me! Tell me where she is! You have to know."

"I'm entering the luminosity of true nature!" he said.

"But we had a deal! Where's Chloé? Stop him! This isn't fair."

"The path of enlightenment isn't always a straight one," Apollinaire explained.

"That doesn't make any sense. None of this does. You're not a twelve-hundred-year-old priest or a two-hundred-year-old poet. You didn't know Picasso, don't know anything about bardos or reincarnation or horoscopes. You're just some old guy in a black robe—and this, there's no way this—" My voice had gone up quite a few octaves, but I was past caring. I pointed at Neil. "There's no way this is anything but some weird guilt dream I'm having, and—" I stared at them. "I have a lot of anxiety right now!"

Apollinaire and Gaétan were smiling at me, all serene and Buddha-like. Apollinaire stood and rested his hand on my shoulder, squeezing harder than I thought necessary, and gave me a stern soul-stare. "Negativity and hatred could block his way to the next life," he stage-whispered. "Think of love and acceptance!"

"You have something to do about this!" I shouted at Gaétan. "This is all your fault!"

Gaétan kept smiling at me, as if he had advanced to another level of awakening and wanted me to come along for the ride. I gave up. There was no point. I stopped, sat down in the circle, grabbed Neil's hand, summoned all the acceptance I could muster, and shut my eyes.

Ever since I started working for Neil, back at the *Georgetown Herald,* I had been nothing but a complete jerk to him. He had given me my first job, a chance to do something that I wanted to do, and I had given him nothing but misery. He had asked for my help, and I used it as a bargaining chip. He tried to be my friend, and I had turned it into some kind of negotiating tool. I had looked down on him, patronized him, treated him like he was a moron, and possibly even killed him, without even saying I was sorry. Acted as if I were some kind of higher being. I knew now I wasn't. I thought I had some kind of divine power, and I didn't. Too late, for both of us, I realized what Gaétan had meant after our escape from Le Bateau-Lavoir. That we all, every person on this planet, came from the same place. I owed him, and everyone else in Georgetown, an apology. If Neil hadn't delivered on a promise, the fault was mine. He was a good person. It was time to let him go.

When I opened my eyes, he was gone. This time, he wasn't coming back. I had nothing but a palm tree print, a kitten poster, and a room full of chicken bones to remember him by. He had made a mess of my apartment, made it impossible for me to paint there, worn my underwear, destroyed my faith in celestial beings, and worse than all that, broken a promise to help me find Chloé. I deserved far worse. And the weirdest thing was that I was going to miss him.

"He's made it to the next level, right?" I asked.

Apollinaire nodded.

I was glad. He deserved it.

It was late, and we all fell asleep. But before I went to bed, I went into the kitchen and found a plate full of unfinished meatballs.

They were delicious.

Seventeen

By the time I woke up, Gaétan and Apollinaire had disappeared. I wandered around the apartment, walking in circles around my couch and coffee table, dodging dirty plates and empty containers of food, wondering what to do. Neil was gone, Gaétan was gone, and with them my last chance at finding Chloé was also gone. I walked until I was dizzy, fighting a sick feeling that there was no point in trying anymore. How did I let this happen? How had everything gone so completely wrong? Eventually, I found myself standing in front of one of Neil's posters. *When life leaves you hanging, don't quit.* I was thinking how it was the dumbest thing I'd ever seen. Then I stopped and thought again. Maybe, just maybe, she was right. Maybe that kitten wasn't so dumb after all.

I had underestimated Neil, and now I might be underestimating that kitten. Perhaps I had also underestimated Google. I decided to take the kitten's advice and give Google another try. Sat down at my computer, flexed my fingers, and turned it on. There were a few emails from my credit card company marked *urgent* but I ignored them, switched to Google, and typed *chloe artist paris* in the search bar. It returned 42,100,000 results in 0.78 seconds. The top three included an electro-minimalist-dance artist named Chloé, a Ukrainian ceramics artist named Chloé, and a fashion designer named Chloé who worked with recycled tires. A scan through the next several pages didn't find anything closer to who I was looking for. I tried several other search terms—*beautiful woman in paris named chloe, artists from paris named chloe, art student named chloe, royal named chloe who is an artist and worked in a restaurant.* Nothing even close. That was okay. Even Google could have bad days.

What else could I search for? I thought I remembered Chloé saying something about Burgundy, although I couldn't remember what it was. The self-anointed "king and queen" had mentioned Burgundy as well. So, I searched *royals from burgundy.* Google spat back *actresses who had worn burgundy-colored gowns to a royal wedding;* something called *Royal Burgundy Bush Bean Seeds* that were described as "vigorous sprouters"; a burgundy, maroon-colored Range Rover, that kind of thing. I was starting to feel like Google's spiders weren't really making an honest effort. Then a small caption near the bottom of the fourth page caught my eye. It read:

The House of Burgundy. List of Living Legitimate Male Capetians. The Capetian dynasty (also known as the House of France) is the largest dynasty in Europe, with over one hundred and twenty living male members descended from the legitimate line. Since the extinction of the House of Courtenay in 1733, the House of Burgundy is the only remaining branch of legitimate Capetian descent.

This looked promising. I bet she was part of the Burgundy dynasty. It looked like a pretty impressive dynasty, and that would be the kind of dynasty she'd be part of.

I discovered that Burgundian kings first ruled France in the sixteenth century. Henry IV was the first Burgundian appointed to be King of France, whose coronation was followed by several weddings, ambushes, slaughters, assassinations, more weddings, a few wars, the taking over of thrones in Spain, Naples, Sicily, a revolution, beheadings, abdication, and, well, it went on and on. The history of the House of Burgundy was interesting, I guess, but not helpful. After reading for twenty minutes, I wasn't even up to the 1600s. I skipped ahead.

A few minutes later, I found fresh hope at the bottom of Wikipedia's House of Burgundy page: a complete list of all one hundred and twenty living members of the Burgundy dynasty. Gratitude, relief, and happiness! This was just what I was looking for. The list included which branch of the family they belonged to, their ages, and where they lived. The Burgundys were spread all over the world, from Singapore to Rio de Janeiro to Brazil, and there was only one living in Paris—a Prince Amaury of Burgundy-Parma, aged thirty-two years. No photo was available, and not much information provided: the scant biography identified the prince as a soldier, businessman, entrepreneur, philanthropist, film producer, and racing car driver. A definite possibility.

After another hour of searching, I found an email address for him, through a business he was connected to. I wrote to him right away, providing a long and detailed explanation of who I was, why I had to find Chloé, and how important it was that he help me do that, right away, please and thank you. As a gesture of goodwill, I added that France would be in much better shape today if the House of Burgundy were still running the country. Then I sat back and waited for his response.

Recent calls
Alan G. (12) 2:10pm

Mother (2) 11:37am

Alan G. (19) Yesterday

Over twenty minutes later, I still hadn't heard back from the prince, so I sent him another email. And another. Ten minutes later, another. Five minutes after that, another. Still nothing. Sent eleven more follow-up emails. Still nothing. I found the phone number to his office and called, but no one answered. Left a message. Explained how urgent this was. Then I sent another email, and another, and called and left another message, but nothing. Then another. After an hour, I started to wonder. What was taking him so long? Was he ignoring me? He must be ignoring me. A dozen, then two or three dozen more emails and probably twenty calls later, I gave up for the night. What the hell was wrong with this guy?

Shortly after I woke up, I started calling and emailing again. If he thought I was just going to give up, he was seriously mistaken. After twenty-seven emails and twelve phone calls, my phone finally rang. It was Alan. I ignored it. Then it rang again. It was Prince Amaury's office.

"*Merde!*" a man shouted into the phone. "Who is this? Why are you harassing us?"

"This is Declan Tucker. To whom am I speaking, please?"

"You know who you are speaking to. This is the office of Prince Amaury of Burgundy-Parma. *Putain!* Stop this harassment immediately or we will call the police."

"I'd like to speak to the prince, please and thank you."

"*Non.* You can't speak to the prince. No one just speaks to the prince. He is the *prince*, you...who are you?"

I repeated my name and summarized the reasons for my call before repeating my request to meet with the prince. "It must be today."

"Excuse me. We are speaking about Prince Amaury of Burgundy-Parma. He doesn't just see anyone, and certainly he will not see you. Stop calling us. Stop emailing. Just stop. Goodbye." He seemed unbalanced. Of the two of us, I was clearly being the most reasonable and diplomatic.

"It is about Chloé, as I have previously stated. And delay is not possible. You must understand, I'm in a hurry."

"That is not my problem. And why do you think the prince knows anything about your, this, Chloé?"

I repeated the story. Despite the fact that I had already explained everything to him in a previous email, so I shouldn't have had to repeat it. Which I didn't even mention.

There was a pause on the other end of the line. "Hold on for a minute."

The phone went quiet, and I waited. Five minutes. Ten minutes. Finally, he came back.

"Describe this Chloé."

I did. He asked me to hold the line again and disappeared. Another five minutes later, he was back.

"The prince is not aware of any Chloé. You have taken enough of his time. Do not call us again."

"He is. I know he is. I'm sure of it."

"He isn't. Now stop calling or we will contact the police."

"The police are sick and tired of me. And I know he knows Chloé."

"He does not."

"Ask him again. He has to know her." I forced myself to keep my voice calm, my octaves low, and maintain my tone of official international diplomat. "This is a matter of some urgency. She is his niece, or a cousin," I guessed, "and her life may be in danger." This was a stretch, I knew, but it did add dramatic effect.

There was a long pause and a longer, louder sigh on the other end of the phone. "Hold for one minute." Four or five minutes later, he returned. "Prince Amaury has agreed to see you. You are very lucky, my friend. Be here at nine in the morning. You will have five minutes. Not a second more."

———

I was kind of hoping Prince Amaury lived in a proper castle. It would have been nice to meet a real, proper royal, unlike the count who just thought he was a king. But he didn't. The prince worked in a bank tower and wore a blue suit with a red tie. His office was big—big enough that I had to raise my voice to return his greeting when I walked in—but it was just an office. No moats, no towers, no crowns. Nothing very royal-like anywhere.

The prince stood up when I walked in. We shook hands and sat down. He looked at me quietly for a moment, then put his palms together as if he were about to ask me to pray. "You are a persistent young man."

Keeping the same international diplomat voice that had worked so well on the phone yesterday, I said, "I'm here on a matter of some importance."

"You seem to believe I know your Chloé. Tell me about this Chloé that I am supposed to know so well."

The prince had big Hollywood eyes and teeth that shone so perfectly they looked like they had been painted on. His hair was thick as rope, every strand in perfect place, his cheekbones male-model high. His forehead had a noble bearing and his chin was strong and determined. Even his voice sounded royal—a deep, steady timber that could have commanded undivided attention from inanimate objects if it tried. All he needed was a beard and a crown and he could have been King Louis XIV.

I crossed my legs. "Chloé is... She's...well, I do not know her last name, exactly. Or where she's from," I said. "I do know she attended École nationale supérieure des Beaux-Arts. Well, she said she did. She worked in a restaurant. And I need to find her. That's all I know. I'm sure she's got some kind of royal lineage. I just know that, somehow. Did you ever get that? That feeling you just know something?" In the face of his big-eyed glare, my voice had lost its international diplomat authority. "Pretty sure she's from Burgundy. She might have said something, or I thought she did, or something close to it. Like you, right? Burgundy? So based on that, I thought you might be able to tell me where she was."

His head tilted to one side. "Based on what?"

I straightened my back and tried to regain my authority. "Based on my assumptions."

"Your assumptions?"

My eyes held his, returning his serious stare with my own. "My assumptions."

The prince rubbed his forehead and sighed. "What does she look like?"

"Blonde-ish. Not too tall. Almond eyes. Round face."

"You just described half the women in France."

What else could I say? Beautiful? Eyes, nose just a bit too... Soft skin? That also sounded like half the women in France. "She's an artist."

He stared at me, waiting for more.

"Shoulder-length hair."

He kept staring. It was getting uncomfortable. I tried to hold my chin up and steady, but I felt like my entire body was fidgeting. "Did I mention almond eyes?" I said. "Actually, Chinese almond eyes."

"Yes. You did mention that." He rubbed his hands together, as if he was trying to milk some piece of relevant information out of me.

"Thin. Pretty thin, anyway."

He thought for a moment or two, turned around and stared out the window, got up, and walked toward the door. "I'd like to help you, but I don't know this person. Your Chloé. My apologies. It's been nice meeting you, but I am a very busy person. Have a good day." He assumed an *I'm sorry* smile and held open the door, waiting for me to leave.

"What about the school? And the restaurant?"

"There are thousands of women like that working in restaurants here. I am sorry. But I am afraid that I'm wasting my time, and yours. I thought maybe I could help...but no."

It wasn't possible. He had to know her. I knew it.

The prince held up a hand, beckoning me to leave. "If you'll excuse me..."

"She likes to go to the Louvre."

"Many artists do. Please..."

I got up to leave. Walked to the door, past him, took a few steps and stopped. Looked back. One last try. The longest of shots, out of pure desperation. "She likes Joy Division."

He was about to shut the door and stopped. Lifted a perfect eyebrow. "Sorry? What was that?"

"She likes Joy Division. I don't know if that helps, but she wore a Joy Division T-shirt."

His *I'm sorry* smile disappeared. "Joy Division?"

"Yes."

"Joy Division," he repeated.

"Yes. Joy Division. Big in the eighties. Do you know them? 'Transmission'?"

"I do know them," he said. "I love Joy Division. 'Transmission.' Are you kidding me? Ian Curtis? Guy was a genius." His face softened. "My favorite is 'Atrocity Exhibition'. You know it?"

"I don't know that one."

"You must hear it! It's the best!"

"I will." He went back to his desk and sat down. "Joy Division. You know what? The girl I remember, the one I think you may be talking about, loved Joy Division. She's the one who told me about them. So maybe. Maybe we are talking about the same person."

"We are. I know we are."

"But the girl I remember wasn't named Chloé and wasn't blonde."

"Okay, well." Maybe it wasn't her?

He picked up an oversize book from his shelf. Old, heavy, and musty-looking, it landed on his desk with a small boom. He went through the index, turning pages, going back to the index, and muttering to himself. "The only photo I have is in this book." He looked through the index again, turned back to another page. Leaned in for a closer look. Turned the book around and pushed it toward me. "Is that her?"

A small family photo, barely a few inches around. Faded. A little person in a large group. But it was her. I knew it was her. She was younger then. Maybe eight? Nine? But she was smiling the same smile. Had the same angelic look. The same eyes. "That's her."

He flipped back to the index. "Her full name is Amelia Celeste Isabella Lisette Chloé Dubois." He leaned closer to the photo. "I remember her now. That Joy Division T-shirt. She wore it to one of our dinners—such a long time ago. Five years? Ten? It was an important occasion, a birthday celebration for one of the elder members of our so-called Capetian Dynasty. A very big deal. Everyone else was in black tie and evening gowns. She wore that T-shirt and ripped jeans. Her parents were so angry and embarrassed." He laughed. "She just sat there, pretending to smile, bored to death. Bored to absolute death. She was right. It was boring."

"I knew it! She told me she had lots of names."

"So. Where is she?" he asked.

Long pause. "What?"

"Can you tell me where she is?" he repeated. "We've been looking all over for her."

"Can I tell you?" What? No. No. I was supposed to be asking that question. Not him. I was supposed to ask *Can you tell me where she is?* and he was supposed to say *Yes* and then this long search would be over and Chloé and I would live happily ever after, blah blah. "But that's why I'm here. I was hoping you could tell me where she is."

His eyes dropped and lips tightened. Shook his head slowly and closed the book. "You don't know?"

"No. I met her for the first time a month or so ago. She disappeared shortly after that. Like I told the man on the phone yesterday, that's why I'm here. I was hoping you would know."

"He didn't tell me that. And I don't know. That is the reason I invited you here, hoping if you did know Amelia—or Chloé—that you could tell us where she might be. She disappeared a few weeks ago," he said. "We believe she ran away from home."

"She did? Really? Why? Why do you think that?"

"We don't know, not with absolute certainty. No one knows. Although, yes, we have suspected there was trouble for some time. You see..." He looked at me, gauging whether he should be telling me more. "There were a lot of rumors about her family, and what little we did know was nasty and sad. You see..."

"But that can't be true. I mean, they have everything! They own Géricaults, a Morris or two, or more, a home in..." I couldn't remember where. What was he trying to say? I was starting to wonder if we really did know the same person. "Morris used to visit them for dinner!"

The prince shook his head. "She told you that? Also, who is Morris?"

"Yes, she did! And I have no idea. She also told me her father is a duke or something. There's nothing nasty or sad about them. They're actual royalty."

He stared at his desk for a few long seconds. "I will tell you something. You know there hasn't been any royalty in France for hundreds of years. But very many families refuse to accept that, even today. They hold onto their old ancestry and titles like it's part of themselves. They try to pretend that one day those titles and riches will be restored, that life will go back to the way it was before the revolution. They have not accepted reality, have not adjusted to the truth. Many of them do not work. They think it's beneath them. And so, they live in poverty."

My visit to the count and countess came to mind. Renting out tours of their castle to cover the bills while they ranted and raved and went slowly mad. But that wasn't the Chloé I knew. Not a chance. "But you can't think Chloé's family is one of those?"

"I'm sorry, out of respect I can't tell you more. But from what I know, I believe it's quite possible she did leave home. We have searched everywhere. The police are looking for her. I have private detectives looking for her, all over France and beyond. No one has found her yet. She seems to have vanished." He rubbed his hands through his hair. "You were the last hope..." He took a deep breath. "This is so extremely distressing."

I couldn't believe it. Chloé living in poverty? Leaving home? It had to be a mistake. What about the art school!

The Géricaults? The dinners with Morris...it couldn't be possible. Could it? And also, to come so close to finding her, and now—nothing. We both gazed out of the window for a few minutes, sharing an unspoken sense of gloom.

"Why wouldn't she tell me?"

He just shook his head. "They're embarrassed."

So maybe she had lied. Maybe she lied to me about who she was for the same reason I lied to her about who I was. Because neither one of us wanted to accept who we were.

"You've searched everywhere?"

He waved a hand at the skyline outside his window. "It's a big city. A big country. We are still searching. Where did you last see her?"

I told him everything I knew, hoping something might help. But while I was talking, I was wondering. If Prince Amaury, with all his money, resources, and royal connections, hadn't been able to find Chloé, what chance did I have? If Interpol, the police, and the prince's private detectives couldn't find her, my Google searches weren't going to get very far.

I needed another plan. Now I knew who she was, even if I still couldn't believe it. But what I really needed to know was where she was, and how I could find her. There was only one possibility left, only one person who might be able to help. And that person was my best friend as well as my enemy: Gaétan.

———

By some strained logic in the universal order of things, young homeless people living in squats are just as hard to find as wealthy people with a royal pedigree. I searched all over for Gaétan, wandering through alleys and going into any squat and hostel I could find. I hung out in Montmartre, hoping he would show up, asked anyone who looked like they might know other homeless people, even went back to the park where he had found me lying on the steel bench that night. Nothing. I ran into a few of my old friends from The Grand, living in new squats and living new lives, but they hadn't seen him either.

That didn't stop me. He had to be here, somewhere, and I would find him. I expanded my search to new areas of Paris, spent hours riding buses and looking through new alleys. After the third day, I was getting desperate. Most people I approached had never heard of him, and the few who had hadn't seen him in weeks. Late on the fourth day someone suggested I check out a new squat that had opened up in the Le Marais area. By then it was late so I went back to the apartment and tried to sleep. I lay in bed, tossed and turned, but I was restless and anxious and found myself sitting at the window waiting until it was light outside.

As soon as the sun came up, I started my search for Gaétan again. Showered, put on some fresh clothes, shaved, and tried to make myself look less vampire-like. I opened the door, stepped outside but stopped because Alan was there.

How long had he been standing at my door? I didn't know and wasn't about to ask. My first reaction was to run, but he was blocking my path and besides I was too tired to run. So I tried to shut the door but he pushed it open with a force I didn't think he had in him, slamming it against the wall. We just stood and glared at each other for a few moments.

"Hi, Declan," he said. His voice sounded different—more Lord Voldemort than neighborhood scrabble enthusiast. "You've been ignoring my calls." His eyes were whiter than I remembered them, and purple-red blood vessels appeared on his oversize neck.

"I was just about to ring you," I said.

"Bullshit. Did you think you could just get out?"

"Out of what? Oh. No. I didn't think that."

"You can't get out. I have you under contract."

"Okay. Well. You're right. I remember that." I was wide-awake now. "I might have to change that contract."

"You can't. It's a fucking contract, you stupid-ass shit." He reached out and grabbed the door so that I couldn't close it again. "What were you thinking? What happened? Did you get a better offer somewhere else?"

"No. That's not it. I didn't think anything."

"Where's all the money you owe me?"

"Oh, that." The invoice. "I don't know where that money is."

"You better find out. Soon."

"Sure, I will. Promise. But now, I just have to—"

"The hell is the matter with you?" He was yelling now, his face close enough to mine that I could smell the coffee on his breath. "I was on your side, you know. I even covered up your bullshit story about growing up in San Francisco. Didn't think I knew about that, did you, Georgetown boy? I did everything for you." He must have seen me grinning. "What the fuck is wrong with you?"

"Nothing is wrong. Everything is really great, thanks for asking."

His hands rolled into fists. "It doesn't matter. You owe me money—for all the press conferences, the parties, all the work I did. You better pay me, or I'll sue your ass off."

"I will pay you." Of course I would. I just had to add thirty-seven thousand Euros to my credit card bill. That bill was so high now it didn't seem real. I was certain there were entire countries that owed less money than I did.

"You're done here. You know that? You're done."

"No, I don't think I'm done."

"You should have stuck to our plan."

"It wasn't my plan. It was your plan." I tried to get around him, but he pushed me back. "I was going to go for a walk."

"You're not going anywhere. You are done. You should have read the contract, you know. You really should have. Isn't your mother a lawyer? How stupid can you be? We have an exclusivity clause. You're mine now. You can't use another agent. No gallery will touch you. And I'm not going to touch you. You're stuck in nowhere land. I'm going to get all my money, and then I'm going let you rot." His breathing got ragged and heavy, and he shut his eyes. When he opened them again, they were bloodshot. "I'm glad I could give you the good news in person."

So my future as an artist was dead, or almost dead. I was stuck in my own art-world bardo, but at that moment I didn't much care. A large part of me was tempted to tell him what I was thinking. To explain why I thought everything was so screwed up. But I was tired and it was complicated, and my personal views on the commercial side of art weren't likely to change his mind. He was leaning so close to my face his eyes were inches from mine and it looked like he was about to punch me, and honestly? It was kind of freaking me out. Also, I really wanted to go and find Gaétan, and he was in my way. So I headbutted him instead.

It was the first headbutt I had tried in my life, and I didn't get much on it. A lack of sleep had thrown my judgment off, and my forehead just kind of brushed his chin. I tried again, pulled my head and shoulders back, and pushed them at his face as fast as I could, but this time I missed altogether. He leaned forward and waved a fist at me and it just missed my chin. I moved closer, grabbed his shoulders, pulled my head back, and this time when I whipped my head forward it made solid contact. Felt his nose hit the top of my head and he cried out in pain and put his hand up to his face, and I could see he was in shock and his nose was bleeding. I pushed him out of the apartment, wrestled my way past him, and ran down the hall and onto the street, and didn't stop running until I was a few blocks away.

Now I just had to find Gaétan.

Eighteen

She called herself Missy Noir. I found her in the Electron Libre, a new art squat in Le Marais. When I walked in the front hall she was dancing by herself, and for a few minutes I just stood and watched. Music that sounded like a mix of hip-hop and French lounge played on a scratchy record player as she shimmied across the room, did a spin-and-shake along the wall, flipped a chair over her head, then set it down and jumped on it all in one perfectly choreographed motion, spun in a circle three times on one foot, threw her head back, and raised her small hands, fingers wide, jazz-style. The music stopped and she opened her eyes, a big grin spread across her face.

"Don't you just love me?" she asked.

I did, wholeheartedly and unconditionally. Missy Noir was just over five feet tall and wore pink jean overalls and leather boots up to her knees. With her head of dyed red-and-black hair, wide eyes, and big red lips she looked like a manga cartoon come to life. She jumped off the chair and walked up to me and peered into my eyes. "Who are you?" she asked. Her voice had a squeaking sound, as if she had just swallowed a balloon full of helium.

"I'm Declan."

She looked me up and down. "What are you doing here?"

"I'm, uh, looking for a friend of mine. His name is Gaétan."

"Who's that?

"He's, well...he's thin, and wears black jeans a lot, and he has this deep voice and hair that goes straight back."

"Oh! You mean the Black guy? The guy that talks really slowww... Like. Every. Word. Is. A. Complete. Sentence?" She mugged a surprisingly good impersonation.

"Yes, that's him. Gaétan. You know him?"

"Yip!"

"Do you know where he is?"

"Yip!"

"Where?"

She shook her head. "That depends."

"On what?"

"On who you are."

"I'm Declan. I'm just a friend."

"Are you a gallery owner?"

"No."

"Are you an agent?"

"No! Do I look like an agent?"

"You don't, but your shoes do." She looked down.

I had forgotten I was wearing shoes I bought on Avenue Montaigne. They looked as out of place here as a Royal Albert tea set. "Well, I'm not."

"Debt collector? Bounty hunter? Probation officer? Process server?"

"I'm not any of those."

She looked me up and down, frowning. Kept staring at my shoes. "Undercover cop?"

"No! We were—are friends. From The Grand Hotel."

"I remember that place. Do you have any ID?"

"I don't have anything."

Finally, she shrugged and smiled. "Okay, then. I can show you where he is."

She walked to a wooden trunk in the corner of the room and pulled out a tall pair of black rubber boots and a yellow helmet with a headlamp, put them on, and threw a backpack over her shoulders. Then Missy Noir nodded at me, walked out of the building and down the street. I followed. She didn't just walk; she strutted, with her head and shoulders swaying back and forth like a gang member looking for trouble. After ten minutes she turned left into a dimly lit alley, turned a corner, and disappeared down an even dimmer street and another alley. It smelled of car fumes and rotting food. Rats ran ahead of us, and a man holding a bottle of gin tried to grab me by the ankles.

"Thanks for doing this," I shouted ahead.

"No problem," she shouted back.

"Where are we going?"

"The catacombs."

"What are the catacombs?"

"You'll see. We'll be there in a minute."

A minute passed, then two. After ten minutes, I was starting to wonder where Missy Noir was going, and if it was a good idea to be following a complete stranger through the dark back alleys of Paris. Then again, I was a stranger to her as well, so I guess we were even.

"So, uh...how long now?"

"Almost there."

A few blocks later, she stopped at a manhole cover. From deep in her backpack she dug out a pair of gloves, put them on, pulled the cover up, and pushed it out of the way.

It rolled a few feet and fell, clanging on the street. Her feet found the first rungs of the ladder and she crawled in. By the time I leaned in and looked down, Missy was already ten feet deep into the earth. She looked up at me.

"Welcome to the catacombs," she called. "The best party place in Paris!" She disappeared into a hole in front of her. It took a few minutes to work my way down the ladder and in front of the tunnel she had crawled in. It was cold, wet, and smelled of mud and limestone. She had told me to stay close, but I couldn't see how I was going to do that. Missy was already fifty yards ahead of me and getting farther and farther away, while I was still struggling to fit inside. Swallowing my rising anxiety, I squeezed my shoulders together, hugged my arms to my chest, and crawled in.

There was just enough room for me to get my hands down and wriggle forward. Everything was darkness, except for the distant light cast by her headlamp, and that was getting dimmer every minute. My hands and knees were bruised and bleeding after the first thirty feet. Every time I looked up I hit my head on the ceiling.

"Missy?" I shouted, trying to sound calm. She was so far ahead of me I could barely see her. "Missy Noir?" *Noir, Noir, Noir* echoed off the stone walls.

"What? Oh, sorry!" She stopped and turned her head around so the headlamp shone back. At least I could see. I crawled forward, trying to keep my head down.

"Where are we?"

"I told you. We're in the catacombs."

I crawled forward a few more feet. "What are they?"

"A bunch of tunnels. There are hundreds of them, all over—well, under—Paris." Then she turned around and crawled. "It's like an underground city. We're going to a place they call the BangBang Room," she shouted back. "He's probably there."

We crawled for another ten feet, turned a corner, and climbed over a pile of rocks into another tunnel. This one was high enough to stand in but sat in water that went up to our knees. That's why she was wearing those boots. Missy Noir started walking and I had no choice but to follow. I'd be completely and forever lost otherwise.

"Sorry about your shoes!"

These shoes had cost me €500, but they were the last thing I was worried about right now. "What are these tunnels for?"

"They're for dead people."

"What? He's not..."

"No! He's not. They *used* to bury people in here. There are something like six million bodies buried in the catacombs. Isn't that interesting?"

I stopped.

She turned around and looked at me. "What?"

"Nothing. Just thinking."

"About what?"

"Different things. But mostly...mostly I'm thinking about being lost in a tunnel with six million dead bodies."

"You're not lost. I'm here!" Missy grinned a big toothy grin, then turned around and kept walking. "Besides, they were buried over two hundred years ago. It's not like they're going to come alive and eat you."

I wished that made me feel better than it did.

It was dry now, and we were in a tunnel that was almost six feet high. We walked past a square decorative display that looked like it was made with human bones. I was too afraid to ask.

"That's Room Z," she said, pointing at a large, dark room with a rounded entranceway big enough for a train to pass through. "It's one of the party rooms. There's another one over there, called the Bunker Under the Mountains, it's a few kilometers away. Up ahead, on the left, is the Monastery of the Bears. It's fun too. But the BangBang Room is the best." The tunnel was large and dry now. The walls were covered in spray paint. We walked into another large room that was lined to the ceiling with skulls and bones. Not painted skulls and bones, either. Skulls and bones.

"By the way, there are a few rules down here. No touching the art. No littering. No fighting, duh. And never speak of the above."

"What's *the above*?"

"You can't talk about what you do above ground, or anyone or anything that is up there or happens up there. Not the news. Not your job. Not even the weather. Down here, there is no such thing as the above."

She waded into a pool of black water. It started ankle-high, but soon we were up to our knees. Then it leveled out and we climbed up a short rock cliff and were on dry rock again. She stopped and poured the water out of her boots. Ten minutes later, the air had turned to thick dust, making it hard to breathe. By now we'd been underground for an hour or two, and my sense of place and direction had disappeared entirely. I couldn't find my way back in a hundred years. I hoped, not for the first time, that Missy Noir knew where she was going.

She stopped in front of a small hole in the tunnel. "He's been down here for weeks. I think something is wrong. He looked depressed last time I saw him."

I'd never seen Gaétan depressed. He didn't seem like the type to get depressed.

"Anyway, this is the hard part."

"This is the hard part?" It couldn't possibly get harder.

"You have to crawl in the shaft. On your back. In that tunnel."

It could get harder.

She pushed her feet inside the tunnel and turned over onto her back. "Don't talk too loud in here," she whispered. "They say making noise could cause a cave-in." Then she shimmied in and disappeared. "Stay close," her whispering voice squeaked out of the hole.

Given that she was about half my size, I had serious doubts about whether I could fit in the same hole. But what choice did I have? If I got lost here, I'd be dead body number six million and one. I bent and squeezed and shoved, tried to pinch my shoulders into my spine, pushed with my fingers, and twisted inch by inch, and finally made it through to an area I could at least turn around in. Now I was headfirst, and I rolled over onto my stomach. Stared ahead into the dark. There was nothing there. Not a splinter of light. Not a sound. Nothing but darkness. "Missy?" I whispered.

Crawling forward, I made my way inch by painfully slow inch, feeling sharp acids crawling up my esophagus. Telling myself to stay calm, to just stay nice and calm, I pushed myself forward. It seemed like I'd been in this small section of tunnel for an hour and only moved a foot or two. The tunnel got smaller and smaller. Everything was stone cold black. "Missy?" I whispered again, slightly louder. Screaming would have felt great right about now, but according to Missy Noir that could cause a cave-in. Missy's light had long since disappeared. It was so dark the air felt like solid matter. But I kept going.

The tunnel opened up a few inches and I got on my knees but hit my head on the ceiling and felt blood dripping and went back to crawling and crawling. Then it closed in again and got smaller and tighter and I was shaking and sweating. My stomach turned into a small lump of quartz. My lips, my fingers, my entire body was shivering. I kept going until I couldn't go any longer, and had to stop because I was shaking too much. I was too afraid and I just couldn't move.

"Missy Noir? You there?" I half whispered, half spoke a few times. Nothing. A few minutes went by, and my efforts to move backward and forward only wedged me in tighter. I was stuck. Pushed, pulled, and wiggled, tried to move but couldn't. There was no sign of Missy, no light, barely enough room to wiggle a finger. I waited for a few minutes, or a few hours, I wasn't sure which. Taking deep breaths, I prayed she'd come back, but she didn't. After one more attempt to move I lost it. I couldn't hold it together any longer, so I just gave up and screamed. Half expected rocks to start crashing around my head, but they didn't. I managed to get my hands over my head and screamed and screamed and listened to the echoes bounce off the walls. I screamed again and waited for the roof to cave in. It didn't, and I screamed louder.

If I was going to die here, I wasn't going to go quietly. I'd rather die quickly in a cave-in than slowly in Missy's own Cask of Amontillado. I screamed until my throat felt scarred. Screamed for Missy, for the police, for my mom, my dad, Gaétan, any friend I ever had. Paused. Listened. Nothing but black silence. Screamed again. Waited. Nothing. My throat felt like it was scraped and bleeding, but that wasn't going to stop me. I was just about to start screaming again when I heard a voice coming out of the dark.

"Croquis?"

That voice. Low and quiet. Serious.

"Croquis? You there?"

I took three deep breaths. "Hi, Gaétan. It's me. I'm here."

"I thought that was you. Why are you screaming?"

"I'm stuck."

"Oh." There was a long silence. "That was a loud scream."

"I don't like being stuck in caves."

"I can tell," he said. "Are you okay?"

"I'm not dead yet, if that's what you mean."

"How did you get here?"

"I was following Missy Noir."

"Well. Just for future reference, you should never do that."

"I'll try to remember that."

"Now grab my hand. It's right in front of you."

I managed to get an arm forward, felt his hand grab mine, and he pulled and pulled and I tried to wiggle and nothing happened. Then he squeezed harder and pulled harder, and I squeezed my shoulders tighter and pushed so hard it hurt but it seemed like I just got wedged in tighter. Gaétan put another hand around mine, and pulled even harder, and just when it felt like my arm was about to come out of its socket I felt myself slide forward. Just an inch or two, but it was something. He kept pulling and I kept wiggling, and I moved another inch, then two. We kept working at it. My shirt ripped, my shoulders were bleeding to the bone, but there was movement. We kept working and were making progress and I had moved maybe six inches. Just when I was starting to think there was a chance I would live through this, that maybe I would get out of here alive, I let go of his hand.

"Why did you let go?" Gaétan asked. His hand was searching for mine. I ignored it.

"I can't do it."

"What? You have to do it. Come, let's get you out of there."

"I can't."

"Why? You just said you don't like getting stuck in caves."

"Because. I just can't."

"I'm not leaving you here. Take my hand." I pushed it away.

"I can't. I can't because of you!"

"Because of me? What are you talking about?"

"Why did you steal Chloé?" I asked.

"Sorry? Steal who? Who is Chloé?"

Liar. As if he didn't know. "From the banquet at The Grand. You know who she is."

"No. I do not. Why are we talking about a Chloé?"

Figured he'd say something like that. I can't believe I thought this guy was a friend. I smiled sarcastically in the dark. "That's bullshit, Gaétan. You know exactly who she is. You sat beside her at the banquet. You left with her. With Chloé. I loved her and you just...forget it. Forget it! Just go. I'm fine."

A long pause. "I'm sorry. I do not recall."

"I'm sorry too. Why don't you just leave?"

"Because you're stuck. I'm helping you get out."

"No thanks. I think I'd rather just die here."

"I don't know her. Honest. I don't remember her."

"Bullshit. Bullshit. Bullshit."

There was a long silence. I was hoping he would leave. Then I could just die, and he could have that on his conscience for the rest of his life. That would teach him a lesson.

"Croquis. You really think I stole this...Chloé? From you?"

"I do think that, because you did."

He sighed. "I thought you would have known."

"Known what?"

"You don't, do you?"

"Don't what?"

"I didn't leave with Chloé. I don't even remember who she is, but I wouldn't leave with her. At least, not the way you seem to think."

"I don't believe you."

"Croquis, you have to know I'm gay. It's not possible for you to not know that."

I had to let that sink in for a minute. "What?"

"I'm gay. Queer. The *G* in LGBTQ. Honestly, how could you not know that?"

"You're gay?" I stopped smiling sarcastically. I did not know he was gay. Never even considered the possibility. Not until he said it. But—yes. It took about three seconds before it became obvious to me. A highlight reel of unmistakable clues ran through my head. He was so organized at the banquet. Understood how to design a room. His costume that night was so ideally suited to the occasion. His clothes—scruffed and worn, but so fitted, and such perfectly styled scruffed and worn—and always with complementary colors. That couldn't be an accident. He was always entertaining, cosmopolitan, empathetic, and intelligent. I was an idiot. I thought that's what all French people were like.

He put his hand out again, and this time I took it. We pulled, pushed, struggled, and strained for a long time, but we did it. I got out. Bruised, bleeding, shivering, still scared to death, but I was out. The tunnel opened up, and I could move again, and saw Gaétan sitting there. A light shone in the distance behind him, throwing him into heavy shadow. The devil's sweet dark angel. My three-time savior. My all-time best friend.

I lay on the ground and tried to stop hyperventilating. "I thought I was going to die."

"You have a habit of almost dying," he said.

My heart rate started to come back to normal. "It's a hobby of mine."

"You should try something else. Like bird-watching, maybe."

"Thanks for saving my life again."

"Always glad to help. Are you okay now? Nothing broken?"

I felt around, but everything seemed miraculously intact. "No. I'm good."

"Now, tell me about your Chloé."

I tried the standard descriptions. Almond eyes. Ripped jeans. Sort of blonde. And got the standard response. So I tried the one thing everyone remembered.

"Now I remember!" He slapped his knees. "The Joy Division! She was on the couch. We were speaking. Such a nice girl."

"Yes. That was her."

"Yes, yes." He thought for a moment. "She told me she was starving. She didn't mean just hungry. She was actually starving. Poor thing, she hadn't eaten for three days before our banquet. A minute after you left she fainted. Didn't you know any of this? We had to carry her out of there. She didn't want to go to the hospital, so we took her back to her place. She was living in another shelter across town. I stayed with her for a few weeks, to make sure she got better. She was very sick."

From a distance, I heard music playing. "Going Underground," by The Jam. A faint light glowed in the rocky distance. I put my head between my knees and tried to think. How could I have missed that? Was I that unaware? That ignorant? How could I have missed the fact that she was starving? At the Louvre, she had swallowed three bagels and cheese in a few minutes, and tossed more in her purse, but I was too focused on myself to give it a moment's thought. She had been anxious and irritated at the party, and I had assumed it was all about me. I really was an idiot. Was there help for that level of imbecility? Was there something like an Alcoholics Anonymous for stupid people? I had a lot of work to do on myself, like a twelve-step program that could stop me from being such a self-centered, dumb, and selfish jerk.

"Do you know where she is now?" I asked.

"No. I've gone to look, but she has vanished."

Gaétan reached out his hands and helped me stand up. "Follow me," he said, and I did. He walked me toward the light. A cavernous room appeared in front of us and I heard loud music and voices and saw candles everywhere.

"Welcome to the BangBang Room."

There were strobe lights and forty or fifty people, about my age, drinking and laughing and dancing. There were all kinds of art pieces, walls covered in graffiti art, mosaics, sculptures of animals and people, and a model of a castle made out of rocks that was over six feet high. There was a gargoyle with a ram's head. I saw a bar made with rocks and barstools also made out of rocks. The smell of incense, pot, and beer mixed with wet stone filled the room. Someone passed me a glass filled with clear liquid, and I had a sip. Straight gin. Ugh.

"Nice place," I said.

Gaétan took a long drink from his glass. "It was better. Before."

"Before what?"

"Before everyone found out about it." His face glowed in the light, and I got a good look at him. Something didn't look right. Gaétan looked pale and thin, even for him. He looked skeletal. His eyes looked lost. "A few years ago, there were just a few of us that knew about this place."

"Then?"

"Then Instagram. Now everybody knows about it. They have guided tours here. It got four and a half stars on Tripadvisor. The underground is no longer underground."

"Can we get out of here?" I asked.

He smiled. "I'd love to get out of here."

Gaétan had a flashlight of his own. He led the way and we went back through an entirely different route than the one I came in. We walked upright the entire time. A half hour later we were pushing another manhole cover out of its place and climbing onto the street. I swore I'd never follow Missy Noir again.

"Where do you want to go?" he asked.

"You look sick, Gaétan. How long have you been down there?"

"It's hard to tell. There's no sun or moon. No clocks. No calendars." He scratched his hair. It stood straight up. "A few weeks? I don't know. You start to feel like a mole rat. I forgot what normal air smelled like."

We walked down the street. The night was cold, and a bit damp, but it felt good to be outside again.

"Where is everybody from The Grand?"

"Who knows? They all vanished. Poof. Spread across Paris and beyond."

"What about Apollinaire?

"He told me he was going to fight in the Greek War of Independence."

"Is there a new one? Or is he fighting in the one that took place two hundred years ago?"

"Two hundred years ago." Gaétan nodded. "Told me he wanted to die in a hail of bullets. He asked me to say goodbye."

"If he has to go, that sounds like a good way to go."

"I agree. For him it's the perfect end."

We kept walking. Not saying much. There was something bothering Gaétan, but I couldn't tell what it was. When he didn't think I was looking, his face would fall and I could see a flash of desperation. No, not desperation, I realized. It was depression. I knew that look. I'd seen that look. On my own face. I went to a psychiatrist for years wearing that look. Before I arrived here, before I found Gaétan and our friends, that was my look.

"What's wrong?" I asked.

"Nothing. Everything is great. I have everything I ever wanted."

I also knew those words, and what they really meant. "So if you don't want to live in the catacombs, and The Grand doesn't exist anymore, what are you going to do? Where are you going to go?"

"Still thinking. I have several options I'm considering carefully."

"Like what?"

"Lots of options. I have many options."

Then he turned around and bowed, formally, stood up straight, and saluted. "It's been great to see you. I have to go." And he walked away, faster, as if he were trying to get away from me.

"What options?" I called out.

He kept walking. It was late now, even by Paris standards, and there weren't any shops open, there weren't even many streetlights on. Everything was strangely quiet. The only sounds were two little dogs barking at each other and Gaétan's shoes scraping on the ancient bricks. Ten feet away. Then twenty feet. Gaétan was turning into another shadow.

"What options?" I shouted.

He kept walking. Where was he going? I tried to catch up to him.

"Wait! Don't go away. Don't. I have an option for you." I needed Gaétan. He was the best friend I'd ever had, and I wasn't going to let him get away again. And also, my plan. My plan couldn't work without him. I couldn't find Chloé without him. And now, now that I knew... "Gaétan! Stop! I have an option for you."

Nineteen

The moonlight bounced off the gray metal of the deserted printing presses. There were twelve of them spread around the room, like a herd of steel dinosaurs frozen in time. A thin coating of dust and spilled ink decorated the broad expanse of the concrete floor. Rolls of white paper sat at the end of the presses, over three feet high and as many feet wide, alone and untouched. The few tables and chairs left behind had yellowed magazines and half-empty cups of coffee sitting on top of them, as if they were waiting for someone to come back and finish them off. It smelled of musty air, mold, concrete, and cold metal. Gaétan and I walked around without speaking, the sound of our still-wet shoes squeaking quietly on the floor.

We went up a flight of stairs and walked past rows of offices, empty except for scattered old shelves, broken desks, and empty filing cabinets. There were faded newspapers lying open on the boardroom tables and curled up on the desks. Indoor windows looked down on the press floor below, where the shepherds would keep watch over their ink-stained flock. Outdoor windows looked down on the other Paris skyline: the one that visitors rarely see, but the one many Parisians see every day. The skyline of factories, warehouses, and abandoned cars, of old apartments, mongrel dogs, and petty criminals, of unsafe streets, faded hopes, and forgotten dreams.

I flicked a few switches on the wall. Scattered light appeared in some of the offices around the floor.

"Electricity?" Gaétan said. "Outrageous, extraordinary luxury."

"What do you think?"

"It's run-down, dirty, broken, and beat-up. It's infested with mice and stinks of mold. Probably condemned, most certainly dangerous." He ran a finger along a banister and came up with a pile of dust. "And therefore perfect. Where are we?"

"It used to be a newspaper called *France Soir*. Closed down in 2011."

Gaétan walked to the window of the office and looked outside. He brushed the grime from the window and turned around. "And why are you showing me around this beautiful old barn?"

"Because it's going to be our new home. This is the plan I was telling you about. It's a place for us—for all of us who don't fit into normal society—to stay. A place where we can live, work, sleep, create art, whatever...argue about suicidal philosophers...in peace. Without agents, public relations firms, galleries, without anyone telling us what kind of art we should be making and what colors we should use. A place where we can live without worrying about getting evicted. It's a sanctuary, a community, an artists' workshop, and a gallery—but a gallery we can call our own. A home we can call our own."

Gaétan looked around, scratching his weeks-old beard. "Our very own Bateau-Lavoir." He stepped over some droppings on the floor. "It even comes with its own mice."

"It's beautiful, isn't it?"

"A home." He leaned on the window ledge, gazing out at the skyline. Thought for a few minutes. "It's nice. Wonderful. Very sweet. I think you'll be happy here."

"Not just me. For you, too. It's for all of us."

He shook his head. "Yes. I understand and thank you. But no, I don't think for me."

"What? But why? It's perfect."

"For you. But maybe not for me. I'm not much of a home person." He wiped dust from the window. "I don't think I could live in one place. But you—and your friends— will enjoy it very much."

I expected he would say this. And I thought I knew why. "I think you could. I've been watching you. You see yourself as some kind of free-spirited, wandering soul, but what I see is a guy who has had enough of moving around. I know the look you're wearing when you think no one is looking. I've lived in that face. It's the face of someone who's lost, who's looked ahead and didn't like what they saw. I think you've had enough of getting evicted from everywhere you settle in and losing everyone you know. You're tired of living on the street, moving from squat to squat. Is that why you moved underground? Because they couldn't evict you from there?"

"No. I moved there because they had free popcorn and a movie theater."

"How old are you now? Twenty-six? Twenty-eight? Not knowing where you'll live tomorrow gets old fast. It's a kids' game. Are you still going to be stealing food when you're thirty?"

He shut his eyes, crossed his arms, and didn't speak for a few minutes. "Even if what you said were true, and it isn't, but if it were—how exactly would this work?"

I went through the entire plan. How this building would have its own workshop and private apartments on the upper floors and a public gallery to sell our art on the main floor. How we'd pool a percentage of the money we made so everyone would have enough to eat, and no one would have to steal or go hungry. I even had plans for health care.

"It is a great plan, my friend," he said. "Very nice, absolutely no question. It is beautiful and inspiring. I love everything about it. Except for, wait, let me think." He sat down at the end of the boardroom table, like he had been appointed the CEO of this abandoned building. "Except for about three hundred and fifty problems. For one"—he lifted a finger—"the police will shut this down as soon as they hear about it. Our government officials are not so hot on squats in Paris anymore."

I sat down at the other end of the table. The chair was broken, and it dropped down until my chin was at the same height as the table. I looked up at Gaétan. "That's the great thing about it. They can't kick us out because we're going to own it. I'm going to buy it."

"Now you're thinking." He snapped his fingers. "Of course. You just buy it."

"Yes."

"Would you mind explaining that particular part of the plan to me once more?"

I stood up. Walked around the table. Explained the plan. His eyes followed me with the hard look of a skeptical shareholder. There was a lot of pressure, but my mom had taught me to be prepared. I talked, talked more, and kept talking. He kept asking questions until he was on his eleventh round of fingers. I answered them. The sun was rising over the scraggly city landscape before we finished.

"Do you have a name for this new home?"

"*Salon des Refusés des Refusés.*"

He shook his head for the hundredth time that night. "*Salon des Refusés des Refusés?*"

"Yes. Do you like it?"

"No."

"No?"

"No, I don't like it. I don't even know what it means."

"It's the exhibition of rejected artworks. Like the one that Apollinaire told us about. But it's been reborn. It's come back. Brand new. Completely reinvented for a new generation of rejected artists, like us, who want to get out from under the thumb of the art establishment. So it's the *Salon des Refusés des Refusés.*"

"It's not a very good name, I don't think."

"It is! It's the second *Salon des Refusés des Refusés.*"

"I know you think that's what it means. But that's not what it means. Maybe your French, it's not so good."

"It doesn't matter what the actual words mean. It's what they say." The name was genius, I thought. How could anyone not love that name? "It's the feeling behind the words. The emotions they evoke."

"I don't think people will feel what you think they will feel. I think they'll just feel like it's a bad name."

"They won't!"

"They will."

"It doesn't matter. It's just a name. What do you think of the idea?"

"The idea?" Another shaking of the head. "It's impossible. You don't have a chance."

"And?"

"And what? It doesn't make sense."

"Obviously. But what do you think?"

"I think you mean well, but I think it's not going to work."

"I know, I know that. But do you like it?"

"No. I think it's a bad plan."

"So you think it could work."

Gaétan took a deep breath, shook his head, and walked to the window. "Here's the real question. I'm guessing, to buy this old building, and bring it up to the most lenient of safety codes, just to make sure it doesn't catch fire or collapse and kill everyone inside it—I'm guessing you'd need perhaps, maybe, ten million euros? Am I close?"

"The real estate agent is asking for twelve million. But you can ask for anything. I'm sure I can get it for less."

"Let's say twelve million. Which brings me to my next question." He raised another finger. "Where does Declan Tucker come up with twelve million?"

I got up and sat on another chair. "Actually, I'm going to need more like twenty-five million. For renovations, maybe a little furniture. Plus, I racked up a lot of expenses on my credit card. I owe them over sixty thousand dollars."

"Whoosh. Well. Of course, I understand." He put his feet on the table and raised another finger. "Another question. How does a young, talented, but not quite—at least, not yet—internationally famous artist...no offence..."

"None taken."

"Come up with twenty-five million euros? I hope you don't think I'm going to finance your madness."

"I don't. No way. I'm not taking any of your money. I wouldn't."

"Good. Because even if I would, I couldn't. I gave it away."

"What?"

"I donated it to a good cause."

"Which one?"

"I gave it to Missy Noir."

"Why?"

"I thought she'd enjoy it more than I would."

In ten seconds, I could have come up with a thousand better places to donate money. But by some weird logic, it made sense. He was right. She would enjoy that money. And she did like helping people, even if she wasn't very good at it. I didn't want it. I had my own plan, which didn't include contributions from anyone. "I'm going to sell a painting for twenty-five million."

Gaétan didn't say anything at first. He looked at me like he was wondering, not for the first time, whether I was completely mad. "You know..." He spoke in the same tone of voice my analyst used when I was veering out of control: a forced calm, trying to pretend whatever I was saying was in the acceptable range of normal human behavior. "You understand there probably aren't more than ten living artists in the world who could sell a work for over a million."

"But there are ten. Why not eleven?"

"Forget it. Forget it! Be reasonable. The whole thing is practically impossible."

"But it's not completely impossible."

"It's very, very, very, very close to impossible."

"Look, if you can believe that Apollinaire is a twelve-hundred-year-old priest who freed a not-quite-dead corpse from the bardo and just went to fight in a two-hundred-year-old war..."

"This is different. There is no financial transaction involved in that particular narrative. No one else has to believe it if they choose not to. Can I at least see the painting you're going to sell for twenty-five million?"

"I haven't done it yet."

Gaétan put his head in his lap. He looked like he was going to curl up in a ball and lie on the floor. But instead he stood up, walked around the table a few times, went back to the window, stared for a few minutes, and turned around. "Croquis, please take this in the best possible way. This is the advice of a friend who truly cares. I want to help you. But I think you have lost your mind."

———

I went to the nearest art store and picked up twelve of the biggest canvases they had in stock. Six feet high by four feet wide. The best you can buy: Old Holland Stretched Claessens Oil-Primed Belgian Linen Canvases. Then I loaded up on other supplies. Several boxes of Sennelier paints, a generous selection of the most expensive brushes they had, four containers of turpentine, a dozen Pilot

Croquis pencils. On the way back to the apartment, I also picked up two cases of tuna. I had everything I needed.

I locked the door when I got home and checked my phone one last time. There were several more calls from Alan, and two calls from the credit card company, but nothing important, so I shut the phone off and put it away. Put on comfortable pants, hung the canvases in the living room, sat down, and stared.

On day one, I just sat on the floor and stared at those canvases.

On days two and three I also sat and stared. Waiting.

On day three, I started painting. Just a few tentative strokes, which I erased immediately.

On day six, I tried again, and once again erased everything I had done.

On days eight and nine, I was starting to worry that it wasn't going to happen. But I knew it would. I just knew it would. This time, the white canvases would not defeat me. I just had to be patient, very patient, more patient than anyone ever had been in the history of the world, more patient than Buddha under the bodhi tree.

On day ten, I had almost given up.

Then it happened.

The muse came.

The real one.

I started painting.

Didn't think, and I didn't have to. It just came, the inspiration flowing out of me like a mighty river. Some omnipotent power had taken over—my muse was in charge. A tiny, almond-eyed angel in a torn Joy Division T-shirt.

For the next fourteen days, I painted.

Three times I woke up with my face on the floor, paintbrush in hand and paint splattered around the room. Stood up and started again.

My breath smelled like a bog and I felt a green, waxy paste growing on the inside of my mouth. My hair was matted together so tightly it was forming dreadlocks. My skin was turning a hard shade of white, closer to the color of bones than flesh. My gums were starting to bleed. I figured I had scurvy and looked around the apartment for something with vitamin C. There wasn't anything. I went back to painting. Despite it all, I felt an unnatural peace. The exhaustion, the hunger, none of that bothered me. Something bigger than me had taken over.

Three weeks and two days later it was over. For twenty-three days I hadn't slept more than a few hours a night. On the twenty-third day, I put my paintbrushes down. I was done. There was nothing left to say that wasn't on those canvases. Everything was there, everything I had ever felt, dreamed, been frightened by and loved, art and life, past, present, and future, genuine and artificial. Everything I wanted to say was there. And, of course, Chloé. Right in the center. My *why*.

I tried to sleep, exhausted beyond exhaustion, but couldn't. I lay in bed, tossed and turned, and after an hour or two gave up and decided to go for a walk. It was light outside. A little sun would be nice. Maybe I could find an orange somewhere to help ward off the scurvy I was pretty sure I had. Showered and brushed my teeth for the first time in three weeks, put on some fresh clothes, and shaved.

Before I left, I wrote a press release, attached a small photograph, and emailed it to every television station, newspaper, and art magazine I could think of.

———

The first call came from *Tableau,* a local art newspaper that billed itself as "The Leading Source of Contemporary Art News Since Forever" and had a pretty popular webcast. They asked if I would be available for an on-camera interview that afternoon. Yes, please.

The interviewer was named Erica Abadabri. She arrived at four o'clock sharp, cameraman and crew in tow, and greeted me with an icy smile. I knew then what a wounded animal felt like when approached by a hungry buzzard. They set up in the former boardroom on the second floor, the same one Gaétan and I had met in when I first tried to rationalize this grand adventure. The next thirty minutes were spent on Erica's hair and makeup. Then, at last, they called me over and sat me down on the couch beside her. I noticed she was being careful to make sure I didn't get too close—I guess she was afraid she might catch something from me. She nodded to the cameraman and a small red light told me we were live.

"*Tableau* has traditionally focused on successful artists. Today, we're doing something different. I'm here with Declan Tucker. Hello, Declan."

"Hello."

"I'd like to start by reading from your press release." She unfolded a paper she had been hiding in her hand, then held it up for the camera. "*Chloé Among the Ruins* is the most important work of art in the history of painting. It is available for twenty-five million euros." She folded the paper and put it away. "That's it."

Alan had taught me the value of a good story in this business, and this was unignorable: it was too dumb to be true. The young, virtually unknown artist who announces he's selling a painting for €25 million was a premade disaster they couldn't look away from.

"Declan." She smiled a perfectly white-toothed smile. "Tell me about your painting."

"Well, there's not much to tell. It's—um—I don't know. It's big, I guess."

"It's a *big* painting." She kept glancing at the camera with a half smirk, as if everyone was in on the joke except me. "Well then. Is that it?"

"I guess. What do you want to know?"

"Is it the most important work of art in the history of painting?"

It was to me. "Absolutely. Not even a question."

"Isn't that something. So, what's it about?"

"I'm not sure it's about anything." I wasn't being coy. I really didn't know what it was about. "I haven't really thought about it that way."

"How have you thought about it?"

"I don't know. How do you think about any painting? How do you think about Picasso's *Les Demoiselles d'Avignon*? It just is. If it makes you feel something, if it speaks to you, great. If it doesn't, that's okay too."

"But, Declan"—her voice took on a smarmy schoolteacher's tone—"*Les Demoiselles d'Avignon* is an historically important painting. You can't possibly be comparing your work to Picasso's. That work was created by one of the world's greatest artists, at the peak of his powers. It was the painting that introduced cubism to the world."

"I'm not comparing it to anything," I said. "But...but it wasn't important when he did it, was it? No one knew what it was. Everyone who saw it said it was garbage. Even his friends. Picasso hid it in his own room for months. He didn't exhibit it for ten years. Didn't sell it for twenty years." I leaned back on the couch. "So far, both of our paintings are going through the exact same trajectory. What does that tell you?"

"What would you say to someone who suggested *Chloé in the Ruins* isn't worth more than a few dollars?"

"*Among* the ruins. And I'd suggest they don't buy it."

"A lot of people are saying it's—well, I didn't say this, but it's been described as unimaginably unimaginative, dull, unfinished, and a lot worse. Crozier claimed it wouldn't get a passing grade as a high school art project. Other critics have lined up behind him. How would you respond to that?"

"They're probably right! But Picasso, Monet, all the Impressionists really, the modernists, the postmodernists, just about every artist who ever painted anything new—they were called similar things. So I suppose I should thank Crozier, and all those critics. They've paid me a huge compliment."

"But they didn't ask for twenty-five million euros."

"No. They sold them for almost nothing. Van Gogh sold one painting in his life, for four hundred francs. Picasso used to sell his work for even less, a few francs, or trade them for food. But those paintings are all worth millions now. Galleries, dealers, agents, investors—they got the money."

"How did you come up with the price?"

"Someone paid forty or fifty million euros for a Koons *Balloon Dog*. I figured *Chloé Among the Ruins* is worth at least half that. So, it's actually a great deal, if you do the math."

"I love Jeffrey Koons's work!"

"If it speaks to you, that's great."

"Can you tell me who Chloé is?"

"She's—she's someone I met in a restaurant. And we..." This was the moment I had been waiting for, and I sat up and looked at the camera. "Chloé? If you're out there, could you—" My voice went up a few octaves, but I stopped and got it under control before I spoke again. "I'm not who I said I was. I'm sorry about everything, I've been a total jerk and I know that, and I just really want to see you. Please, call me. You know where I am. If you could..."

"What?"

"Nothing. Sorry, totally got distracted there."

"You can tell us. Just what?"

"No. Just forget it."

"I'm sure everyone would love to hear it. What?"

I took a breath and leaned back, smiled, and waited for the dead air to have its effect.

"Well, then. Fine. Fine. Can we see your painting now?"

I had planned on showing it today, but, well, she was just being so annoying that I changed my mind. "No. I don't think so."

"You don't think so?"

"I think I'll just keep it under wraps."

Her eyes opened wide and she stared at me. I couldn't tell if she was thinking about wrapping her hands around my neck or punching me in the face.

"Why can't we see it?"

"You've seen the photograph."

"But it's not..."

"You can see it at our opening. The grand debut is just ten days away."

She repeated the question several times, getting increasingly hostile. It must have been hard on her. She couldn't make sarcastic jokes about a painting she couldn't see. But it was too late, and I wasn't going to change my mind. Finally, she gave up and left.

There were six more interviews over the next three days. Articles were printed, reprinted, and appeared everywhere. It seemed like every art publication, television channel, radio station, and newspaper were in a race to see who could publish the most hostile review or wittiest insult. My painting was, in those highbrowed artistic circles where tall foreheads prevailed, a sad, pathetic example of everything that was wrong with art today. It was atrocious, vile, and rotten to its oil-based core: an absolute disgrace. One of the critics wrote that it was a pitiful and despicable piece of fecal matter conceived by an inerudite amateur who should be sold for scrap, or better yet, burned and forgotten.

As I had hoped, all that negative publicity from the art world establishment did its magic with the underground artists in the city. If the establishment hated it that much, they thought, my painting must be good. Fringe artists, writers, and guests in art squats from around the city and beyond stopped by to check it out. Most of my old friends from The Grand wandered in. Some of the people I'd seen in squats around the city and the catacombs dropped by. Missy Noir paid a visit. She was driving a Lamborghini. They all looked around the place, and most of them liked what they saw. A few asked if they could join us. The *Salon des Refusés des Refusés* started to grow.

A few days later, eight of the artists from The Grand had moved in. Eleven artists I had never met joined them shortly thereafter. They hung work on the gallery level, took up rooms on the second and third floors, and made themselves at home. The more the critics piled on *Chloé*, the more artists moved in. After a few days, there were twenty-eight artists living here and thirty-nine pieces on the wall. With Gaétan's design aesthetics, and a lot of heavy lifting and deep cleaning from our new residents and myself, the abandoned newspaper building had been transformed into a beautiful contemporary art gallery.

The *Salon des Refusés des Refusés'* grand opening was on the same day as Art Basel's. Before we had opened the doors, the lineup of visitors outside our building stretched for three blocks.

Twenty

Gaetan and I stood by the window in one of the second-floor offices, watching the events unfold below. *Chloé Among the Ruins* anchored the gallery on the far wall. Sixty-eight paintings, installations, and short films were spread over the rest of the room. We opened the doors at ten o'clock and the crowds started pushing their way in. By eleven, it was packed. The visitors had to push, shove, and squeeze to get where they wanted to go, and the place they wanted to go the most was in front of *Chloé* where they stood three, six, then eight rows deep. It wasn't as big as a *Mona Lisa* crowd, but it was big. My painting had become famous. It was so awful that everyone just had to see it.

The crowds kept coming, pushing, and shoving their way in front of *Chloé* until it looked like a mosh pit. They stood, shook their heads, pointed, joked, had their laughs. They took their photos in front of it while making funny faces. I heard "*Chloé Among the Ruins?* More like Chloé Among the Crap!" eleven times.

"I think they will learn to like it," Gaétan said. "It's ahead of its time."

"They really hate it now," I said, "but after a hundred years maybe they'll realize they don't really hate it. They'll just kind of hate it."

Eventually, the crowds moved on from *Chloé* and started looking at the other works in the gallery. There was a totally different reaction—serious conversations, heads nodding, compliments, and enthusiasm. More often than not, they bought one or two of them. Perhaps, in part, because they seemed like such a bargain in comparison—far under €25 million. And also because they were brilliant. The walls were full of original, innovative, beautiful work. Our residents were true artists. By midafternoon, almost everything was sold out.

"This is unbelievable. Outrageous," Gaétan said. "Croquis, look what you've done. This is impossible. A gallery selling everything—except your work, of course—during its grand opening. I bet it's never happened before." He hugged me from behind. "Was this your plan all along?"

"No," I said. "I really wanted to sell my painting. I owe a lot of money on my credit card."

"I'm sorry your painting didn't sell."

"Well, maybe it was overpriced."

"Maybe, just by a million or two. Also, and don't say I didn't tell you, but I did."

"I know. A Croquis is a bourgeois pencil..."

"You should have used a Staedtler. I told you."

It was after midnight before all the visitors left. The doors closed. The walls were bare, except for *Chloé Among the Ruins.* The artists and residents walked around in a kind of dumb shock. We had done it on our own, and we did it all outside of the art world establishment, without paying the agents, auction houses, and galleries. We had stuck a finger in the establishment's eye. There was a celebration. We all sat in a big circle and drank a lot of wine and shouted a lot of cheers-to-us. There was a lot of talk about changing the world and setting new paradigms. And later, even a little arguing about ancient philosophers, just for old times' sake. We were together again.

An hour or two later, everyone went to bed. I sat on the floor underneath *Chloé Among the Ruins*. After a day of surround-sound noise, the quiet felt heavy and soft, like a pile of ultra-plush cashmere blankets. The moon looked down on me, a little shining sliver in a universe of darkness.

Nothing had changed and everything had changed. No one bought *Chloé Among the Ruins,* of course. Everyone had come to have a laugh at that impetuous, unknown artist who dared to ask €25 million for his painting. But they bought the other work. With no agents or galleries to pay, our artists did very well. They wouldn't have to steal groceries again for a long time. The *Salon des Refusés des Refusés* had generated so much good press about its artists and co-op model that the government wouldn't dare shut it down. Everything worked out pretty much as I had hoped, except for one thing. I truly believed that Chloé would show up. She didn't. It seemed like everyone in Paris had come except her. So even if the entire plan had worked, it felt like nothing had worked. I had achieved almost everything I wanted, but the one thing I didn't was almost everything to me. And that sucked.

It was time to move on. I didn't believe I was the world's greatest artist anymore. Wasn't going to become famous, set new paradigms, or start a new movement. Didn't believe my paintings had divine power anymore. I wasn't even sure if they were any good. If they couldn't bring Chloé back, they couldn't be that good. Now I had to face the truth, and a cold, hard reality check was long overdue. Gaétan could take care of the *Salon des Refusés des Refusés,* but I couldn't stay if Chloé wasn't here. I needed to find something new. Needed a plan B for my life. But what? What would Declan do next?

I could go back to Georgetown. I missed that place. I knew many of the problems I had there were a lot of my own doing, that I could have worked a little harder at being friendly. Maybe I could get my job back at the *Georgetown Herald* and spend the next fifty years paying off my credit card. Or find something new. I could become a hedge fund manager, maybe. Whatever they did. Or I could go into business, work my way up the ladder, create some nice-looking PowerPoint presentations. They all sounded like good plans. But if they were such good plans, why did I feel so sick while I was thinking about them?

My body felt too heavy to move. I was nodding off to sleep on the floor when, a little after 3:00 a.m., the front door swung open, creaking and complaining like it was about to come apart. Someone was standing at the entrance. From my vantage point—I was on the other side of the floor, a long way away, and with the moon providing backlighting, all I could see was a dark outline. Whoever it was looked like they were in pain. An elderly, bent figure, dressed in ill-fitting clothes, leaning to one side and limping, walked slowly toward me.

Was it Apollinaire? I really needed a little Apollinaire right now. A little surrealism, perhaps a horoscope reading, a tarot card or two, someone to take me out of myself and tell me what was going wrong with my life and why my stars weren't lining up and how my enlightenment needed to be more enlightened—or something like that. Something to explain why, after all my careful planning, my almond-eyed angel Chloé hadn't appeared as I was so certain she would. Where was she? Why hadn't she come? What happened to my divine power? Then the figure that was stumbling so slowly across the floor looked sideways and the moon hit her face.

Her hair was straggly and unwashed. She walked so slowly and her back was so bent over she looked like an old lady with advanced osteoporosis. She came a foot closer, and I saw her caved-in eyes. They looked like black holes. Her skin was a whiter shade of pale than I had ever seen on anyone. She had lost weight, and she didn't have much weight to lose in the first place. Chloé was wearing her Joy Division T-shirt, but now it was more gray than white. She looked up, saw me, and I thought she tried to wave, but it was hard to tell, and she stumbled forward a few steps before finally just giving up and sitting down on the floor, looking at her feet. She sat there, unmoving, as if she were waiting for the world to end.

I jumped up and ran to her, helped her up. She looked and felt like she weighed about sixty pounds. She smelled like a back alley. Her teeth had a yellow coating surrounded by black rings, and her hair was almost entirely matted together. I got her over to a couch and laid her down. She offered a gutted hello and a weak attempt at a smile. Then I ran and found water and a few leftover baguettes and cheese. She drank, lay back, sat up, drank more, then took a few small bites of a baguette and nodded a silent thanks. She lay down and started talking, but the words were jumbled together and unintelligible. I just listened. Five minutes later she closed her eyes and fell asleep.

There wasn't much for me to do but watch her and that's what I did. She slept, I stared. There wasn't much there, a skeleton's shadow of the Chloé I knew, but she was the most beautiful skeleton's shadow I had ever seen. I found a blanket and laid it over her. The blanket fell off and I put it back on. There was a lot of mumbling and a few quiet cries, like she was having nightmares. I probably should have called an ambulance, but I couldn't let her go again, so I told myself she wouldn't want to wake up in a cold hospital. Then—an hour later? Two? Six? I must have fallen asleep, because I remember waking up and she was sitting on the couch looking up at the painting behind us. *Chloé Among the Ruins.*

"Good morning," I said.

"Is it morning?" she said. A faint, dry whisper.

"I don't know, actually."

"What's that?"

"It's just a painting I did."

"Is that me?" she asked.

"Yes."

She smiled, her glassy red eyes just a little clearer. "I remember that."

Neither one of us said anything for a few minutes.

"Who are you?" I asked.

"I don't know." She looked at me, then out the window. She lay down again. "I'm not who I said I am."

"Neither am I. I'm not who I said I am either."

"I know," she said.

"Do you want more food? Water?"

She nodded. There was bread, cheese, and water in the kitchen and for a few more minutes all she did was eat. Then she smiled and fell asleep again. The sun had started to shine in the windows and before long we saw a crowd of people hanging around outside. Gaétan explained to them that we were sold out, and asked them to come back in a few weeks. Then he put a sign on the door and everyone left, mumbling to themselves.

I carried Chloé up to my room on the second floor and shut the door. She slept for another six hours. It took a few more baguettes and two triple espressos, but by evening she was starting to look like the human Chloé again. She asked if there was a toothbrush she could borrow. I let her use mine.

"I supposed you're probably wondering..." she said.

"No, no. I wasn't."

"You weren't?"

"Okay, honestly? I was wondering. I haven't been thinking about anything else. You don't have to tell me, and you're still too weak, so it should probably wait. But yes. I was wondering."

She drank more coffee. "Do you remember when we met at the restaurant?"

Did I remember? Every second. Every millisecond, in high-definition super-slow motion.

"I told you I was going to school at École nationale supérieure des Beaux-Arts."

"Yes."

"But I wasn't. I mean, I was. Then I wasn't. I stopped going when I got sick."

"I'm sorry."

"I got sick and stopped going to school, and to work. You know I worked at the restaurant. I worked there in the day, when I wasn't at school, and in the evenings a lot, and I worked at a steel factory at night, and I, I just worked so much." Her eyes shut, then popped open again. "But I had a breakdown, I guess. It was too much, I was so tired, and so anxious and afraid that I wouldn't be able to keep it all up, and I couldn't, I tried so hard, but I couldn't. I left home one morning and never went back." She was quiet for a few minutes, and I thought she was falling asleep. "Do you remember when we met at the Louvre? I was sleeping in a park. I hadn't eaten in two days. You must have wondered, didn't you? Why I looked like that?"

I hadn't wondered. Had thought she looked perfect. How oblivious could I be?

"You asked me questions about my family and everything, and you were just being kind, I know, but I was afraid and embarrassed. Afraid you'd find out the truth. That's why I ran away. And then, at the party, it was the same thing. I was so afraid, I thought you knew I was lying, you must have known, so I kind of freaked out on you. I'm sorry. It wasn't my best moment."

"Why didn't you tell me?"

"I know you think we have money, but we don't. I lied because I was embarrassed."

"But that didn't matter to me. And besides, I told you I didn't have any money anyway. There was no reason to be embarrassed."

She told me, in a broken, faraway voice that stopped and paused every few minutes, who her family had been two or three hundred years ago. Long before she came along. Several horses, acres of land, a castle. Titles. Thirteen-course dinners with maids and butlers. Hunting with the king. Then the revolution happened, and it all went away. Some members of the family survived by selling land, jewels, and relying on the kindness of their extended family and royal friends who had somehow managed to hang onto their wealth. Some, like Prince Amaury, became successful on their own. Most didn't. Most, including Chloé and her family, sank into poverty.

"No Géricaults?"

"No Géricaults. No nothing. I made it all up. I've been making it up all my life. You know, I grew up listening to story after story about the glorious Burgundys. How we were part of the Bonaparte family, how I am the great-great-great-whatever-granddaughter of Emperor Napoleon, and how we were descendants of Louis XIV, how our family goes back to Spanish nobility." She put the coffee down, lay back on the couch, and shut her eyes. "But we had nothing, and we were ashamed. We were embarrassed that we couldn't afford to live in a castle, but meanwhile, we couldn't even afford food.

"Eventually, my father shut down. He sat alone in his room day after day, shouting at voices inside his head. My mother drank all day, pretending everything was okay until she passed out on the floor. I was the only one working, the only one bringing any money in, to pay the bills and buy the groceries for all of us, but I couldn't. I couldn't hold it together." There were tears falling from her eyes, and she wiped them with her worn T-shirt. "I was so tired, so tired.

And one day, something went wrong inside me and I just couldn't do it. I was broken. That's when I left."

"I'm sorry. I'm sorry all that happened to you. I'm sorry I didn't even notice, that I didn't even help you. I have no excuses."

"I left my parents. I don't know what's happened to them."

All I could do was hold her hands while she cried, burying her face in the couch.

"This is piggy of me, but do you have any more food? Anything?" I ran and grabbed more food, plus some more water and brought it back. She propped her head on her arm and ate quietly for a few minutes. "I'd give anything to have been born into a normal family with normal parents. To have nothing to complain about but too much homework and strict curfews."

All the time I had been telling her I was eating out of soup kitchens and living on the street, she really was starving. All the time I had pretended to have nothing, she really did have nothing. Which made me the biggest jerk ever to come out of Georgetown, the biggest jerk in all of Paris, and in the running for the biggest jerk in history. I felt like crawling into a hole under the earth and staying there forever. I kept apologizing for being such a jerk.

"I saw you interviewed on TV." She smiled. "You were kind of being a jerk."

"I've been a jerk for a long time. But I'm trying to get better."

"You're not a jerk. The only real jerks are the people who don't think they're jerks." She took another bite and swallowed quickly. "You did have money. I could tell...those jeans. Your hands. Poor people don't have hands like that. And so, I wondered, why would you lie?"

"Because I was an idiot. I'm still an idiot, but also I was an idiot."

"I don't think so. That's not why."

It was my turn to tell the truth. "I didn't grow up in San Francisco. I grew up in a small town, and we were, well, comfortable, actually very well-off. And...I never ran away, or joined a carnival, or anything like. My dad never left us."

"But why lie about that?"

"I was embarrassed. About being so spoiled. And even worse, about being so, so nothing. And..." I shook my head. "Nobody wants to hear about a rich kid who grew up in a normal, middle-class family. I don't have a drug problem, I don't hate my parents, I don't have an incurable disease. I'm just a boring guy with a bad attitude."

"That's not it. That's not all it was. You have something you're not telling me."

Yes, they were there. She was right. "I do have issues. My wires didn't fuse, I guess."

"You don't have to do this alone, you know."

"You're right. And I am. I'm going to get help."

She smiled at me, and that smile turned over my universe. It made me think everything was okay. That I was okay. If Chloé liked me, I couldn't be nearly as bad as I thought I was.

She finished eating and brushed crumbs off her lap. "I wanted to tell you. At the Louvre that day. But I couldn't. It was—it is—I felt like it was my fault. I didn't want anyone to know who I really was. I was afraid. But when I heard what you'd done, that you painted that"—she nodded at the painting—"I had to come and see you. I think what you did was so..."

"Do you want to sleep?" I asked.

"I think I better. Sorry about this." She lay down on the couch. "Do you know of any place I can stay? I'm running out of alleys to sleep in."

"This is your lucky day. We have a few luxury suites still available in this exclusive hotel. Featuring lumpy mattresses, occasional electricity, and cold running water."

She was asleep before I finished the sentence.

———

Two weeks after the gallery showing, the Paris city council legalized our squat, calling it a "place of collective creation." I suppose they had realized that art squats like ours could bring in more tourists. The *Salon des Refusés des Refusés* was officially official. We could stay, create, exhibit, and live as we wanted without worrying about being evicted. They even paid for the construction required to bring it up to code. Before long we had almost sixty artists living in our luxurious suites.

It's been over a year since our grand opening, and the *Salon des Refusés des Refusés* has continued to grow. Rent has remained stable at twenty-four baguettes, salted butter, and a nice selection of cheese, or some reasonable facsimile. Gaétan settled in as the building manager; turned out he was a homebody after all. Chloé stayed with us, and went back to school, thanks to generous contributions from Prince

Amaury. I was painting again. I may not have been brilliant, or genius, or set new paradigms, but I was pretty good, and getting better. And since my work had somehow brought Chloé back, I would never question my divine power again.

No one ever did buy *Chloé Among the Ruins*.

I wouldn't have sold it anyway.

Now I know why da Vinci never sold the *Mona Lisa*.

THE END

Acknowledgements

I am forever grateful for the ongoing patience, support, inspiration, and encouragement of Ann. Thank you to Diane Young who edited an early draft of this novel and to Lianne Fontaine who copy edited it. And a special thanks to my art history professor Hayden B.J. Maginnis, who taught me how to see.

Copyright

This is a work of fiction. Names, characters, places, and incidents are products of the author's imagination or are used fictitiously and are not to be construed as real. Any resemblance to actual events, locales, organizations, or persons, living or dead, is entirely coincidental.

www.ingramcontent.com/pod-product-compliance
Lightning Source LLC
Chambersburg PA
CBHW070411310726

48977CB00003B/638